AROUND THE
WAY GIRLS 6

AROUND THE WAY GIRLS 6

MEISHA CAMM,
MARK ANTHONY,
RAHSAAN ALI

www.urbanbooks.net

Urban Books
1199 Straight Path
West Babylon, NY 11704

Around the Way Girls 6 copyright © 2009 Meisha Camm, Mark
Anthony, Rahsaan Ali

All rights reserved. No part of this book may be reproduced in any
form or by any means without prior consent of the Publisher, excepting
brief quotes used in reviews.

ISBN-13: 978-1-60162-153-5
ISBN-10: 1-60162-153-1

First Printing July 2009
Printed in the United States of America

10 9 8 7 6 5 4 3 2

*This is a work of fiction. Any references or similarities to actual
events, real people, living, or dead, or to real locales are intended
to give the novel a sense of reality. Any similarity in other names,
characters, places, and incidents is entirely coincidental.*

Distributed by Kensington Publishing Corp.
Submit Wholesale Orders to:
Kensington Publishing Corp.
C/O Penguin Group (USA) Inc.
Attention: Order Processing
405 Murray Hill Parkway
East Rutherford, NJ 07073-2316
Phone: 1-800-526-0275
Fax: 1-800-227-9604

AROUND THE WAY GIRLS 6

THE PACT

By Meisha Camm

Acknowledgments

I want to thank Jesus Christ for giving me this gift of writing. With the power of prayer and determination, anything is possible.

The easiest part of a book is actually writing it. I have learned that struggle, hard work, and patience are three vital elements in the process of becoming successful.

Thank you to Carl Weber, Natalie Weber, and the Urban Books family for believing in my work, once again.

Most importantly, a special thanks goes out to all of the fans. Thank you for the feedback and encouragement.

Thank you to my parents, Rodney and Shelly Camm, my daughter, Shamaya, and my sister, Melanie, for the encouragement and support. To Jessica Tilles and Niko Hamm, thank you for pushing and pushing me to write to the best of my ability, and critiquing my work.

To my friends and family, Mr. and Mrs. Ballinger, Tiffany Ballinger, Carla Harrison, Malita Manning, Daneisha Elsbery, Kisha Bailey, Vickie Kennedy, Janie Harrison, Aquita Roberts, Raena and Steven Simmons, Darlene Epps-Minor, Danene Taylor, Kisha Dodson, Tracy Davis, Chrissy Smith, Sara Schiable, Linda Potts, Pat Howell, Kisha Powell, Vera Redd, the entire Wade family, Darrick Person, Calvin Hatcher, and Renee Bobbs, thank you for your kinds words of encouragement.

To the online writing groups, Real Sista Writers and Writers–Rx, thank you for always sending me important information pertaining to the book world. A special thanks to Gevell Wagner for taking the time out to read my work.

To Nikki Turner, Tobias Fox, Edwin and Earnest McNair, Michael Baisden, Shannon Holmes, Zane, and Mary Monroe, thank you for steering me in the right direction.

Chapter 1

"What did you see, Yana?" Ma screamed at me with a pair of sharp scissors in her left hand and a clump of my hair in the right hand.

Out of the corner of my eye, I caught a glimpse of one of the kitchen knives in her pocket. Plus, I noticed the curling iron was at its highest temperature. "I didn't see anything," I whimpered, looking at her through the bathroom mirror, hoping she would believe me.

"I overheard you talking on the phone to Kiki," she insisted before letting go of my hair and smacking me across the face.

"All I told Kiki was to be home before the sun comes down, because we know how you are about us coming home late," I explained while she cut large clumps of my hair.

After my lips stopped moving, it took her no time to snip two more clumps. Ma knew, more than anything, I cared a lot about my hair.

"Being bald is going to be a great look for you in school," Ma announced with an attitude as she continued to cut. "Now, unless you don't want to be completely bald and have a five-inch scar down your rosy cheeks, tell me right now what you saw," Ma demanded, the blade of the knife in position to cut my cheek.

"Okay, I'll tell you. I saw Pop."

"Where did you see him?"

"Umm . . ."

"Wrong answer," Ma commented before burning my neck with the scorching-hot curling iron.

"Please, stop," I begged.

"Girl, that's what you get for lying to me. Now, I'm going to ask you one more time. Where have you seen your daddy?"

"I saw him at the Laundromat. He was with another woman and a baby who looked just like Kiki when she was a baby. Pop saw me and acted as if he didn't even know me. I'm sorry, Ma. I'm so sorry," I explained, tears streaming down my face from the aching pain of the burn.

"No, your father is supposed to be here with us eating dinner, and he's with another woman. I stood in line for two hours at the fish market to cook his favorite tonight," she screamed, running to her bedroom.

I followed behind her. "Ma, put the gun down, please," I begged.

"This is your father's fault. How could he do this to me? I'm not going to be stuck taking care of his damn kids by myself," she screamed. Ma shoved me out of the bedroom and tried to shut the door, but I got my fingers caught.

"Don't do this. Kiki and I love you so much," I said, while she repeatedly slammed the door against my fingers for me to let go. The pain was too much, so I let go. The door slammed shut, and I heard a shot.

The alarm clock went off, and I woke in a cold sweat, relieved. I was just dreaming. Now, I had to get up and make breakfast for Kiki, Teresa, and me before the bus came.

"Teresa, Kiki, get up. The bus is coming in thirty minutes!" I assured them.

* * *

Each day at 3:45 on the dot, the bus driver, Ms. Grey, kicked my baby sister, Keisha, who went by the nickname Kiki, Teresa, and me, along with eight other kids, off the bus in front of Browns Park.

Living in the heart of Norfolk, Virginia in one of the worst housing projects hasn't been easy. My mother never took us anywhere outside of the city of Norfolk. Mrs. Smith, an English teacher, always talked about collecting seashells along the sands of Virginia Beach. According to her, the drive was only about twenty minutes away from the middle school.

Teresa, Kiki, and I took a deep breath, holding each other's hands, wondering if we could get to our building without getting killed. Six months ago, Jeremiah, a kid in my class, got shot by a stray bullet. Three days before that, I had accidentally dropped my lunch tray, and all the kids laughed at me while I was trying to get tomato sauce and mozzarella cheese off my sneakers with napkins. Jeremiah came and helped me pick up the lunch off the floor.

"Ma?" I called out after we all went into the apartment. I listened to hear if her TV was still on in her bedroom. Usually around this time, she was getting ready to watch *The Jerry Springer Show*, her all-time favorite talk show.

"What's for dinner?" Teresa asked while taking her book bag off her shoulders.

"Chicken fingers and fries, I guess."

"Don't worry, Yana, your mother is coming back. She always does," Teresa reassured me, giving me a hug.

Three years ago, Ma adopted Teresa. Her parents and baby brother were killed by a fire in the building next to us, and none of her other family members could take her in. Ma was real good friends with her mother, Ms. Cooper, and felt adopting Teresa would bring extra money in the house. And so Teresa became a sister to Kiki and me. Being nosy, I heard Ma talking on the phone a couple of times to a lawyer about suing the city over the faulty electrical wiring that caused the fire.

"Thanks." I walked into the kitchen and preheated the oven three hundred and fifty degrees to bake the chicken fingers and fries.

Ma taught me at an early age to cook basic stuff like pancakes, eggs, toast, chicken fingers, fish sticks, fries, Oodles of Noodles, and Pop-Tarts.

On the refrigerator, I caught a glimpse of a picture of Ma, Teresa, Kiki, and me two years ago at the carnival in the parking lot of Military Circle Mall. We were proud to hold up our bags of blueberry cotton candy and cherry-flavored snow cones. Those we were the days when she was happy and healthy. Ma had the body of a supermodel, brown skin, dark brown eyes, and long jet-black hair, which she loved to part down the middle.

Ma wanted more for us girls than the average. She made us read so many books and also the dictionary. In return, I got joked every day at school for talking proper like a white girl. Teresa and Kiki found books to be boring, but me, I could spend hours in a library.

Ma believed Pop was coming back to live with us so we could all be a family for a long time. Finally, one night, after a long screaming match in which Ma got two black eyes and a broken nose, Pop told her it was over and he would never marry her. After that, Pop just came and went as he pleased, disrespecting Ma to the point where he even spat in her face, calling her out of her name. Ma's name was Helen, but I heard *bitch* and *ho* more often. I cried myself to sleep so many nights wondering how he could treat her like that. She loved him so much.

Ma loved showing us old pictures of Pop. His name was Peter Johnson. Back in high school, all the girls wanted to be with him for being the star wrestler. With light brown eyes, curly hair, and an award-winning smile, he used to be a fit six-foot-two. Now, he was overweight, potbellied, and had blood-shot-red eyes. When he did come around, if he wasn't holding an ice-cold Michelob in a brown paper bag, I wondered if something was wrong with him.

After doing homework, fixing dinner, and washing dishes, I cleaned up the apartment. I found six dirty needles and discovered Ma's drug stash. While brushing my teeth, I watched the drugs flush down the toilet, hoping Ma would get help.

I was tired and climbed into the third twin bed. It was tight in the bedroom, but we managed to make do. As long as we had each other, we were fine.

Chapter 2

"Yana, wake up!" Ma demanded, smacking me in the face. She had all the lights turned on in the bedroom.

At first, the lights were blurring my vision. The alarm clock read 2:15 in the morning, and Teresa and Kiki lay still in their own twin beds, probably scared to death.

"Ma, what's wrong?" I pleaded, barely recognizing her. She had lost at least another fifteen pounds.

"Where is it?"

"Where's what?"

"The stash, Yana. Where is it? You're the only one who cleans up this shithole!"

"Ma, I don't—"

Ma didn't even let me finish. She grabbed a baseball bat and hit me on the left side of my jaw. Then she picked me up and pinned me against the wall.

"I'm going to ask you one more time—Where is the fucking stash?"

"I don't know," I whispered, barely able to speak, and terrified to tell her the truth.

Ma threw me down on the floor and kicked me in the stomach so many times, I lost count. Teresa and Kiki were begging her to stop.

"What? You don't think I know that you want me to stop shooting?" she asked, waiting for an answer.

"I don't know," I responded, not wanting to get hit with the bat again, hoping my jaw wasn't broken. Usually, Teresa, Kiki, and I got smacked in the face or a hit upside the head a few times for talking back, but she'd never beaten me like this.

"Yana, you must think I'm stupid to not realize that. I'm so sick and tired of you leaving brochures about drug rehab places and side effects of drugs. Don't leave that crap around my house no more." Ma poked my temples with her finger.

"Okay, Ma, I will stop."

"I'll stop using when the fuck I get ready. I can't prove it, but I know you took my stash. Next time, leave my shit alone. Y'all better be happy I'm getting a check for each one of you; otherwise all of you would be at an orphanage or homeless shelter somewhere. Yana, do you know what it feels like to have withdrawals?"

"No," I replied, my hands clenching my stomach.

"It feels as if I'm going to fucking die. Now, because of your dumb ass I have to go out and get some more," she yelled at the top of her lungs, leaving our bedroom and storming down the hallway.

When the front door slammed shut, Teresa and Kiki fell to their knees, crying over me.

Chapter 3

"What are you here for?" the receptionist asked, rolling her eyes at me and acting as if I was bothering her.

"Umm, I need to see a doctor, please," I responded, bundled up into my purple coat, and a scarf protecting my face. Teresa and Kiki wanted to come, but I made them go to school, since I didn't want to piss Ma off and get my ass beat again. Even though the phone was disconnected at home, I still didn't want to take any chances of the school trying to contact Ma if all of us skipped school.

"Take a number and get your mother to fill out these forms please. Where is your mother at?"

"She got caught trying to find a place to park, but she should be coming in any minute now," I explained, lying through my teeth. I turned to look out of the window, hoping to make the excuse look convincing. I had taken two different buses to reach the Brambleton Avenue free health clinic.

"You're number forty-five. It's probably going to be three hours before you're seen." She handed me a bunch of forms.

"Yes, ma'am. Thank you."

"You're welcome. I love a child who shows some respect

for their elders. In that case, I'll get the doctor to take you in right away, baby. Once your momma comes in the door, I'll show her to where you are." The receptionist pressed a button on her phone, and the next thing I knew, a nurse called my name on the other side of the building.

Chapter 4

The nurse, Ms. Carver, shut the patient room door behind her and started asking me a lot of questions, which I barely knew the answer to. Luckily, most of her questions required a yes or no. After Ma got hooked on drugs, she stopped taking us to the doctor and the dentist. She didn't go herself either. Too scared to give them any real information about me, I used the name Donna Martin.

"So, Donna, what brings you here at the clinic this morning?" Ms. Carver asked after taking my temperature, heart rate, and blood pressure. This lady was nice to me, but she reeked of smoke and cheap perfume from the dollar store.

"My jaw and stomach are very sore."

"How did you get so sore?" Pen in hand, Ms. Carver was ready to write down everything I said.

"The next apartment over from us has a huge dog named Baxter. Yesterday, while I was coming out of my apartment, which is on the second floor, he spotted me, started barking, and ran in my direction. I was so scared that I started running, lost my balance, fell down the stairs, and landed on my stomach."

"Honey, let me take a look at the damage. Please remove your scarf and coat," she instructed.

"Okay."

Ms. Carver gave me a dreadful look after I let her look at all of the bruises. She put her trembling hands on her mouth. "Donna, are you sure you received this from a fall down the stairs?"

"Yes. This is what landing on concrete can do to you."

"Can I ask you something?"

"Yeah." I started copping an attitude, not knowing what was going to happen next. I just wanted to see if there were any broken bones.

"Did someone do this to you?"

"No," I blurted out.

"Baby, no fall from the stairs did this to you. It looks as if someone beat the hell out of you. Tell me who did this to you. Donna, you don't deserve this."

"No one. Please help me. My stomach is killing me, and my jaw feels as if it's barely holding on."

"Donna—if that's even your name—as a healthcare professional, it's my duty professionally and ethically to report this to Social Services." She picked up the phone and began dialing a number.

"Please, Ms. Carver, don't call Social Services. I have my little sister and Teresa to watch over. I'll tell you anything you want to know. Please, I'm begging you not to break up my family. We can't go to foster care." I got on my hands and knees, with my head at the top of her left shoe.

Chapter 5

After talking to Ms. Carver for a little over an hour and pouring out my heart to her about Teresa, Kiki, Ma's drug abuse, and Pop not being around, she reluctantly decided to not call Social Services, but gave me plenty of names and numbers of centers that Kiki, Teresa, and I could go to.

Ms. Carver walked back into my room, where I waited on the results of the X-rays, a Cherry Coke in one hand and lemon cookies in the other.

"Yana, thank the Lord, nothing is broken. The doctor is going to come to examine you to see if we can give you something for the pain. We have free samples here at the clinic I can give you."

"Is he going to call Social Services?" I asked, my lip poked out.

"No. I told him I ruled out abuse. But if I ever see you back here or in the streets looking like this again, I will report it to Social Services. You're only thirteen years old, really just a young girl, and at a vulnerable age where you need your mother the most. She's just using you as a punching bag because a man doesn't want her. Remember, you don't have to take her shit. Please excuse me for cursing.

"I'm going to give you my number. Call me anytime you need me. In return, I will need something from you."

"I don't have any money right now. I can pay you back with my lunch money."

"Baby, I don't want your lunch money. What I want in return is for you to promise me that you won't turn to drugs and follow in your mother's footsteps. I want you to make something of yourself." She grabbed my hand and gave me a gentle hug. "I promise." I wrapped myself in her arms and hoped Ma would never beat me again.

Chapter 6

By the age of sixteen, I painfully realized the only thing my mother loved was my father, and the only thing he loved was the streets and alcohol. Growing up, I did any and everything to impress her, but good grades, acting in plays, and receiving awards did nothing to faze her. God forbid if my father was upset with her; she'd barely speak to Kiki, Teresa, and me.

If only Pop loved Ma the way she needed to be loved, our lives would have been totally different. To cope with the pain of loving a man who didn't love her back, my mother went on several drug binges, and her drugs of choice were now heroin and crack. On average, four or five days would go by and we wouldn't see her. The longest she was ever gone for was sixteen days.

As the years went on, Ma lingered in the apartment on the first and the fifteenth of the month to collect her checks, and she'd occasionally throw me a fifty-dollar bill to buy food. She never used the food stamps on food. Apparently Ton, her supplier, took that as payment as well.

"Do you think we'll end up like Ma?" Kiki asked, clutching to her blanket with holes in it.

"No, we won't end up like her. Go to sleep. You know Ma

doesn't like to hear us make a sound when Uncle Fred is around," I explained, my lips quivering. Around nineteen times and counting, the lights had been cut off due to Ma not paying the bills. Three days ago, the heat was cut off, and Ma's only backup plan seemed to be a guy named Fred, who she made the three of us call *Uncle* Fred.

"She took both of the space heaters for herself. We're going to freeze tonight," Teresa whispered.

"Yeah, Ma and Uncle Fred are nice and warm in her bedroom," I stated.

That night, I couldn't barely sleep because Ma was making so many moans. We could hear her bed shake when they were having sex.

Chapter 7

Two years later Teresa and I graduated from Booker T. Washington High School. With the help of guidance counselors, Teresa and I were able to get into Hampton University on scholarships and school loans. Not wanting to leave Kiki behind with Ma, we'd planned on getting an apartment together. It was always going to be a battle getting Ma to let go of Kiki, since she still got a check for her. Plus, a large settlement was brewing for the death of Teresa's family, and Ma had her eyes on that too. For Teresa and me, the money train was going to run out in a month.

Neither Ma nor Pop showed up to my high school graduation. I guess they just didn't care. Kiki tried her best to keep our spirits up that day. I didn't allow myself to break down. All I knew was, I had to get from under Ma's grip and make something of myself and keep the promise to Ms. Carver.

Through the years, Ms. Carver was our role model as well as a mother, protector, and a friend. She was the one who uncovered a lot of scholarships for Teresa and me, saying, "There are a lot of free grants out there. All you have to do is apply for them."

In return for her kindness, I never wanted to let her down. She was so happy to meet Teresa and Kiki that very first time. On weekends, she bought us pizza, took us to the movies, the mall, the zoo, and treated us to manicures and pedicures. But most important, she taught us how to conduct ourselves as ladies.

Ma, ever since the first day she laid eyes on Ms. Carver, was always rude to her. Even though she treated us like shit, I could tell she was jealous of our newfound friend. A tiny part of me had Ms. Carver come around, just to get a reaction out of Ma, because I knew it bothered her. Someone else was stepping on her territory.

With my relentless nagging, Ms. Carver decided to quit that nasty habit of smoking, putting at least ten more years on her life. Now, I can't imagine how we lived without her.

There was a knock on the door. I didn't think nothing of it, because it was around the time that Uncle Fred usually showed his face.

"Ms. Carver, what are you doing here?" I asked after hugging her. I was so glad to see her.

"Hey, baby. How are you doing?"

"I'm good."

"Where's Kiki and Teresa hiding?"

"They're 'sleep. Those two can't stay awake for nothing." I giggled.

"Please go get your mother for me," she told me.

"All right."

After I knocked on her bedroom door several times, Ma came out to the living room.

"Well, if it isn't Carver gracing us with her presence. What could you possibly want at this time of night?" Ma coughed. For the last five days, she'd been wearing the same stain-covered shirt.

"This time of night and day has been a usual routine for you," Ms. Carver responded.

Ma laughed. "Oh, you finally figured it out."

"Yes, I have. I hired a private investigator to see exactly

where my husband has been spending so much time at. Helen, you knew this whole time and wasn't woman enough to tell me. You smile in my face while stabbing me in the back by screwing my husband."

"I didn't even know who you were until Fred told me about you."

"It's *Fredrick*," Ms. Carver corrected her.

"Well, round here, Fredrick likes to be called cougar in the bed. The funniest part of this whole situation is, Fred pays my bills, and you take my kids out and spend money on them. Money from your household is being trickled down to my household. By the way, in your living room, those pastel purple drapes are ugly."

Ms. Carver hit Ma so hard, she knocked her down. "Keep talking. I've had enough of your mouth. You may think you can bully these girls around, but you won't do the same to me." She smacked Ma in the face.

Ma quickly ran into the kitchen and got her knife. "Bitch, come on," Ma egged her on, knife in hand.

I came between them, not wanting either one to get hurt, and was trying my best to not get cut.

"The punch was for beating these girls down on a daily basis. The smack was for you screwing my husband. Stay away from him." Ms. Carver went up close to Ma.

"Please, Ma," I pleaded, "put the knife down before someone gets hurt."

Both of them continued to go at each other. The next thing I know, the knife grazed my arm, and blood was all over the living room carpet.

"Yana, baby, are you all right? Do you need to go to the hospital?" Ms. Carver asked, snapping out of her trance of kicking Ma's behind.

"I will be okay," I assured her. I quickly washed the cut off.

Ma was still trying to take swings at Ms. Carver. She didn't even care that she cut me. I was glad Kiki and Teresa slept through all the commotion, because they didn't need to see this.

"Call me if you need me. Yana, I'm so sorry about all of this. I never meant for you to get hurt," Ms. Carver said.

"Get the fuck out of my house!" Ma screamed. "These girls only have one mother, and it's not you. Come around here again, and I'll call the cops on you. You're not the first or the last married woman who's been cheated on."

"These girls are better off with me. You heard what I said— Stay away from my husband!" Ms. Carver walked out the door.

That night, I tossed and turned in my bed thinking about how small the world is.

Ma had no remorse for sleeping with Ms. Carver's husband. As long as Uncle Fred was giving her money, she would continue to sleep with him.

Ms. Carver was too nice of a person to be dealing with this. Despite everything that happened that night, I still wanted her in our lives.

Chapter 8

Kiki, Teresa and I weren't little girls anymore. Even though my hair was kinky, curly, and knotty, I used a straightening comb faithfully every week to tame it to being straight. Now it came down to my shoulders. Flipping through old pictures, I realized how beautiful Ma used to be, and where I got my brown-sugar skin tone and Coca-Cola-bottle shape. Now, her eyes looked sunken, and she was literally skin and bones, and had nasty sores all over her body.

Teresa kept her hair short and had an almond skin tone that was smooth to the touch. With her small waist and thick behind, guys went crazy for her.

Kiki was the wild one out of the bunch and was constantly dyeing her hair black, blond, red, or autumn brown. I was surprised her hair hadn't fallen out yet. She had her heart set on going to hair school and then opening up her own shop. She was thin but still carried a nice shape with her dark skin tone, which she got from Pop's side of the family. She looked just like him; there was no way he could deny her.

Lately, I'd been hearing a lot of talk from her about getting breast implants. Watching BET videos and mainly listening to Ma made her think she needed bigger melons. I told her to hold off until she got older, because she still might be grow-ing.

Over the years, Ma became harsher with us, not so much her hands but with her words. She stopped putting her hands on all of us once I took a stand and smacked her back after she smacked me because I forgot to tell her that Pop had called. I'd smacked her so hard, she tumbled into the dining room table and fell to the floor. Kiki and Teresa were too scared to stand up to her to let her know that those days of beating us were over, but I wasn't, and she knew it.

One thing Ma and I had in common was our feistiness. When she was at the apartment, we constantly heard that all men wanted were to use us for our bodies and go to the next one. My hate and resentment for Ma became stronger be-cause she loved to do anything to make us as miserable as she was.

Being the social butterflies that they were, Kiki and Teresa were too embarrassed to bring friends and guys over to the apartment. I either had my nose in a book, or was too wor-ried about putting food on the table, making sure the bills were paid on time, and finding bargains for clothes for the small amount of money Ma gave us for it.

When Ma realized that she never had to get off Section 8, she refused to get a job. Her job was getting Pop to come back to her.

Chapter 9

Determined to celebrate our high school graduation in style, I planned a fun night. As a graduation present, Ms. Carver set up a four-hour stroll with a limousine. After the principal called my name and Teresa's to walk across the stage and receive our high school diplomas, her mouth was the loudest I heard.

Last year, I'd started working part-time at Up Against the Wall, a trendy clothing store in Military Circle Mall. With four months of my paychecks, I'd managed to save money for tickets for the Nas concert at the Norfolk Scope tonight. Most of our friends were going. Plus, I was able to buy outfits fit for the occasion for Teresa, Kiki, and myself. Not being able to afford the real thing, I bought Gucci, Fendi, and Iceberg knockoffs.

God must have answered my prayer, because Ma was nowhere to be found while we were getting ready. We had less than an hour before the limousine would be waiting downstairs for us.

I'd picked up a black Iceberg dress for Kiki with open-toe heels, and a red purse to add color. Deep down, I knew she was going to be a trendsetter.

Teresa was excited about her brown Fendi shirt and matching skirt set, with cream heels and clutch bag to match. I chose to wear a grey Iceberg shirt and matching jeans, black Nike DC sneakers, and a black bag.

Tonight, I knew we were going to receive lots of attention, and I wanted the least of it. Trusting men was becoming an issue for me, so I had never let one get too close. Besides, I was too busy trying to figure out a better life for the three of us.

I was the first one ready and plopped myself next to the window to see when the limo would be pulling up to our apartment building. The phone rang. I was surprised it was even on. "Hello," I answered.

"Can I speak to Ms. Yana Parker, please?"

"Yes. This is she."

"Hi. This is Leonard, your limousine driver for the evening. I will be arriving in the next fifteen minutes," he responded.

I could hear the radio playing in the background. "Cool. We will be ready. Thank you. Bye-bye." *It must be nice to have a cell phone*, I thought, looking out of the window again.

"Teresa, Kiki, come on, let's go downstairs. The limo driver is going to be pulling up." Those two loved eyeing themselves in the mirror, and I didn't want it to make us late for tonight's festivities.

"Give us five more minutes," they insisted in unison.

The stretch white limousine was decked out with a car phone, radio, a CD player and a mini-bar. We were all going to feel like stars for the night. Teresa and Kiki poked their heads out of the roof window and started waving to people walking on the street.

"Yana, I thought we were heading to the concert," Teresa said after taking a seat next to me. "Why is the driver getting on the highway?"

I giggled. "I have a surprise for you two."

Kiki took her head out of the window. "What is it?"

"Do what you do best."

"What's that?" Teresa asked.

"Sit back and ride," I stated, cracking up with laughter.

Kiki poked her lip out. "Yana, stop playing."

"Kiki, pick your lip up. We're going to Red Lobster on Independence Boulevard in Virginia Beach."

"You mean the restaurant with the TV commercial about those shrimp we see all the time?" Teresa inquired.

"Yes." I nodded.

"Wow! I can't believe you're taking us there," Kiki added in disbelief.

"It will be good for us to get out of Norfolk, for a change of scenery."

"Red Lobster, here we come!" Teresa shouted.

After a thirty-five-minute wait, the anticipation of eating and the Nas concert was building up in all of us. Seeing it would be our first time there, we didn't know what to expect.

"Parker party of three, please," the hostess announced on the intercom.

"Come on, y'all," I stated, leading the pack.

"Right this way, ladies," the waiter suggested. "Hi. My name is Armando, and I'll be your waiter for the night. Tonight's special is almond-crusted trout and Asian glazed salmon." After we were seated in a spacious booth, he commented, "I must say, all of you ladies look so beautiful tonight."

"Thank you. We're celebrating our high school graduation," I responded with a huge grin on my face, pointing to Teresa and myself.

"Congratulations. What school did you graduate from?"

"Booker T. Washington High School," I blurted out.

"I'm going to do my best to start your night off right. What can I get everyone to start off for your drinks?"

"A Coke for me," I said.

"In your commercial, what is the drink called with the frozen strawberries?" Kiki asked.

"It's the strawberry daiquiri. It will come in handy, with such a hot night."

The temperature went into the low 90's today and the humidity wasn't going anywhere.

"A non-alcoholic one."

"Yeah, I want that," Kiki said.

"Lemonade for me," Teresa said.

A couple minutes later Armando returned. "Ladies, here are your drinks and cheddar biscuits. Are you ready to order?"

"Yes, we all want the fried shrimp, popcorn shrimp, and French fries combination," I responded.

"Great. Would you like salads or coleslaw with your meal?"

"A salad with ranch dressing for me. Plus, for an appetizer, we would like two orders of clam strips with lots of cocktail sauce."

"Coleslaw," Teresa and Kiki said in unison.

"All right, I'll get these orders going for you, ladies. It shouldn't be more than twenty minutes." Armando collected the menus from us.

We didn't bother to even look at them, because we knew what we wanted as soon as we hit the front door.

"Is anyone sitting here?" a voice inquired after our food arrived at the table.

It was none other than Nathan, a guy from around the neighborhood. He was at least six feet, had pearly white teeth, bulging muscles, and the skin tone of a Mounds coconut bar. Ever since we were in the seventh grade together, he had been trying to pursue me. I did have a small crush on him, but didn't want to bring him in my world of drama and pain, so I pushed him away.

Nathan worked out relentlessly and was even a quarterback on the high school football team. All of a sudden, he dropped out in junior year. The rumor around the school was, he was selling drugs. From the way he was decked out in Iceberg from head to toe, and his platinum cross necklace and bracelet to match, I wouldn't have been surprised if the rumor was true.

"Hey, Nathan," I responded.

"How are y'all ladies doing tonight?" he asked, rubbing his two hands together, his eyes all on me.

"We're fine," Teresa said.

"Yana, it was a lovely thing to see you walk across the stage today."

"Thanks."

"Did you just get here?" Kiki nudged me in the leg.

"Nah, me and my boys just got finished eating a ton of crab legs. We were sitting on the other side of the restaurant. Yeah, in a little while, we're heading to the Nas concert."

"We're going too."

"Maybe I'll see you there. Yana, I gotta run, but I went ahead and took care of the whole bill, and the tip."

"Thank you." No one had ever done anything like that for me, and I thought it was way over the top.

"Yana, call me," he added with a cocky attitude. He jotted his number down on a crisp hundred-dollar bill and handed it to me, not wanting to let go of my hand.

"I will."

"Bye for now. Here's a little change, just in case you ladies wanted something to eat or drink at the concert," Nathan explained, just as his cell phone started to vibrate. Then he headed to the foyer of the restaurant and walked out.

Nas gave a hell of a show. Thousands of people, along with Teresa, Kiki, and me, were singing to the songs. My favorite was "If I Ruled the World," featuring Lauryn Hill.

We ran into Nathan, but he was drunk, and too many girls

were up in his face. I thought to myself while riding back home, *I may call him, but do I really want to even think about getting involved with a guy who sells drugs?*

Kiki and Teresa wasted no time talking to guys, getting numbers and giving out theirs. The concert ran over, and I didn't want us to take the bus home. So, with the extra money that I had left over because Nathan took care of the restaurant tab, I paid for an extra hour ride around the city in the limousine before we went home.

"Y'all, I had the best time and will never forget this day," Teresa announced, nearly drenched in sweat.

"Me too." Kiki smiled.

"We have to go out more often," I said as I put the key in the apartment door.

As soon as I walked in, I heard a loud noise, almost as if a body was slammed against the wall. Ma and Pop were fighting again—more like Pop was beating the hell out of Ma, and she was just taking it.

Once again, I heard him slam her body up against the wall. Ma wasn't aware that I knew she had a stolen loaded 9 mm with a silencer hidden in the pantry in a bag of sugar on the top shelf. With crooks breaking in these apartments almost every other night, she had to get some type of protection. Kiki and Teresa froze at the front door. I motioned for them to come in quietly, and I gently shut the door.

Since I was tall enough, I quickly grabbed the gun from the bag of sugar, and hid it behind my back. Ma's bedroom door was halfway cracked.

Pop screamed at the top of his lungs, "Bitch, I'm tired of you following me everywhere I go! Look at you—you're fucking pathetic! These girls are all going to grow up just like you—a straight-up ho." He punched Ma in the face so hard, I saw her blood splatter on the wall.

"Why do you still come around here?" Ma pleaded.

"If I don't have shit else to do, then of course I'll come to get some free pussy, food, and beer. You tried to trap me by having Yana. Bitch, you knew we were just fooling around, and you tried to ruin my life. Next thing I know, Kiki comes along . . . if she is even mine."

"They're your kids. I have never slept with nobody else." Ma tried to wipe the blood off her face with her hands.

"Yana is mine; but Kiki ain't mine. I ain't taking care of no kids that ain't mine."

"You don't take care of Yana," Ma whimpered.

"I've been telling you for years—I'm not the marrying type or the family man."

"Listen, baby, they all will be leaving eventually to go off to college. After they're gone, it can just be you and I, just like old times."

"You will never be my woman ever again. I don't want a cracked-out needle-shooting ho!" Pop picked up the iron off the ironing board and hit Ma on the right side of her head, and she collapsed on the floor and lay there unconscious.

I was hoping she wasn't dead. "Don't put your hands on Ma anymore," I declared, taking a stand and entering into the room. By this time, I could hear Teresa and Kiki nudging closer and closer to the bedroom.

"Stay the hell out of this, Yana. This is between me and your momma." The blood-drenched iron in his left hand in position to hit her again, he turned around to face me.

"Leave her alone," Kiki hissed, her and Teresa standing behind me for cover.

"All you ever do is beat on Ma, spit on her, and put her down. All she wants is to make you feel good. She loves you more than she loves herself and us put together. Ma would do anything for you.

"Pop, you were never a real daddy to us. I don't even know why we call by the name *Pop*. We should be calling you by your real name, *Pete*, like everybody else calls you," I yelled.

"It's not my job to be your daddy. Didn't nobody tell your

hardheaded momma to have y'all. The truth be told, I wanted to get rid of both of y'all because I didn't want no kids." Pop smirked with a devilish grin.

I knew exactly how Pop operated. He was feeling challenged by me. I refused to let him break me down as he had done to Ma over and over again. "Huh? You wanted to get rid of us? What have you done to contribute to society?"

"Girl, what the hell are you talking about? I can't even understand what you're saying. I been told your momma to stop wasting her time, and stop letting y'all read books with big words in them. In case you haven't figured it out, folks don't talk like that around here," Pop screamed, his foul breath reeking of alcohol.

I was getting a kick out of getting under his skin. "My point exactly, Pete. Your ass is fucking lazy! You've been in and out of jail for years. Yeah, you say you don't want a job. The truth is, you can't get a job. Once employers figure you can't read, who the hell would want to hire you, a forty-year-old illiterate drunk." I laughed.

"Shut up!"

"Go ahead, Pop, there's a book on top of the bed. Read the first sentence. Can you even sound out the first word? Years ago, Ma begged you to take a class for illiterate people. Are you able to say the word *il-lit-er-ate*? After a while, she stopped trying because every time she asked, instead of a simple no, she would get a smack in the face or on the lip. I was young, but I remember more than you think."

"Your momma must have taught you to have a nasty attitude. Once I get done with her, you won't have a momma to teach you anything no more," Pop responded with embarrassment and rage. He turned around to hit her in the head once again.

I knew he wasn't going to stop. Closing my eyes, I fired two shots. Within seconds, I'd gathered enough courage to open my eyes, only to find Pop lying on the floor. One shot went in between his eyes, and the other shot went into his throat. He had a look of disbelief on his face I will never forget.

For at least thirty minutes, I sat on the bed holding Kiki and Teresa in my arms while all of us were crying. I'd killed my father. Nothing was going to bring him back. Worst of all, Ma would never forgive me for taking away the only love of her life.

Anger, sadness, relief, shame, and fear consumed my body. I felt anger because Pop never told us once that he loved us. Not even one hug or kiss of fatherly affection. Sadness lingered in my heart because he was gone forever. Relief surfaced because I knew he could never put his hands on Ma again; shame, for the way Pop treated all of us, especially my mother. A real man can't possibly treat the woman in his life in such a disrespectful way. Fear came tumbling down in my mind because I didn't want Ma or the police finding out.

Not to mention, my life was only just beginning. I didn't want to go to jail for someone who didn't give a shit about me. What if I had to spend the rest of my life in a jail cell fantasizing about what I *could* have become?

Thankfully, Ma was still unconscious. Since the gun had a silencer on it, it was more than likely that no one heard any gunshots.

"What are we going to do now?" Kiki whimpered, dried tears on her face and her nose running.

"Kiki, get a towel to wipe Pop's blood up. Once you're finished, get a knife and try your best to get the bullets out. Then pick up that can of paint from under the sink in the kitchen and quickly touch up the two bulletholes in the wall."

"Okay," she responded quickly, and went into action.

"Teresa, go into the pantry and get as many trash bags as you can, so we can wrap Pop's body up. His body is too big to fit into two bags, so cut the ends of the bags. After we cover up his whole body, we can tie the ends of the trash bags into knots."

"Where are we going to take him?" she asked.

"Behind the building . . . there's a deep forest where no one hardly goes. We can take him out there and dig a hole. I'm going to get that medium-size shovel that Ma uses to plant flowerpots on the patio.

"Since the apartment is the first floor, we can use the back door to get out. Once I start digging, you two can be the lookout for me." I rummaged through Pop's pants pockets to get his ID. If someone found his body, without an ID, it would be harder to identify him. I made a mental note to throw his ID into the Dumpster, but first I needed a pair a scissors.

After we finished our tasks, I got up the nerve to check on Ma. Her frail body lay on the floor. She was still breathing. I picked up a pillow off her bed and placed it under her head. Ma despised hospitals. There had been plenty of times I begged her to go after Pop gave her a beating, but she always refused. Even though Ma knew she needed the medical attention, she didn't want Social Services or the police getting involved in our lives.

We carried Pop's heavy body into the woods. It was a humid night, and the mosquitoes were out to feast upon anyone they could get close to. Adrenaline and fear gave us the strength to carry him the forty yards from the building. He was every bit of two hundred and thirty pounds. Thankfully, we didn't spot anyone.

Kiki was the lookout for me. "How much longer are you going to dig?"

"Just a few more digs." I wiped the sweat from my face. "How long have I been digging?" I asked, wishing we had another shovel.

Teresa looked at her watch. "Over an hour."

Once I finished, we pushed Pop's body into the hole. Then I started to fill the hole with dirt. We all started to cry again. It was so final. Pop was really gone. I couldn't believe that I killed him. Was I going to hell? Would I have bad luck for the rest of my life? Would I feel the evil presence of him everywhere I went? Many thoughts, questions, and potential outcomes raced through my mind.

Finally, I patted down the dirt-filled hole and instructed Teresa and Kiki to sit down on the ground. I wanted them to hear me out. At the least, I owed them an explanation for my actions. I sat on the ground next to them and held their hands.

"Kiki, Teresa, I don't blame you if you hate me for the rest of your lives. I was so sick and tired of seeing Ma take those beatings over and over again," I whimpered, tears streaming down my face. "For years, you two couldn't see it, but I had a lot of hate and resentment in my heart"—I pointed to my heart—"for this man."

"You did what you had to do." Teresa squeezed my hand, letting me know she was on my side.

I looked at her. "Especially you, Teresa, you've been through enough already, with your family being gone."

"Kiki and you are all the family I got, and all the family I need. Yana, I know you'll always look out for both of us and give me your last if I needed it. Tonight, you took me out when you could have kept the money or spent it on yourself. That's love right there," she said, tears in her eyes.

"Sorry to say, but with him gone, we will all be better off." Kiki shook her head from side to side. "The other day, I overheard him and Ma talking about Teresa's settlement. I got the feeling that was another reason for him to stick around the house—to cash in and benefit from the money. How could a man be so evil and not give a fuck about nobody?"

"Neither of you have to worry about that. In four months, Teresa will be eighteen, and the money will go to her . . . little does Ma's money-hungry ass know. Let's worry about that later. From this day forth, we have a pact that is unbreakable. I love you two with all my heart. No matter where life takes us, we will always be there for each other. We will never discuss with anyone, or utter another word about what happened tonight. Agreed?"

"Agreed," Teresa and Kiki announced in unison with low voices.

We stood up and gave one another hugs.

On the way back to the apartment, I wrapped the pieces of Pop's newly cut up ID in a small black plastic bag and threw it in the Dumpster, and tossed his wallet in there. The only thing in it was a stale piece of Wrigley's spearmint gum and an old scratched-out lottery ticket.

Chapter 10

Halfway to the back door of the apartment building, a familiar voice called out, gently clapping his hands, "Job well done, girls."

It was Ton, our mother's drug supplier. Through the years, we saw him way more often than Pop. Ma certainly was a loyal customer. Plus, he'd seen Ma hit me around a few times. Though he was usually nice to us, deep down, I despised him for giving Ma heroin and crack. She was literally dying before our eyes, while his drug empire was getting bigger and stronger. Yeah, Ma only put a small sum in building his money, but think of her, times thousands of other people who had also been with him for years.

Ton was dressed in Enyce and smelled of Issey Miyake. Bald and about five foot nine, I'd guess he was in the mid-thirties.

When I'd first met him as a little girl, I worked up the nerve to ask, "Why do you go by the name *Ton*? He explained growing up as a fat kid wasn't easy, and that the neighborhood kids came up with the nickname.

"What are you talking about?" I inquired, trying my best to play it off, even though I was carrying a shovel in my right hand. Kiki and Teresa didn't dare say anything. Suddenly, I had the urge to pee in my pants.

"Well, let me see, Yana. I'm guessing your father is in the ground in a freshly dug hole. Before y'all came home, I stopped by to drop off some *candy* to your mother and other loyal fans. When I got to the apartment, your pops and her were going at it as usual. After I finished my errands in the building, I had to take a piss and ran to the back of the building, where I saw the three of you carrying out something.

"Listen, you don't have to explain. I thought your pops was a piece of shit anyway. Everyone knew how much your mother loved him. She used candy to ease the pain of her heart. Now, being the businessman that I am, I'm sure we can all make some type of arrangement where everyone can be happy." Ton winked at me out of his right eye. "Ladies, please step into my office," he broadcasted, leading us back to where Pop's body was.

While we were walking back, I was getting more worried about Ma. *Did she wake up yet?*

"What do you want, Ton?" I inquired, giving Kiki and Teresa a look to not say a word.

We weren't going to admit to anything. I'd watched too many crime and court shows that perpetrated time and time again, it's not what you know, it's what you can prove. Deep down, I felt responsible for dragging them into this mess. I tried my best to stay calm. To make him go away, and ensure the safety of my sisters, I was willing to fuck him. That's probably what he wanted anyway. Just one night, I was hoping.

"All I want is a small arrangement among the four of us. You see, girls, tonight was a celebration. It will be my last night."

Teresa and Kiki looked terrified and confused.

I just wanted to appease his request, so we could get the hell on with our lives. "Last night for what?" I questioned with a touch of irritation, not liking when people talk to me in riddles.

"It's my last night to make drop-offs for my fans. Plus, I won't be directly be taking care of anyone who don't want to pay, or people I have problems with, if you know what I mean."

"Where do we fit in?" I inquired with my hands up. My skin was getting sticky from sweating so much.

"This is the first night that y'all have ever killed. It certainly won't be your last. As a payment, for my hush-hush, I want the three of you to get rid of a few of my enemies. Think of it as you all cleaning up the city streets. No one will ever guess three girls from the hood will be my best assassins.

"Now, first thing is first. Go check on one of my best fans, your mother." Then he added, "In two days, meet me at the public library in JANAF at ten o'clock in the morning."

"We won't kill for you," I shot back at him. I couldn't believe he asked us to do something so evil and vicious.

"These people you want to kill have families," Kiki told him. "What about them?"

"Cut it with the questions. I'm going to be the only one asking questions right now. Is it cool to do what I have asked of you, or do I need to go to the cops to confirm my suspicions that y'all brutally killed your father?" he asked while pressing the numbers, 9-1-1, into his cell phone.

"Put the phone down," I said. "It won't be necessary. We will be there."

"Good deal. See you then. By the way, pack a few bags. Y'all need to get out of the hood for a while."

"So we are clear, how many little favors are we required to do?"

"Just a few." Ton motioned for us to walk back to the building. He walked us back to our apartment, shook each of our hands, and left.

I didn't know how to take him. All I wanted to do was take a hot shower and have some time to think. My life was turning into a bigger nightmare.

Teresa shook her head. "I can't kill innocent people."

"I don't either," I said to her, "but we need to weigh our options."

"Going to jail isn't an option for any one of us. Maybe we should leave and move to California. It's way on the other side of the United States, and no one will know us."

"With what money can we get to California?" I had to remind her. "Teresa, we have full scholarship at Hampton University. I didn't work so hard for A's and B's to end up like Ma or in a jail cell."

"You're right," she said.

"Let's do what Ton wants and move on with our lives," Kiki said. "I can't take this pressure of him going to the cops."

"So are you all in agreement to go along with Ton's plan?"

"Yes," Teresa and Kiki said, nodding their heads.

Chapter 11

Sleep didn't come for any of us that night. We spent the wee hours of the morning cleaning off Ma, slowly placing her onto her bed, watching over her, and making sure there wasn't anything else to clean up.

Ma woke up the next morning in her bed with the worst headache. Teresa had her usual pain medication and an ice-cold Pepsi waiting by the nightstand by the bed for her. By this time, we'd washed her face to get off the caked blood. While Teresa and I entertained Ma, Kiki went to wash our clothes from last night at the corner Laundromat. I didn't want to give Ma any hints as to the true events of last night.

Getting out of the bed to use the bathroom, she asked, "What happened? Did you see your father leave?"

"Ma, we didn't see him. We came back from the concert, and you were on the floor covered in blood. Pop was gone."

"Damn it," she said through slightly cracked bathroom door. "I made your father so angry. The last thing I remember is him hitting me with the iron. He has never done that before."

After brushing her teeth and coming out of the bathroom, Ma gently rubbed the bright red gash on the side of her head. She turned to look at the bloody iron on the floor. She opened her can of soda to take the painkillers.

"How do you feel?" I asked her.

"Clean off that iron for me. I need a hit. Girl, you got any money? It's going to be another seven days before those checks reach the mailbox."

I shrugged my shoulders. "Ma, I don't have any money." I headed to the bathroom and reached for the nearest wash-cloth to wipe off the iron.

"I'm sure that nurse friend of yours gave y'all something for graduating."

"Did you give us anything?" I was still angry and hurt at the fact that she didn't even congratulate Teresa and me. Now, she was begging us for money that someone else gave us. Besides, it wasn't unusual these days for the two of us to go at it on a regular basis.

"Anyway, what time did y'all fast-ass tails get in here last night?" Ma asked, completely ignoring my last comment.

"Around midnight," Teresa said.

I came out of the bathroom. "On Monday, we're going on a college seminar trip," I said, changing the subject. "I would like to take Kiki with us."

"Where are you going?"

"Hampton," I answered.

"Good. It's about time. Y'all need to get the hell up out my house. As long as you have Teresa back in a month, that's fine." She looked right into Teresa's eyes. "A court-appointed attorney wants to talk to you."

"For what?" Teresa asked.

"That money is coming soon, and it's all due to me. I've been taking care of your ass all these years when I could've left you out on the street. All you have to do is tell the man how good I've been taking care of you. That's all. Now, leave me alone. I've got to take a shower, shoot up, and find your father. I messed up big this time. I'm going to fix his favorite tonight—fried fish and okra with buttermilk mashed pota-toes," she announced, heading back into the bathroom.

Chapter 12

As planned, Ton picked us up at the library on time. Not knowing how truly long we'd be gone, we packed a few bags. Yesterday, I wanted to call Ms. Carver and let her know what was going on. I knew she wouldn't have hesitated to get me the best lawyer. But instead of having the police and the courts dangle my life before my eyes, I took a chance with Ton.

"Morning, ladies," he greeted us as we hopped into a beat-up green Dodge Neon.

"Hey," Kiki and Teresa responded.

"Good morning," I said. "So where are we going, and for how long?"

"Yana, be patient. First, we're going to grab breakfast from Waffle House. We'll eat at my house. Teresa, I want you to be the one to go in, order the food, and pay." Ton reached in his pocket for a twenty-dollar bill.

Ton's house, located near Lynnhaven Parkway in Virginia Beach, was in a new development named Acredale Estates. It was a huge six-bedroom, four-bathroom that included a spacious kitchen, office, fish tank, swimming pool, Jacuzzi, sunroom, and a big backyard with a fence, not to mention a sophisticated security system, and four ferocious dogs.

I could tell he took much pride in his 52-inch television. It was one of the first things he mentioned about the house. He was trying to play it cool, but he got excited showing off his toys that he had in the three-car garage—two Kawasaki motor-cycles, a pair of Jet Skis, a walnut-brown 4-door Lexus and black Jaguar with rims.

I guess this is what all that drug money went to, I thought. "You have a nice home," I stated as we were eating breakfast in the kitchen. Kiki and Teresa were starting to relax, but I continued to have my guard up.

"This is the kind of house you see on that show for the rich and famous." Teresa was amazed at the size of the home.

Ma never wanted and couldn't afford a house. She said it was too much responsibility. As I thought of Ma's remarks, I realized all she wanted was to be close to Pop, even if that meant keeping us in a drug-infested building. I was hoping that none of us would turn out to be as selfish.

We were never close to Ma's family. They lived in the Ghent area of Norfolk and had high hopes for Ma. She would have been following in her mother's footsteps as a service representative in the Social Security Administration. According to Ma, government jobs were hard to come by. Her parents disowned her after they saw she wasn't going to leave Pop and get off welfare. When our more-than-absent grand-parents did visit us, they turned their noses up at us, looking at Kiki and me as evil spawns.

Five years ago, our maternal grandmother died of ovarian cancer. Instead of going to the funeral to pay her respects, Ma was walking the streets looking for Pop because they'd had a fight the night before. Since then, we haven't heard from the grandfather at all. Even holiday cards stopped coming.

Pop's family was even more dysfunctional. His mother died of a drug overdose, and his father was in Greensville Correctional Center, serving a life sentence for murder. From what Ma told me, Pop had a sister that wanted nothing to do with him. After all these years, she probably didn't even know about us.

"I know I got a gorgeous house. I'm not done picking out a few more pieces of furniture though," he said, cutting his waffle with a knife.

After we finished eating, Ton directed us back into the living room. "Let's get down to business," he declared. "For the next three weeks, I'm going to train each of you to kill with a gun. On July Fourth weekend, there's going to be a huge blowout party at Powder, a club along the oceanfront. A lot of out-of-towners will be in the area. Your targets are going to be Juan and Rick." Ton showed us two surveillance pictures.

My stomach was queasy as we began to take orders from him. I still couldn't believe we were going through with it. Killing innocent people wasn't supposed to be on the list of accomplishments. "Is the club twenty-one and up?" I asked. "If so, how are we going to get in?"

"Leave that up to me. Each one of y'all are getting fake ID's." He reached for a camera on the coffee table. "Say cheese!"

"I want my picture to look cute." Kiki giggled after posing for the camera.

"Yes, it will. Kiki, I want you to work on makeup, outfits, wigs, and hairstyles for the three of you. It's your thing." Ton smirked.

"Teresa, you're the man magnet. I want you and Kiki to start being regulars at the club. When it goes down, someone is less likely to think anything. Does anyone have questions?"

"I don't have a question," Teresa announced, "but I do have a comment."

Ton nodded. "Go ahead, I'm listening."

"I can't do this. I don't know if I'll be able to live with myself, knowing we killed innocent people."

"These people aren't innocent."

"That's what you say. I don't think I can go on with the rest of my life with their blood on my hands," Kiki told him.

"Ladies, your decision. Remember, every decision you make has consequences. Now, let's take a trip to the nearest police station."

"No, let me talk to them privately," I begged. "Give us a minute."

"Take all the time you need," Ton insisted before heading to the bathroom.

"I won't do this," Kiki said, crying.

"I'm scared," Teresa whimpered.

"We've come too far to go to jail over Pop, who didn't even care about us or love us. If anything happens, I will take the blame for Pop's death and the lives that Ton wants us to end."

"You can't do that," Teresa pleaded.

"Two is better than none of us making a better life for ourselves. Promise me that you'll let me take the blame."

"Okay," they agreed in unison.

Ton came back into the living room. "So . . . have you reached a final decision?"

"Yes, we'll do it," I announced.

"Good. Now, let's back down to business. Yana, you're the thinker of the group. After Kiki and Teresa have gone to the club a few times, I want you to go to stake out the place. Here is a layout of the club. You can see where the bathrooms, bars, stairs, chairs, tables, pool tables, and the dance floor are." Ton directed us to the easel.

"Wow, it's a big club," I said.

"That's my point exactly. Y'all have plenty of space to work your magic. Next, we're going to work on getting driver's licenses. Study the book carefully. Y'all only have two days to read before we go to take the test." Ton handed each of us a driver's manual. "Today and every day, we will practice with guns—I prefer guns with silencers."

I said, "Why choose us? You could have walked away from what you thought you saw. You could have gotten professionals."

"Two days ago, I saw an opportunity. Not to mention, I can train y'all the way I want. Here's five hundred dollars for each of you. Teresa and Yana, save it for those books you're going to need at Hampton. I hear they cost a lot. Kiki, don't spend it all in one day. We have a lot to get through today. Let's go to Lynnhaven Mall for a shopping spree. Remind me to pick up cell phones for y'all. All I ask for in return is your loyalty." He dangled his car keys in his hand after he gave us the money.

On the way there, I thought, *Ton knows a lot about us.*

Chapter 13

At the DMV, Kiki and I passed our drivers' written and driving tests on the first try, but it took Teresa three tries, I guess because she was so nervous. Ton had been making us drive everywhere we went now.

A week had passed since we left the apartment. We were at the gun range practicing shooting on everything from a .22-caliber pistol to a shotgun. The bigger the gun fired, the bigger the sound. Even with the hearing protection, it killed my ears, leaving a nagging ringing in my ear. Every time I aimed at a target, I thought about Pop and the horrible things he'd done to Ma.

"Come on, Kiki, you got to at least try to shoot the gun," Ton told her. "It's the smallest one they have in the place."

"I can't," she said, sobbing.

This was our fourth day here, and Ton did the same thing, trying to steer Kiki to shoot the gun.

"Try one time." I stood behind her and gently rubbed her shoulders to relax her.

"Okay, I will," she said reluctantly, and fired the .22 pistol one time.

Next thing I know, she collapsed on the ground.

After five minutes of uncertainty and fear, not knowing if she was going to get up or not, Kiki finally woke up.

"What happened?" she whispered, her head in my lap.

"You fainted. We're getting out of here," I told her.

Ton and I picked her up.

I made sure my wig wasn't falling out of place. Every time the four of us ventured out, it was in disguise.

After getting back to Ton's place, we laid Kiki on the grey leather couch. She began to cry even more. I knew why she was crying. We all knew why she was crying. With everything going on and being at Ton's mercy, one of us was bound to break down at some point.

"Listen up, Kiki can't be shooter. I get that now. I don't want you to be in this kind of state. Baby girl, just be a lookout for Teresa and Yana, all right," Ton said, sounding genuinely concerned about her.

"Okay," she said, nodding her head.

"Y'all go ahead and take a dip in the pool. Maybe it will help everyone to relax. I know these few days haven't been easy for any of you. Especially for you, Yana. I know your mother gave you a hard time, always beating the hell out of you, and didn't give a damn about who saw.

"Whatever you're thinking, I'm not the monster you think I am. Our lives have similar stories. My pops used to beat me, too, coming home from a bad day at work or drunk from a bar. One day, just like you, I took a stand for him beating on my mother. Unfortunately, my moms was standing right there and saw me stab him. The same day, she disowned me at the age of eleven. Too young to get charged with any real crime, I was shipped off to a juvenile detention home for boys. I never looked at women quite the same, until I was adopted by a woman named Dottie, who gave me a good home," he explained, not shedding one tear.

Kiki, Teresa, and I just started sobbing. It was somewhat

comforting to know someone could relate to what we'd been through all these years.

I was tired after two hours in the pool. (Bathing suits were among the many outfits Ton picked up for us at the mall.)

Later on that night, Ton fired up the grill for a backyard feast. We had barbecue ribs and chicken, grilled shrimp, steak, baked potatoes, and corn on the cob. For dessert, we pigged out on a sweet watermelon.

After everyone had gone to sleep, I stayed up thinking. *Maybe Ton isn't so bad*. Each one of us was given our own rooms to sleep in. The beds were all king-size and totally different from the cramped twin beds at Ma's house. I was hoping we would never have to go back there. At this point, I didn't care about her deadline for having Teresa back.

Chapter 14

July Fourth weekend came too quickly. Ton made us practice the plan five times. The .22-caliber pistols with silencers were tucked tightly in the crotch of Teresa's and my
panties, as we drove in the Honda Accord he had given us to
drive. The both of us were wearing black leather pants. Her
bebe top was purple, and mine was red. Kiki, on the other
hand, had her ass and titties hanging out in a Fendi dress.

Lights, camera, action, I thought as we approached the
club.

About forty people were ahead of us in line. While we waited,
Kiki, Teresa, and I were making small talk. During this whole
process, Ton had insisted that we not disguise ourselves, so
we could blend in with the crowd.

"'Sup, Ms. Lady," the security guard recited to me, as he
did to the other women in front of us.

Ton approached him after leaving his Jaguar with valet
parking. He loved that car and washed it every chance he
got. "What's up?"

"Hey, Ton, the boss told me you would be coming through
tonight."

"Yeah, it's Fourth of July weekend, and I came to have
some fun." Ton grinned, pointing to Kiki.

"I hear that. Come right on in." Miles moved the red velvet rope to allow Ton in.

"All right, these three ladies, let them through. Man, they're the first three good-looking things I've seen tonight. It's been a hell of a day." Ton handed Miles a hundred-dollar bill and pointed to us.

"Thanks." I smiled at Ton.

"Sure. Girls, step right in," Miles told us, and we walked in.

Ton spotted some of his friends and started talking to them.

It was blazing hot inside the dark club, because so many people were in there. "Ruff Ryders' Anthem" was playing so loud, I could barely hear. Kiki went straight to the bar, two guys in hot pursuit of her ass, and people were getting pissy drunk.

Teresa walked around while I went to the bathroom. After I got into the bathroom stall, I gently pulled the gun from my panty crotch and placed it in my handbag. When I came out, Teresa went in and did the same thing.

An hour had passed, and people continued to bump into me. After forty-five minutes in the building, Kiki was to step outside the club and calmly walk back to the car and wait for us.

I looked at my watch. We had ten minutes to go. Even though Teresa and I were on opposite sides of the club, we kept close eye contact with each other. I waved to her like a girlfriend I hadn't seen in a while, to give the cue to get the guns in position and finish the job. Juan and Rick were on opposite sides of the club. Rick was standing by the pool area with an entourage of ten people, including half-naked girls. His back was turned to me, and he was laughing.

I aimed at his heart and pulled the trigger. Then I kept walking. Teresa was walking back to the entrance of the club. *Did Teresa get Juan?* I thought.

I found Ton holding a drink in his hand and bobbing his

head to the music. He was still talking to his friends. I moved in closer toward him and shot him in his lower chest. Out of the corner of my eye, I saw Ton fall to his knees.

The double doors of the entrance were in sight now. We finally walked out of the building, took a deep breath, and continued to walk to the car.

Kiki had already started the Honda. "Y'all made it!" she said as I shut the passenger door.

I looked at Teresa. "Did you get Juan?"

"I shot him in the back of his head."

"I got both Rick and Ton!" I declared. "We did it!" I announced as Kiki was approaching Interstate 64. *Now we can move on with our lives.*

Chapter 15

"Sh! Sh! I need to hear this," I said to Kiki and Teresa, pointing to the television.

"*This is Mya Roland, reporting live for News Channel 13. I am standing in front of the popular club, Powder, by the oceanfront. Last night, two men, Juan Martinez and Rick Soleth, were gunned down in the club, and a third was severely wounded. The police have not yet released his name. Dozens of club patrons have been questioned, and the police have not yet come up with any leads. The club owner has assured me he will be stepping up security to prevent this from happening again. Both Martinez and Soleth were facing federal drug charges. We will definitely be following this case. This is Mya Roland, reporting live from Virginia Beach. Back to you, Nancy.*"

Kiki and Teresa begged me to turn the channel back to BET so they could watch videos. We all felt a huge weight had been lifted off our shoulders. Still, a part of us felt bad.

Those men probably had families, I thought, my head down as I sat in the chair. "I'm glad nobody thinks anything."

"When can we go back to Ton's house?" Kiki asked

"When he calls." I quickly took a peek at my cell phone to

see if I had missed any calls. We were crashing at the Clarion Hotel, off Bonney Road in Virginia Beach.

To get our minds off the murders, we grabbed most of our clothes and belongings from the apartment. Luckily, Ma wasn't there. She did leave Teresa a note to call the lawyer, and to let her know if we spot Pop. Driving away, I didn't bother to look back.

Next, we drove to Hampton University to take a tour of the campus. It turned out Teresa, Kiki, and I would be staying with each other in a nearby three-bedroom apartment. Another student was supposed to stay with us but dropped out at the last minute. The apartment was small, but I was grateful for anything.

Thankfully, our grants and scholarships would be taking care of the rent, books, and the tuition. Teresa's major was education, and mine was pre-law. All we had to do was hold up our end of the bargain and at least maintain a 2.0 average. Of course, Teresa and I were going to make higher grades than that, since our goal was to consistently stay on the A and B grade average.

We needed so much stuff to make our apartment feel like a real home, but didn't have enough money to buy what we wanted. For example, furniture, lamps, just to name a few, were on my wish list.

On the drive back to Virginia Beach, I was thinking about where I could get a job. Once school started, I would be quitting Up Against the Wall. We decided to go to Burger King for my favorite comfort food—a Coke, bacon cheeseburger, and an order of onion rings with lots of ketchup.

Finally, we headed over to Wal-Mart to pick up some needed school supplies. School didn't start for another month, but I wanted to be ahead of the game.

My cell phone rang. It was now ten o'clock in the evening.

I looked at the caller ID. It was you know who. "Hello," I answered.

"Hey. Are y'all all right?" Ton asked.

"We're fine. How about you?"

"I'm good. I was just checking on you. Enjoy your evening," Ton said.

"Okay, you too," I replied, and pressed the end button on the phone.

Chapter 16

The remark, *enjoy your evening*, was the code for us to come back to the house in four days, to let the heat of the situation die down.

We spent the next four days at the indoor hotel pool, shopping a little, opening bank accounts, and going to the movies. No Ma in my ear, no stress, just the way I liked it.

On the way to Waffle House, we picked up a late breakfast for the three of us. It was going on noon.

The week before the shooting, when the girls went to sleep, Ton and I would sit in the sunroom and talk. He even showed me his extensive gun collection in the basement. His real name was Lucas Costen, and he was thirty-four years old. He was the only child and vaguely remembered the family that did come around his mother's house. Ton refused to ever look at, or talk to, his mother again. His hatred was much deeper than mine for Ma.

He'd been selling drugs since the age of sixteen, along with Rick and Juan. His clients ranged from people like Ma, to college students, to prominent judges, attorneys, politicians, and doctors. His adopted mother, Dottie, acted as if she didn't know anything and didn't even question it when he paid off the mortgage on her house. She was in denial.

Rick, Juan, and Ton had a drug ring that went sour. Some low-level soldiers, as Ton called them, were running their mouths in Rick and Juan's camp. Federal indictments were about to drop, and Ton didn't want to have his operation exposed. With Juan and Rick out of the way, Ton stood to inherit their clients and even more money.

I kept this tidbit of information to myself to protect Kiki and Teresa. What they didn't know wouldn't hurt them. I had to admit, Ton was growing on me. Teresa and Kiki were probably noticing the chemistry between us.

Ton greeted us at the door with open arms, giving each of us hugs.

I noticed the prescription on the coffee table. "Where did I hit you?"

"You got me right below the shoulder. The cops were trying to get me to crack at the hospital. Of course, I didn't tell them anything. Yesterday, my man Camron dropped me off at my house. The Jaguar came back to the house two days ago. I didn't want it sitting at the club."

"How did the staff treat you?"

"A'ight. Juan and Rick were rushed to the same hospital, Virginia Beach General. I sent my condolences to both of their families." He took off his T-shirt and pointed to the gauze pads on his right shoulder.

It turned out Rick was recently married and had a six-month-old son. Juan had five kids, three girls and two boys. He wasn't married, but he had extended family and relatives living in the area.

"I'm so glad this is over. Ton, we're going to start packing our bags. I'm eager to get back to the school so we can start setting things up in the apartment with the little bit of stuff we have. Could you take us to the bus station so we can catch a ride to Hampton?"

"That won't be necessary." Ton dangled some keys. "See that Nissan Altima sitting outside in the driveway? Y'all can have it, along with the gold Acura Legend and the navy blue Toyota 4Runner."

We did notice the cars and the truck, but we figured they belonged to him and his friends. Kiki quickly grabbed the keys and was heading to the door to give the Acura Legend a test-drive.

"Not so fast, ladies. I'm not done. Kiki, I want you to stay with Teresa and Yana and finish high school near them. The closest one is Kecoughtan High School. After you finish, I paid for you to enroll in Ghent Beauty School. It's a highly recommended school. You know, maybe one day you could open up your own shop.

"For the three of you, I went to Haynes and picked out three bedroom sets, couch, loveseat, recliner, entertainment set, and dinette set for the apartment. Jot down the address, and it will be there in two days.

"I almost forgot. I also bought a bookcase for all those books y'all need. I picked out most of the stuff myself. I got pretty good taste in the furniture department.

"Ladies, thank you for everything. I'm not going to lie—I'm sad to see y'all go." Ton handed each of us an envelope with five thousand dollars.

I made a mental note to put the money into my savings account. All of us gave him hugs, again. He held me the tightest. Teresa, Kiki, and I were jumping up for joy. Teresa quickly wrote down the address and gave it to him. Kiki wanted the Acura Legend, and Teresa wanted the red Nissan Altima, so I was gladly stuck with the Toyota 4Runner. Ton wasn't going to hear any complaints out of me.

"Before I fall out from this shoulder pain, I have one more surprise for you ladies. Step into the dining room."

With all of the excitement, we all forgot about the breakfast from the Waffle House.

Ton was a man who listened, and went into action. In our conversations, he'd uncovered that we loved Jamaican food. Montego's, a well-known restaurant, catered a feast for us. He had a buffet with steamed fish, roti, dumplings, jerk chicken, curry chicken and shrimp, beef patties, oxtail, rice and peas, and cabbage prepared just for us. Along with Jamaican punch, we had a rum cake for our sweet tooth. Rum cake was Ton's favorite dessert.

The food was delicious. Ton packed most of it up to take to Hampton with us. We all ate so much that I needed a nap. Ton didn't have much of an appetite because of the medicine he was on. Instead, he was drinking shots of cognac throughout the day.

After we all talked about the future and cleaned up the kitchen, Kiki and Teresa were heading out. I decided to stay with him for a little while. Ton was beginning to look pitiful because of the pain. After saying our goodbyes to Kiki and Teresa, we decided to watch television in the living room.

After flopping down on the couch, I sipped on a cold glass of punch. *Maybe, I shouldn't have eaten that second piece of rum cake*, I thought, feeling on my stuffed stomach. Suddenly, I thought of Ma and how she must be worried to death about Pop. For the rest of my life, I'd have to look her in the face and lie to her about where he really was, though he was only forty yards away from her. A long time ago, I'd promised myself to never let the love I have for a man consume my life.

"Why the long face? You miss Kiki and Teresa already?" Ton gently placed his hand on my leg.

"Nope, it's not that. Even though Ma doesn't care about us, I still take care about her. We all do. With us leaving, I have to admit, I will worry about her."

"Yana, that's one of the things I love about you. Girl, you got a big heart."

"Thank you." I smiled, not knowing what to say next.

"Your mother is a survivor. She will be all right. Let me cheer you up."

Ton surfed the TV channels and landed on UPN, which was featuring an old episode of *Good Times*, the hilarious episode where J.J hooked up with this guy named Sweet Daddy, a gangster in the community. Sweet Daddy wanted J.J. to give him his liver, but J.J. refused.

After the yawns kept coming over and over again from Ton and I, we both drifted off to sleep.

Chapter 17

"Wake up! Wake up!"

"What's wrong?" I asked. Ton was sweating and looked pale.

"My stomach is killing me," he said, almost out of breath, his hands clenching his stomach.

I quickly grabbed the prescription bottle. My plan was to look on the Internet for the side effects of 800 milligrams of Motrin, an ibuprofen, but the bottle said it all. "How many shots of cognac did you have today?"

"I don't know. Eight or nine, I guess. Why?"

"When taking this medicine, you're not supposed to drink because it can cause intestinal bleeding—I'm calling the ambulance." I ran to get the cordless phone from out of the dining room, almost tripping on the dumbbell in my way.

He started throwing up blood. "Oh shit! Am I going to die?"

"Not on my watch. The ambulance is on its way. Whatever you do, keep your eyes open. I can't lose you now."

"I'll try."

As soon as Ton's lips stopped moving, he lost consciousness.

* * *

"Where am I?" Ton asked, lifting his head up.

"You're in the hospital. *Sh!* Don't say anything, and don't try to get up. You're too weak. The nurses just got finished running more tests. Your blood is hard to get out. You have rolling veins, so the nurse had to get it from your hand. The doctor will be in here soon."

"How long have I been here?"

"Three days."

"Have you been staying here with me all this time?"

"Yes. Right in that burgundy recliner chair in the corner of the room. It wasn't too bad. I left once to go get registered for my classes and talk to my guidance counselor. Kiki and Teresa stayed here to keep you company. I thought about leaving one of your friends a message, but I didn't know anyone's phone number. Then I thought, maybe you didn't want anyone to know where you were. Thankfully, you're going to be fine. Just do me one favor," I urged, rubbing the top of his head.

"What's that?"

"Follow the directions on the prescription bottles. You can't have any alcohol for several weeks, and the doctors will be sending you to a specialist to look at your progress."

Just then, there was a knock on the door.

"Come in," I said.

"Good morning, Mr. Costen. I'm Doctor Vinson. It's a sure good thing your wife got you here just in time. How are you feeling?"

"My stomach feels as if it's on fire."

"When you arrived here, things didn't look so great. You bled out internally, and we had to do emergency surgery to repair the interior lining of your gastrointestinal tract and esophagus. Alcohol can be consumed after thirty days. For two weeks, lay off the spicy foods. I want you to give the lining of your esophagus time to heal, so I don't want you to suffer any kind of irritation."

"Will do, Doc." Ton nodded.

Before leaving the room, Doctor Vinson shook Ton's hand and mine.

Ton smirked. *"Wife?"*

"Please. I don't have any ulterior motives. From watching Lifetime movies, when you say that you're the wife, people move into action. I would have said anything to keep you alive," I explained.

"It's cool. You did what you had to do. Thanks for saving my life. You're my angel in disguise," he said, holding my left hand.

For the next two weeks, Ton was on a strict diet, along with his medications. We mainly ate a lot of soup and bread, like the doctor recommended. His shoulder was healing as well. Kiki and Teresa came by to help me take care of him and were relieved to see he was regaining his strength. Most nights, I stayed with him. The girls didn't mind at all. They were rather happy to see I was starting to really like Ton.

Besides, they'd found their own friends. Teresa met a guy named Will, a sophomore majoring in biochemistry. His dream was to find a cure for common diseases, such as cancer and AIDS—and to get inside her pants

Kiki found Carlos at the Coliseum Mall, a senior cutie who went to her new high school. He was all she ever talked about. More importantly, we were all happy, and that's what really mattered to me.

"Yo, the movie *Belly* is playing tonight. Let's check it out. I've been in this house way too long. I got to get out," Ton said from the master bedroom, sounding much better.

"Sure." I put the English literature book I was reading atop the rest of the two hundred dollars worth of books I needed for the semester.

"Plus, I'm in the need of seafood. I'm taking you to the Aberdeen Barn tonight. I don't express my feelings to many people. Thanks again for saving my life and taking such good care of me. I really appreciate it."

"You're welcome. All you asked for is loyalty, right? You would have done the same for me. I'm just happy you're going to be okay," I responded, tears in my eyes.

Ton pulled me close and gently kissed me. His tongue felt tender against mine.

"Yana, I'm really feeling you. Let me into your heart. I promise I won't break it," he whispered into my left ear, and then started nibbling on it.

"I'm scared." I turned my head the other way and pulled away from him.

"Don't be. You want me, and I definitely want you. Stop fighting it." He pulled me back closer to him.

"What do I have to offer you?" Truthfully, all I had was the clothes on my back.

"I'm not worried about that, Yana. You got goals, and you're determined to make something of yourself. Material things, I'm not the least bit worried about."

Ton started feeling on my thighs, as we looked into each other's eyes. He pulled my jeans shorts off, revealing my mango-colored thong. My legs wide open. Ton slightly bit my thighs. It was making me wet, and he knew it. I didn't want him to stop but was too scared to say anything.

Next, he licked his two fingers and ran them along the outside of my pussy. Then he took his tongue and licked along the outside of my pussy. Finally, his tongue found its way to my clit, flicking it back and forth. It felt wet and warm, and I began to get a tingling feeling. He started licking the side of my neck, while maneuvering to take off my matching bra.

Both of his hands were massaging my breasts now. First softly then hard. I loved the combination. It didn't take long for his tongue to find his way to my left breast. Back and forth, he would lick my clit and then my breast, making me more wet. Not only was Ton fucking my body, he was also fucking my mind.

"Let me love you, Yana." He kept licking my clit.

"Yes."

"Come in my mouth," he said over and over again, relentlessly licking my clit.

Suddenly, a burst of pleasure swarmed around the stroke of his tongue and my clit.

"Did you come?" he asked.

"Yeah," I responded out of breath.

He picked me up, and we kissed the entire way up the stairs. When we got to the bedroom, Ton gently laid me on the bed, grabbed a condom from the drawer, and slipped it on. "I've been thinking about this for a long time, Yana," he whispered into my ear while lying on top of me.

"Ton, I have to tell you something."

"What, baby?"

"Umm . . . I'm a virgin."

"I'm honored to be your first. Don't worry, I'll make it memorable. So far, I haven't gotten any complaints in the dick department," he assured me while entering my pussy.

At first it hurt, but once I started getting wet, I wanted to feel more of those deep thrusts. We started kissing again.

Ton motioned for me to pin my legs back as he ran his thumb against my clit and continued to give me those strokes. "Yana, baby, I'm coming. Shit! Damn! You feel so good!"

Little did he know, I came again too. *Pretty good for a first-timer*, I thought as Ton still lay on top of me.

Chapter 18

"Do you want me to drive?" I inquired.

"Nah, I'll drive," Ton said. "I have a very special guest coming with us tonight, if you don't mind."

"Not at all. I'm quite curious about the people in your life." I hopped into the passenger seat of the Jaguar.

We ended up in Lawndale, a middle-class neighborhood located near Norfolk State University. The good thing about this area was it sat off to the side, so the traffic from the school didn't come this way.

Ton unlocked the door with the key to enter the house.

"Hey, baby." Dottie, his adopted mother, greeted us with hugs.

"Hello, Ms. Woods," I said, taking a look at the house. She had the living room and kitchen walls decked out with pictures of Ton.

"Honey, you are beautiful. Welcome to my home. It's nice to meet you."

"Yes, ma'am. Thank you. It's nice to meet you as well."

"Lucas, I packed a peach cobbler to take with you back to the house."

"Thanks, Ma. Let's get going. I made reservations."

* * *

At the restaurant, Dottie and I talked about everything. I didn't mind her asking me a lot of questions, so I dabbled into my childhood. She was a very nice lady. She told me her husband left her because she wasn't able to have children of her own. She picked up the pieces and decided to adopt. Even though she went through tons of red tape, she finally was able to get Lucas.

She asked me about the future and was proud to know I was going to major in pre-law. To be honest, I wanted to be a voice for the people, poor people, that is. The ones who couldn't really afford law services.

I didn't answer any of Dottie's questions about Ton's hospital stay, owing to Ton nudging me in the leg. Ton played it down to a mere tummy ache. He told me afterward that one of her good friends was in the same emergency room that particular night and let her know he was there.

On the way to the movie theater, he shared with me that he didn't want her worrying about him, and that in the near future, he planned to retire her from a janitorial supervisor position at Old Dominion University.

"Do you want anything from the concession stand?" Ton asked as we entered the building. "I'm getting a small bag of popcorn."

"Yeah, I'll just take a box of Raisinets. I'm still stuffed from the broiled seafood platter," I answered as we stood in line to buy the movie tickets. Plus, I wanted to save room for some of his mother's peach cobbler and a scoop of vanilla ice cream.

"Do you want some of my Raisinets?" I asked as we took our seats in theater number nine.

"Nah, baby, I'm highly allergic to raisins. The doctors told Dottie just a small hint of a raisin would stop my breathing."

"Wow!" I expressed as the movie credits starting playing.

*   *   *

Belly was worth every penny. It showed the value of true friendship and love. Even if you are the most successful person, if there's no one to share it with, it can get lonely at the top.

Before heading home, Ton bought me the movie soundtrack. I loved that song, "Here Comes the Boom," by Sean Paul, Mr. Vegas, and DMX.

Chapter 19

"Rise and shine, Yana," Ton declared as he opened the curtains, allowing the sunshine to greet me in the bed. "I ran your bath water."

"Good morning," I responded, running to the bathroom to pee and brush my teeth.

"Breakfast is downstairs," he explained.

I turned around to look inside the Jacuzzi tub, only to discover pink rose petals and bubbles.

Ton started taking off the wife-beater I had slept in the night before, his own. Next, he removed my panties. Then I took off his shorts and boxers. Ton didn't have a shirt on.

"Climb in," he said, reaching his hand out for me.

I nestled into a sitting position in front of Ton. Ton had taken all of the stiffness out of my muscles three weeks ago by making me come over and over again. Since then, we'd been going at it like rabbits. Ton had taught me a few tricks. He rubbed my shoulders.

"What are your plans for today?" I asked, while his hands explored my body.

"You," he answered, one hand on my clit and another on my nipples.

After he made me come, I returned the favor by sucking

his dick. Ton loved for me to lick the tip while I stroked the bottom. Plus, he liked it when I deep-throated him. What drove him wild was sliding his dick up and down the middle of my breasts while I sucked the top of it. Watching me, Ton's dick got harder as I did it over and over again.

Missing Kiki and Teresa was taking a toll on me. For so long, all I'd cared about was making sure they were okay. Still, I called every day to check up on them. I knew how to be there for them and tried my best to keep us all on the right track, but falling in love with a man was unknown territory for me.

Last night, I had yet another nightmare about Ma stabbing me because I'd flushed her drugs down the toilet or hid them from her. At times, I couldn't even concentrate on my homework. Plenty of times, I sought refuge in Ton's arms, and he did his best to console me.

"Ton?" I asked, opening the door with groceries in my hand. We were tired of eating out. I planned to make spaghetti with meatballs, heat up a few pieces of garlic bread in the oven, and whip up a salad with Peppercorn Ranch dressing.

"Baby, I'm in the kitchen," he announced.

"Hey," I greeted him.

"Let me help you with all those groceries." Ton kissed me and grabbed the two bags out of my hand.

"Thanks."

"Are you cooking tonight?" he asked with a grin on his face.

"Yes." I giggled back. I noticed someone with headphones getting a can of Sprite out of the refrigerator.

"Yana, this is Nathan, my son," Ton said with a proud grin.

It was none other than Nathan from my high school. The same one who had been eyeing me for a while. This was an awkward situation. "You didn't tell me you had a son," I stated in his ear in a low tone.

"You didn't ask. It was a touchy situation. Nathan was born when I was sixteen. After me and his mother split, she wouldn't let me see him, which hurt my heart to the core. About five years ago, we started getting close again after he saw the games his mother was playing. He made his own decision to see me. Now he works for me. The business has to stay in the family," he expressed, still whispering.

"Pops, this is the lady you've been telling me about?" Nathan took off his headphones.

"Yes," he answered, standing next to me.

Now I understood where Nathan got his cockiness from. I'd never bothered to call him back, because Ton stepped into my life.

"This is Yana, the girl I've been telling you about since middle school," Nathan explained, shaking his head.

"Man, I'm sorry. I didn't think she was the same one."

"Pops, how many girls named Yana do you know?"

"I'll leave so you two can talk. Nathan, I didn't know you were his son," I explained before rummaging through my purse for the keys. I couldn't help but wonder if Ton knew the whole time I was the one Nathan had been talking about for all those school years. The last thing I wanted to do was to come between their relationship as father and son.

At least Ton cared about his child. My parents couldn't have cared less if I had died.

"Yana, it's cool. You gave him a chance first. I lost," Nathan responded

I walked out of the kitchen, hoping Nathan wouldn't sabotage my relationship with Ton. Only time was going to tell how all of this was going to play out, but my plan definitely wasn't to get involved in a love triangle with a father and son.

I discovered Ton had two sides. One side was kind, sweet, humorous, down-to-earth, and caring. The other side was the one I was first introduced to—the coldhearted, backstabbing, I-want-it-my-way, fuck-the-world type. Some days, I didn't know which side I was going to see. Today, he let me know he would backstab his own son to get what he wanted. Ton had known me since I was a young girl. I wondered, *How long has he been peeping me out?*

Two weeks later, Ton and Nathan got into an argument about a drug deal gone bad. Ton had lost money, and in his eyes, it could have been prevented if Nathan had made better decisions. Was that truly the issue, or were they getting into it because of me?

Chapter 20

It took some adjustment, but school was a breeze for me; first semester, that is. Right now, we were on Christmas break. Teresa and I met a lot of people who were trying to be somebody in life. We appreciated positive people around us, especially Ms. Carver, because it made us want to strive to accomplish our goals. Both of us worked in the bookstore to earn extra money. Plus, I hadn't even started pinching off the five thousand dollars Ton gave each of us.

Three months ago, I broke down and gave Ma my cell phone number only. She was crying and hysterical about Pop missing. She even went to some of his drinking buddies to plead with them to see if he was all right. They hadn't seen him either. She wasn't going to go to the police and file a missing person's report.

To our surprise, she had taken Pop missing as a sign that their relationship was over. Ma, being the jealous type, had convinced herself that he ran off with another woman. In September, she'd entered a drug treatment program. She claimed she was making good progress and vowed to stop using her body to pay for drugs. The program encouraged family members to join in on counseling sessions, but so far none of us bothered to show up. For so long, Ma used all three of us as pawns to manipulate the welfare system. So many nights we went hungry. And holidays were the worst. At times, we didn't even have soap or toilet paper because she'd decided to shoot or smoke the money up.

Kiki and Teresa were starting to let their anger and resentment go and were entertaining the idea of possibly giving Ma the chance to come back into their lives. They'd convinced me to have a face-to-face with her. Mine was still built up inside of me. Deep down, I truly felt the only thing she'd want was money.

We were on our way to see Ma and the so-called progress she'd made. Even though no one had said it yet, our visits to her hell hole apartment were going to be few and far between. We lived different lives now, and that's the way we planned to keep it.

Teresa turned the key and opened the door. The apartment was spotless and smelled of a clean, fresh breeze.

"Get in here and sit y'all asses down on the couch," Ma ordered from the kitchen.

Here we go again, I thought.

Ma had gained at least ten pounds, her hair looked healthier, and those sores had faded away. Not to mention, she had a smile on her face. It had been years since she'd cracked a grin for us. I had to admit, I was surprised how great she looked. She looked like Ma of old.

After the three of us sat down with attitudes, Ma got on her knees in front of us.

"Hate, disgust, shame, sadness, heartache, pain, and cruelty are all words that come to mind for the way I treated y'all all these years, Especially you, Yana. With all my heart, I'm truly sorry. It's hard to believe, but I'm getting clean for good.

"I realized your father leaving is the best thing that could have happened to me. A huge weight has been lifted off my shoulders. My parents have started talking to me again. I feel

like I've accomplished something with the treatment center."
She reached for a piece of paper on top of the television. It
was a certificate of completion. She'd been clean for ninety
days.

"I hate you," I hissed.

"You used us. All you cared about was money. Mommy
would be ashamed for the way you treated us. I thought you
adopted me because you really cared about me," Teresa
spat back, tears in her eyes.

"Yana was there. Ma, you weren't. You were always gone,"
Kiki told her. "The streets and Pop were always more important than the three of us."

"Girls, I know it's going to take some time to—"

I cut her off. "A long time or maybe never. We would have
been better off with Ms. Carver, but you refused to let her
take us in and continued to fuck her husband for money."
The hatred I had for her was deep. It hurt so bad.

She reached out to us. "Will you ever forgive me?"

"I don't know," Kiki answered.

"Maybe."

"Hell no. I'm ready to leave. Let's go. I feel like I'm suffo-
cating in here," I declared before we got up from the couch to
leave.

"Yana, Teresa, Kiki, please give me five more minutes,"
Ma pleaded.

"You got a minute. Hurry up," I told her, my arms folded.

"In time, you all will see. I'm getting help because I want
my three precious daughters back. Those drugs were killing
me. I don't want to die with a needle in one arm and a crack
pipe in my hand. Girls, you are worth much more to me than
that."

"Time's up," I replied, and we all walked out the front door.

Chapter 21

Getting Blizzard Treats at Dairy Queen cheered us up. My favorite was the blueberry cheesecake. That day, we decided not to talk about Ma anymore. I promised myself, if I ever did have kids, I would never treat them the way Ma treated us. There's a difference between discipline and outright cruelty to children.

One good thing about her treatment was that she had forgotten all about Teresa's settlement. The city was found negligent, and Teresa was awarded $1.5 million. Kiki and I tried to talk her out of it, but she split the money three ways with us. A teller at the bank recommended we open money market accounts, so we did. I strongly advised Teresa and Kiki to save the money for our future. Teresa decided to give Ms. Carver one hundred thousand dollars for being there for us.

Fulfilling a longtime dream, we flew to Orlando, Florida, along with Ms. Carver, to spend the Christmas holiday in Disney World. We had a blast. Our favorite theme park was the Magic Kingdom.

I missed Ton a lot during this time. A week before Thanksgiving he'd confessed that he loved me, and I told him the same. It was long overdue.

Ton used the Christmas holiday to get closer to Nathan. I

was glad to hear they were trying to patch things up. Nathan became interested in a girl named Sheena. It didn't help that she resembled me quite a bit.

Instead of waiting until after Christmas to give me my gift, Ton gave it to me before I left. It was an oval-shaped 2-carat diamond pendant with matching 1-carat earrings. I gave Ton the latest DJ equipment. As a hobby, he liked to mix tapes.

Kiki, Teresa, and I rang in the New Year with Ma's parents, Richard and Harriet Madison. They'd called and begged us to come over. Ma had moved out of the projects and moved in with them. She needed a new environment.

We talked for hours about our whole lives. We discovered that Pop didn't want them having a relationship with us, and Ma just followed his orders. Not wanting to make matters worse, they stayed away.

With the help of everybody's encouragement and love, and with Ma's determination, she had a fighting chance to beat her drug addictions. More importantly, they welcomed Teresa with open arms and accepted her as a granddaughter too.

Since then, every Sunday we went over to their house for dinner at three in the afternoon. I had to admit, these gatherings definitely brought us closer together, and I felt as if I'd gained two more loved ones—my grandparents. Ma was actually interested in what was going on in our lives. Through therapy, she was learning to try to not control us anymore. Besides, she couldn't anyway.

Chapter 22

"You love me, right?" Ton inquired after we celebrated Valentine's Day together by me just riding him.

"Of course." I reassured him with a kiss.

"I need you to do something for me."

"Whatever you need. I'm listening."

"As you know, I got the Tidewater area on lock. Everyone is buying my magic. I'm trying to step into the game in the city of Richmond."

"I don't mind making drops for you."

"Nah, that's not it. What I need is for you to round up the girls and take out a major player named Henry Rickson, aka Conrad." Ton jumped out of the bed and reached in his briefcase to show me a picture of him.

"I thought the murders were over," I hissed at him. "You know Juan's daughter goes to Hampton University. Last semester, she was in my biology class. I had to look at her every Tuesday and Thursday knowing what we did to her father." My stomach started to turn.

"Don't let it get to you. I got to them before they got to me. I really need you to do this for me."

"You said, I quote, 'Only a few had to be taken care of.' " I let out a sigh. My heart started racing. I couldn't believe Ton was asking me to do this again.

"Yana, *a few* doesn't mean *two*. Besides, if you want to get technical, you only killed one person for me. Hear me out. Once you get Conrad, there's only five more men I need you to take out for now. These men cover D.C., Baltimore, Philadelphia, Charlotte, and Miami. I haven't set my eyes on New York City . . . yet."

"I have to go out of town? What if I get caught?"

"Baby, you mean all three of you. Y'all got clean rap sheets. If one of you was to get caught, only a few years behind bars is the worst you would be facing. Plus, I would hire the best lawyer. I can't go to jail. I've got eight felonies in the five cities I've just mentioned. There are no more chances for me," he expressed, caressing my face.

I screamed, "So you would let me go to prison?"

"I wouldn't let you go there. That's up to the judge and the court system. If you do the murders right, you won't have to worry about getting caught."

"Hmm, another tidbit I didn't know about—you and your extended criminal record. We already killed people for you, and you want us to do it six more times, making it sound as if you're ordering vacation spots. I have a conscience. I can't do it anymore, Ton. I'm sorry." I got up from the bed.

"Yana, you will be sorry if this plan doesn't go through. Power and respect is all I got in this world. What will truly be sorry is your mother finding out where your pops really is the whole time she was looking for him. I don't want to ruin your newfound relationship with her or your grandparents. So I'm not going to hit you or disrespect you. I leave you with a choice." Ton walked out of the bedroom and into the bathroom.

"All right. I'll do it only on one condition."

"What's that?"

"Leave Kiki and Teresa out of this. I'll go alone. There's still one thing I really need to know."

"Agreed. You can go alone, as long as the job gets done without baggage following you." Ton nodded his head. "What else do you want to know?"

"Since we're being honest here—Did you know I was the Yana that Nathan was referring to?"

"Yeah, I knew. Nathan doesn't deserve you. He tends to think with his dick instead of his head. You don't need a man like that in your life. For years, Nathan told me how you would come to school hiding black eyes and mysterious bruises. I felt bad. With your mother being a client, and me popping in and out of her apartment to make drop-offs to see what's really going on, I put the pieces together. If anything, you should be thanking me for taking you out of a bad situation. Plus, I rescued your sisters too. For that, you owe me, Yana."

"How could you do that to your son?" I asked, shaking my head in disbelief.

"I love my son, but we have more of a friendship than a father-and-son relationship. Shit, I'd barely turned sixteen when he came along. I'm not concerned about him right now. Our goal is to take over the world."

"You mean *your* goal," I spat back.

"Now, be focused on the task at hand. I don't have time for you to make mistakes or be stressed about what-ifs and regrets. Everything that I will get, Yana, you will benefit from," he said, ignoring my last comment.

"Ton, this is fucking it. I'm going to have seven murders on my hands because of you."

"No more, I promise—I love to hear you curse. It turns me on. Now bend over and give me a double dose of your pussy." Ton motioned me to get into a doggy-style position on the carpet.

* * *

Later on that same night, I heard Ton talking in his sleep about trying to take over the West Coast. *When is this going to stop?*

I slowly realized I was in love with a monster that only cared about himself. Deep down, I felt Ton didn't give a shit about me. Instead, he wanted to use me as an assassin. Even though I was the one that came up with the idea of shooting him to make it look as if he was a target too, he still had the nerve to threaten me about Ma and my grandparents. Despite everything, I still loved him and was ready to do anything for him.

I tossed and turned through the night and kept thinking, *Am I just following Ma's footsteps?*

Chapter 23

Ton was excited about turning thirty-five and threw a huge birthday bash at Club Icon in Chesapeake. All his friends were there. Kiki and Teresa came too.

The whole night, I kept rubbing up against his dick. Truthfully, he was just happy because he was about to, slowly but surely, take over the East Coast with his "drugs, money, and respect."

With midterms coming up, I'd decided to call it a night at one in the morning, and waited for him at the house. While I was turning the channel to watch *Martin*, Ton walked in.

"Hey, baby." Ton greeted me with a kiss in the living room. His breath smelled of alcohol. He was drunk.

"Hi," I responded and smiled.

"Thanks for such a great birthday. Baby, I gotta admit, you can cook. How did you know fried chicken, baked beans, and macaroni and cheese was my favorite meal?" he asked, tickling me.

"Dottie told me," I said, giggling.

"I bet she told you a lot." He lifted me up and carried me to the dining room table.

"What are you doing?" I asked, still giggling.

"Getting the rest of my birthday present." He took off the

big T-shirt I was wearing, only to discover I didn't have on a bra or panties. That seemed to make Ton's dick even harder.

"You want me?" I asked, looking into his eyes and taking off his belt, willing to get into any position he wanted to fuck me in.

His jeans and boxer shorts fell to his knees. "Yes, baby." He started feeling my wet pussy. Next, Ton watched me play with myself. Those two fingers I used, he gladly licked. Then his python entered in with force.

"Hurry up. It's starting to hurt," I spat at him.

"Just give me five more minutes."

After two hours of trying every position we knew, my pussy was bone-dry and aching. Ton finally admitted he couldn't come. Maybe it was the alcohol.

After I "stroked his ego," we took a shower together.

"All that work has got me hungry," Ton said after I gave him a massage. "Can you heat up a plate for me?"

"Okay."

"Baby, cut me a piece of that rum cake you bought. I want to try it."

"Sure." I gave him a kiss and a hug. "Meet you downstairs."

"Whoa, I'm stuffed." Ton rubbed his stomach as he leaned back in his chair.

"You should be, after everything you ate." I yawned. The clock read four in the morning.

"I'm going to sleep for the rest of the day."

"I'm sleepy too. I see you really like rum cake."

"It was tasty—"Ton tried to talk, but his face started to turn blue, and he was having trouble breathing.

"Ton, what's wrong?"

He pointed to his chest and mumbled something.

I could barely hear him. "What did you say, baby?"

After a couple minutes of struggle, Ton lay motionless on the kitchen floor. I quickly dialed 9-1-1.

Next, I called Dottie, and within ten minutes, she came rushing over to her son's side. "What happened?" Dottie demanded to know while the paramedics were taking Ton's vital signs.

"I don't know. He came home from the club drunk, we talked, he ate, and we were about to go to sleep," I answered, tears in my eyes.

One paramedic asked, "Do you know if he's allergic to anything?"

Dottie quickly pointed out, "Yes, he's highly allergic to raisins."

"Oh no! Raisins were in the rum cake I bought him for his birthday. He ate three pieces. I didn't know. Ton never told me he was allergic to raisins." I started bawling.

The paramedics tried to revive Ton, but it was too late. He was gone.

Dottie fell on her hands and knees and wept for hours.

"Dottie, I'm so sorry."

"Honey, it's all right. You didn't know. Ton never told anyone he was allergic to raisins. He had a bad reaction at lunch one day at school when he was a teenager. Some kids joked him for the rest of the school year about being allergic to raisins. Maybe he was embarrassed. I don't know." Dottie sobbed. "I can't believe he's gone, girl."

After countless questions from the police detectives and talking to Dottie, the cops ruled out foul play and it was considered accidental death. I was exhausted, but felt free from the grips of Ton's demands. I had played the role of the broken-hearted girlfriend to a T. With the extra rum I'd added to the cake to make it moist, Ton wasn't able to taste the raisins.

Kiki and Teresa rushed over to help me get most of my

things. Dottie completely understood I didn't feel comfortable staying in the house that night.

"Did they buy it?" Kiki asked as we got back to the apartment in Hampton.

"I think so," I told her.

"I'm just glad he's out of the way." Teresa shook her head.

Ton, not grateful for what he already had, paid the ultimate price—his life. It was clear to me that he didn't give a fuck about nobody but himself.

I refused to ever be like my mother and do whatever the man I loved said to do. Besides, I couldn't bear to think of all the families that would have been affected by those murders.

A week later, the funeral took place at Mount Vernon Church in Norfolk. I didn't have the heart to tell Nathan the truth about his father.

As it turned out, Ton had twenty properties, five vehicles, one boat, and a gym. He mostly left everything to Nathan and Dottie, except the house, which had a "for sale" sign in the front yard, furniture included, and the two cars and the truck that Kiki, Teresa, and I drove.

Now we could finally move on with our lives.

At an offer I couldn't refuse, I'd sold Ton's house.

Epilogue

Five years later, after two relapses, Ma was completely drug-free and living on her own. We were all able to mend our relationship with her. My grandparents and she came to our college graduation at Hampton University. She'd even started dating again. My grandparents were more than grateful to have all of us in their lives.

To this day, as far as Teresa, Kiki, and I knew, Pop's body still lay in the back of the old apartment building we once lived in.

Ms. Carver was now the director of the free health clinic on Brambleton Avenue. We talked on a weekly basis. She divorced Uncle Fred. Ms. Carver was so proud of our accomplishments, she gave Teresa and me a graduation party, and was also happy to know that Ma had gotten her act together. Ms. Carver admitted to smoking a cigarette from time to time when stressed.

Kiki, deciding college wasn't the route for her, went to Ghent Beauty School. After she received her license, she opened her own shop and became one of the most known and wanted hairstylists in the Tidewater area of Virginia. It was crazy to see women waiting for hours to get into her chair. She had a cozy two-bedroom condo in downtown Norfolk.

Teresa became a kindergarten teacher after graduating from Hampton, and she loved it. Her longtime boyfriend, Carlos, and her got married last summer, bought a house in Chesapeake, and had a baby girl named Maya, whose great-grandmother, Harriet, had the pleasure of being the proud babysitter.

With my degree in pre-law from Hampton University, I attended law school at Regent University. I finally passed the bar on my second try and was now the assistant district attorney for the city of Norfolk, specializing in child neglect and abuse. I'd also bought a three-bedroom house in Virginia Beach. I now had a new love in my life named Kurt, and we were taking it slow.

Teresa, Kiki, and I continued to remain close—nothing or no one could ever change that—and still carried on the tradition of going to our grandparents' house every Sunday for dinner.

CONNIE'S CARTEL

By Mark Anthony

Chapter 1

How the Cartel Was Formed . . .

August 1997

"Miss, can I have a word with you?"

I knew the voice was directed at me, but I paid it no mind. I said to my homegirl Monya, who I always called Money, "Money, fuck that nigga! Just keep walking." My heart was pounding from nervousness as we walked out of Macy's in Queens Center Mall. Me and my girl had just finished boosting, so we didn't have no time for bullshit.

The persistent dude asked, "Ma, I can't talk to you for a minute?"

"Nah, that's a'ight, sweetie, we good. We in a hurry."

Money turned around and noticed that the dude was still following us. "GG, he kinda cute," she said in a devilish tone.

"Money, I said, 'Fuck that nigga!' We gots to keep it moving!"

I was always on point and about my business, but Money was always about chasing dick. So it didn't surprise me when she stopped and gave the dark-skin cutie some play.

"So what's good wit' y'all? Y'all track stars or what? Why y'all running from me?"

"'Cause we got moves to make!" I said with all kinds of attitude. Right off the bat, as soon as the nigga opened his mouth, I could tell he was corny. He was cute, but the mutha-fucka was corny, and there was no need in wasting all of our time.

"Oh, y'all got moves to make? Like what?"

"Like none of your gotdamn business! Money, come on, let's go!"

"Don't pay her no mind," Money diplomatically explained to the dude. "She just stressing over some shit. But, yeah, we do have moves to make. We heading to The Tunnel later on, and it's getting late, so we trying to hurry up."

"Oh, okay, okay. The Tunnel? So that's what's up. So can I get your name and your number real quick? I'll holla at you later, and maybe I can slide through and buy y'all some drinks or something."

"Uhhh, NO!"

"GG, calm down. Look, don't pay her no mind. My name is Monya, and that's my girl GG. What's your name, sweetie?"

The dark-skin dude smiled and licked his lips. He came across as cocky as shit. The truth was, he was cute, but he wasn't no LL Cool J or Tyson Beckford, so he needed to knock it off with the lip-licking. *Corny muthafucka!* I thought to myself, shaking my head.

Money looked like she was about to start with a bunch of small talk, so I had to cut that shit short before it started. "Money, give the nigga your number and let's *goooo!* Got-damn!"

Just as Money was about to give dude her number, two other guys walked up to where we were all standing. My first thought was, it was some of Pete's cornball-ass friends, but it only took just a quick moment to realize what was really up.

Dude reached into his shirt and pulled out a badge that was dangling from a chain. "Yo, sorry, ma, but I gotta place y'all under arrest for shoplifting." He calmly whipped out a pair of handcuffs and placed them on Money's wrists.

One of the other guys that had approached us instructed me to turn around and place my arms behind my back, and he quickly placed handcuffs on me too.

"Ain't this a bitch!" I shouted out loud. "What the fuck you mean, you arresting us for shoplifting? We ain't do shit!" I screamed as loud as I could, purposely trying to cause a scene in the crowded mall.

"Miss, just calm down and take a walk with us to the back, and we'll straighten this out," one of the cops said to me.

"Man, fuck that! I ain't walking nowhere, and there ain't shit that needs to be straightened out! All I know is, you better get these tight-ass handcuffs off of me and my girl, or else there's gonna be a problem!"

The third cop, who hadn't placed handcuffs on anybody, opened the oversized Coach bags that me and Money had and began rummaging through them.

"What the fuck are you doing? Did I say it was okay for you to look in my shit like that? I know my rights, and you ain't allowed to illegally search my shit like that!" I screamed and talked as tough as I could, but those cops wasn't trying to hear shit.

Before I knew what was what, me and Money were sitting in some back office in Macy's waiting on two uniformed cops to come scoop us up and take us to the precinct.

"Money, the next time I tell your ass something, you better fucking listen to me! This is some bullshit!" I said to Money.

The truth of the matter was, it wasn't Money's fault that we'd gotten arrested. Nah. We got arrested because all of that boosting shit was old and tired. We were sixteen now and had been boosting since we were thirteen. And whenever you overdo some shit and wear out your welcome with a hustle, it usually means it's the start of your downfall. And, Lord knows, I was more than bored with boosting. Not to mention, it wasn't providing me the high lifestyle I wanted to live.

Later that night, at about one in the morning, me and

Money were transported from the precinct to Central Booking on Queens Boulevard, where we were put in a holding cell and had to wait to see a judge before we could be released.

"You know we supposed to be at The Tunnel right fucking now laid up in VIP with Mase? You do know that?" Money said to me.

Money was beyond aggravated, and so was I.

"Look at this muthafucka!" I said to her.

We both shook our heads as we saw Pete dressed in a correction officer's uniform. He was the one who'd arrested us.

"Oh, that's our boy! The toy cop!" Money shouted from the bench she was sitting on.

We both started laughing.

"What the fuck are you doing in here? You mean, you ain't a real cop?" I asked as I stood at the front of the cell and spoke to Pete through the bars. He walked up to our cell. "Nah, I'm a C.O."

"Yo, this is really some bullshit! Money, this nigga really is a toy cop. Let me guess. This is your real toy-cop job, and working at Macy's is just your side toy-cop hustle . . . so you can pay for the extra cable channels and shit, right?" I burst out laughing.

At that point I was so frustrated, I couldn't help but try and make myself laugh.

"Y'all two got jokes. And I see you still on that nonfriendly shit that you was on earlier," Pete replied.

"Nigga, please," I replied.

The cell we were in was packed with chicks in there for all kinds of shit, from prostitution to drug possession, you name it. Pete motioned for me to come closer to the cell bars then said to me in a whispering tone, "Let me put you up on something real quick. All that from earlier was just me doing my job, but on the real, I really did wanna get at you. I mean, your girl is cute and all that, but I wanted to holla at you, so I'm just saying . . ."

Oh my God! This nigga is so fucking corny! I thought to myself. I literally wanted to scream. Being the natural-born hustler that I was, I thought quickly on my feet. I knew I could get something out of this situation. "Word? Okay, okay." I smiled and nodded my head.

"So I tell you what—I know there's only one judge working on the weekends, and I ain't trying to sit up in this cell for another twelve hours. My fucking feet is killing me! So if you can work it out for me and my girl to jump ahead of all these chicks and see the judge within the next hour, then me and you might be able to work something out between us when you get off. You feel me?"

Pete's eyes immediately shifted to me to see if I was being straight up. Then he nodded his head and he stepped back about two feet or so from the cell just so he could get a better look at me with my Alicia Keys beauty and my Alicia Keys body to match.

"That's what's up? Okay, no doubt. I got y'all."

Half an hour later, me and Money were walking out of Central Booking as free women. We were issued a desk appearance ticket and told to stay out of trouble for the next six months, and then we were sent on our way.

Little did I know it at the time, but getting caught shoplifting earlier that day and, more specifically, meeting Pete the toy cop, would forever change my life.

Chapter 2

*W*HACK!
That was the sound I heard coming from the top of the steps that led to the basement apartment that me and Money shared with our other homegirl, Saleeta.

Then the next thing we heard, Saleeta was screaming for her life, and then there was a vicious rumbling sound of her body tumbling head over heels down all thirteen steps before she finally came to a crashing stop on the basement floor.

"Don't you ever fucking do no shit like that! You hear me, bitch?" Rahmel barked, pressing his size thirteen Nike Air into Saleeta's throat.

I had been sitting down on the sofa watching videos, and Money was in her room lying down, but we both went charging to Saleeta's aid.

"Rahmel, get off of her. What is wrong witchu?" I yelled as I tried my hardest to push him away from Saleeta.

"Fuck this trick-ass disrespectful bitch!" Rahmel continued to apply pressure to Saleeta's throat. I was sure she was gonna pass out at any second. I pushed and punched his muscular six-foot four-inch frame, but that wasn't having any effect on him.

All Money and I could do was plead for him to stop. But before we knew what was what, Rahmel had pulled a .45-caliber handgun from his waistband and rammed it into Saleeta's mouth, drawing blood in the process. He scooped her up by one hand and held her up against the wall and was ready to blow her brains out.

Thankfully, just at that moment, our landlord burst open the first-floor door that separated his part of the house from our apartment and stormed down the steps. "Connie! What the hell is going on in here?" he yelled. "I done told y'all about keeping up all this damn noise at all times in the morning."

Why Mr. Robinson always thought I was the ringleader and cause of the commotion is beyond me, but he would always come after me for the explanation.

As soon as he was able to see all of us, he immediately knew what was up.

"Old man, just mind your fucking business and go back upstairs!" Rahmel shouted.

"Muthafucka, is you crazy? Running up in my shit, breaking up shit, and you gonna tell me to mind my business? Nigga, I'm sixty-eight years old, but I guarantee you if you don't take your hands from around that girl I'll kill you my damn self! Now try me if you wanna!" Mr. Robinson, like a real OG, reached in his pocket and pulled out a snub-nosed .38. "I'm from the old school! Y'all little punk-ass niggas ain't shit!"

I couldn't help but almost laugh, but at the same time, I was impressed with Mr. Robinson's gangsta.

Rahmel looked at Mr. Robinson with a screw face, and then he mushed Saleeta to the floor and stormed outta the house.

After making sure that Saleeta was all right, Mr. Robinson again singled me out and told me that if we was gonna be bringing thugs to the house, disrespecting his shit, then we all was gonna have to find another place to live.

I calmed him down, assuring him that we would pay to get his stairs and the holes in the wall fixed before the week was out.

"All right. I mean, don't get me wrong. Y'all are all nice young ladies, and I wanna give y'all a chance to get on your feet and make it, but I'm just getting too old for any bullshit."

Money was consoling Saleeta.

"No, no, you're absolutely right," I told him. "I promise you, there won't be any more problems."

As soon as Mr. Robinson was gone and out of earshot, I let loose. "See, this is some bullshit! Saleeta, let me guess—You ain't make that nigga enough money tonight up in the strip club, so he beat your ass?"

Through pain and tears, Saleeta explained that she was in the strip club trying to hustle and make as much money as she could so she was naturally hollering at all of the dudes that came through the spot. She'd made the mistake of hollering at one dude who was a pimp, but she had no idea.

So, Shamel, Saleeta's pimp, looked at that as the ultimate sign of disrespect and beat her ass, to make sure she wasn't on no slick shit, trying to leave him for another "Daddy."

"See, this is exactly what I'm talking about! This is some bitch-assness that we be dealing with and putting up with. Last week me and Money got arrested for boosting, this week, Saleeta, you getting your ass kicked by Rahmel. And for what? For fucking bullshit pennies. This shit is ending tonight! Word is bond. The last thing I know I want is to be like my no-good-ass moms, out there at thirty-*fucking*-five, still chasing nutsacks, and dropping it like it's hot up in the clubs. And why? 'Cause she ain't got no paper. And so she out there hoping a nigga will sponsor her ass and take care of her. But to hell with all of that shit! Money, how much paper you got?"

"I got about three stacks."

"Good. And I got two stacks. Saleeta, what about you?"

"I got a little over two stacks."

I paused and I thought to myself for a minute, nodding my head. Then I went and poured myself a drink. When I returned back to the couch, I told Money to grab a piece of paper and a pen, and for her and Saleeta to grab a seat and meet me at the kitchen table.

After we sat down, I began to draw out a diagram that had an organizational chart with the names Sing Sing, Nassau County, and Rikers Island. These were different jails, but the jails also represented different territories. At the box on the top of the chart, I put my name, Connie. To the right of my box and just below it, I put Money's name in the box. And to the left of my box and just below it, I put Saleeta's name in the box. And at the very top of the paper, above my name, I wrote in big, bold letters—CONNIE'S CARTEL.

"What the fuck is this?" Money asked.

"This right here is the fucking blueprint! Ya heard me?" I looked at everyone in the face.

"Now I been thinking about this shit for a minute now, but with all the bullshit that's been going on, it's like now is the time to move on this shit and get it done. A'ight, this is the thing. We all know how to hustle and get money, and we all been getting our little money. But it's time for us to really get this paper and end all the bullshit. I mean, Saleeta, your moms let her boyfriend fuck you crazy since you was seven years old, and now that's why you're so fucked up! Money, your mom's been on crack since the shit came out, and since before you was born, and that's why you so fucked up! And my ass ain't no better. My moms abandoned my ass at two years old, and I been bounced around the foster care system like a fucking ping-pong ball, and that's why I'm so fucked up! But y'all know what? Don't nobody give a fuck about that shit. That shit is in the past, so from right here, right now, we making a pact to forget about all the bullshit, and the only thing we concerning ourselves with is getting this bread. 'Cause once we got the bread, then the bullshit will go away. So from now on, it's money over bullshit, and it's money over niggas!"

Saleeta and Money both nodded their heads. They continued to look at me to see exactly where I was going with what I was saying.

"Now here's the thing. If we wanna get paid, then we gots to control some shit. Saleeta, you doing the prostitution and stripping, but you don't control that, so you getting hit off with pennies. Me and Money boosting, but we don't own the fucking stores or the fucking malls, so we just getting hit off with pennies too. Now I was thinking about the drug game. We all done did runs outta state for niggas and got hit off with pennies, but even with that shit, we ain't never controlled no shit. But we can get in this drug game right now and fucking murder the game. I'm telling y'all."

Saleeta immediately replied that she was down for whatever because she was definitely tired of the bullshit she was going through. Money also was down for whatever, but the thing that she didn't understand was exactly how I was planning on the three of us controlling the drug game.

"See, here's the thing. We all sixteen-year-old chicks, so we can't take over the street side of the drug game and control that, but we can control the shit that seems the least desirable. And what I mean is, we can easily control the drugs inside the jails. And that's why on this paper I got Nassau County Correctional Facility, Rikers Island, and Sing Sing. Those are the three joints we gonna control for right now, and then we gonna fucking grow from there."

Saleeta and Money both looked at me as if to say they couldn't believe the bullshit I was on.

"Y'all looking at me like I'm on some bullshit, right?"

They didn't answer and just looked at me.

Before they could speak, I told them I would be right back. I walked into my bedroom. After a few minutes, I came back to the kitchen table and slapped a badge on the table. "You fucking think I'm bullshitting now?" I asked.

"Oh shit! GG, that shit ain't fucking real, is it?" Saleeta asked.

"Gimme that shit. Let me see it." Money snatched the badge and began examining it.

"Y'all think I'm bullshitting, but I'm not. And I'm telling y'all, give me a few weeks and I'll have a driver's license with a last name on it that matches the name plate underneath this badge."

"Saleeta, this shit is real." Money handed the badge to Saleeta.

Of course they were curious about how I had gotten my hands on a real-life law enforcement badge. But I was no dummy. I knew I had to keep my mouth shut about the shit, or else I'd risk my empire crumbling before I even had a chance to build it.

"I got it, and that's all that matters, and what that means is that I can basically go on my drug runs to re-up and shit and not have to worry about a gotdamn thing if the cops stop me. Is this shit crazy or what?"

"Wow! GG, you are so outta control, and I love the fuck outta you for it!" Money said.

"But here's the thing. I just wanna know—Are y'all wit' me on this Connie's Cartel shit or not? I mean, I want y'all to help me build it, but I'm building it with or without y'all, so a bitch needs to know."

Without hesitation, Saleeta and Money both told me that they were more than down.

"Okay, no doubt. That's what I'm talking about. There's just two things I want y'all to remember and for us to agree on. Number one is, don't nobody get greedy, and number two is, no matter what the fuck may go down, don't nobody open up their mouth and snitch about shit. We clear on that?"

Saleeta and Money both nodded in agreement, and with that, Connie's Cartel was started.

The following week I was planning on buying a pound of weed with the $7,000 we had combined, bagging that shit up, and have it distributed inside the jails. It was gonna be a beautiful thing, because the retail value for drugs inside the prisons was like four times what it was on the street. So I knew we were about to cake off lovely.

Chapter 3

"You outside? Okay, I'll be there in a minute," I said to Pete. I hung up my cell phone. I slipped on my four-inch black heels that went so good with my tight jeans and my black wife-beater. I stared at myself in the mirror for a quick second before heading outside to meet him.

"What's up, mama?" Pete leaned over and attempted to give me a kiss.

"Look, can we drive please. I told you I ain't trying to do all that kissy-kissy lovey-dovey shit out in public."

Pete looked at me, a smirk plastered on his face, and just nodded. "So no public affection?"

"Exactly. No public affection. I ain't into that," I replied with a bunch of attitude.

The truth be told, I was into public affection, as long as it was with the right dude. But Pete was far from the right dude. The nigga was twice my age, married with children, still corny, and he just came across as trying too fucking hard to have a swagger that just wasn't natural.

The thing was, from the first phone conversation Pete and I had, the day after he had gotten me locked up, I knew his ass was "vic material."

As we drove down my block and turned on to Hollis Avenue, I asked, "So where we going?"

"To the *tellie*," Pete replied with one hand on the steering wheel, trying extremely too hard to profile with a gangsta lean. "Yo, this shit right here is a pussy muthafucking magnet! Word is bond!" Pete turned the volume up so that everyone could hear the music blasting from his car.

I have to admit, as corny as his ass was, he was the only person I knew who was pushing a convertible Jaguar. The car was off the hook, and everyone on the streets took notice as we drove by.

"Ain't nobody even feeling yo' cocky ass like that," I joked.

"Yeah, I'm really feeling myself right now, but you might wanna play your cards right. These young niggas ain't got shit on me, and they can't do shit for you."

On some level Pete was right. I mean, I knew that he could do shit for me if I played my cards right, and in fact he had already started doing shit for me. Today, though, I was gonna make him step his game up.

"Yup. And them old-ass broads ain't got shit on this tight-ass pussy right here," I said, running my hand between my crotch.

"Wow! That's what the fuck I'm talking about!"

I got Pete's ass open.

Just then we pulled in the parking lot of the Kew Motor Inn. Before we could even close the door to our room and get settled in, Pete had dropped his pants and was all over me. He quickly threw me on the bed, unbuttoned my jeans, and peeled them off of me.

I purposely didn't wear any panties because the other day he told me that he liked when women didn't wear panties.

"I see you was paying attention." Pete smiled and buried his face in my pussy, working his tongue on my clit.

"Ahhhh shit! I love the way you eat this pussy."

Pete definitely knew how to eat the lining out of a pussy.

When his tongue was on my clit and he had a finger inside my pussy, that nigga might as well have been Denzel Washington or some shit because, at those moments, he definitely had it going on.

He repeatedly flicked his tongue on my clit. "You gonna cum for me, baby?"

"Yessss! Yessss!" I screamed with my eyes closed.

About one minute later, my legs were shaking, and my whole body was trembling, as I came hard.

"Oh shit! Pete, what the hell do you be doing to me?" I asked, giggling at the same time.

"Ain't nobody ever eat your pussy like I do, right?"

I shook my head no.

Pete had me take off my wife-beater, so he could suck on my titties, and before I could blink, the nigga had flipped me around onto my stomach, slid on a condom, and was fucking the shit outta me from behind.

I was always vocal when I had sex, but with Pete, I stepped up the theatrics on purpose, just to boost his ego. I was screaming and panting and carrying on, and I knew I had him thinking that he was truly murdering shit like a porno star.

"Oh yeah, baby," I screamed. "Fuck me! Take this pussy, baby! Take it!"

Pete was grunting and pumping and working his dick as hard as he could. He was working with a little something so it was all good, and plus, I loved getting fucked in that position.

"Ahh shit, I'm getting ready to nut, baby," Pete hollered.

I reached my right arm back to grip Pete's thigh and I pulled him closer to me so that he could pull out when he came. He had all of his body weight pressed against my ass and in seconds he was filing up his condom with cum.

"Your pussy is so gotdamn tight. I love that shit," Pete said, breathing heavily as he lay next to me.

Pete had brought a bottle of Bacardi and a two-liter bottle

of Coke, which was in a bag resting on the floor. I got up and poured me a drink and reached into my bag and got a Newport to smoke.

"So, Pete, what's the deal? We gonna get this bread or what?"

Pete smiled as he sat up. He took the condom off then stood up. He grabbed hold of his jeans, made his way over to me, and poured a drink for himself. "Let me show you something." Pete reached into his pants pocket and pulled out a wad of cash. "You see this shit?" he said. "You see that car we was driving in? A nigga don't get this shit off my C.O. salary, you feel me?"

I felt everything that Pete was saying. As far as my scheme to hustle drugs into the jails, I knew that Pete was 'bout it and would be down for whatever from the first night I'd kicked the idea to him and he gave me that badge.

"GG, you get the work, and I gotchu. Forty dollars for every hundred is what I need, and I gotchu on this."

I took a pull from my cigarette and smiled. I knew I had to use what I had to get what I wanted. I thought to myself, *As long as Pete comes through for me on his end of the deal, then he would be able to practically own this pussy of mine.*

Chapter 4

Even though I was only sixteen, I carried myself in a much more mature manner. And, depending on how I was dressed, I could easily have passed for an eighteen to twenty-five-year-old woman. It was never a problem for me to get inside of the hottest club, order drinks, or pretty much do anything the average sixteen-year-old just couldn't do.

I had a passion for partying and usually went out partying at least three nights a week in Manhattan. Matter of fact, it was my love for partying that caused me to drop out of Jamaica High School at the tender age of fifteen. I mean, who had time for school or for waking up at seven o'clock in the morning and going to homeroom? I sure as hell didn't. Usually my nights of partying included me coming home at five o'clock in the morning either drunk as hell, high as a kite, or a combination of the two. And that's, of course, if I made it back home at all, because many nights I would leave the club and head to a hotel or to the house or apartment to fuck some nigga I'd met that same night. So, needless to say, by seven o'clock in the morning, I was usually in no condition to be getting up going to any fucking school.

Without a doubt, out of all nights, I loved partying on Tuesday night the most. Tuesday night was industry night, when all of the major record labels would have album release parties for different artists who had new albums coming out. It was at one of those industry parties that I'd met this hustler from Harlem named Minnesota.

With my butterscotch complexion and fat ass, it was nothing for me to attract ballers, record executives, or athletes. I looked good as hell, and I had the sophisticated swagger to match.

I knew exactly how to work my shit. I wasn't like the majority of thirsty bitches who would have their hat in hand begging for dough, expecting a nigga to trick on them as soon as he met them. I was on the opposite end. I would never ask for shit, and I think that's the reason I would always get hit off with money from all of the dudes I fucked with.

Although I hadn't spoken to Minnesota in about six months, I knew he'd be happy to hear from me when I called him and asked him to come to Queens and see me. And I was right. We spoke on the phone for about fifteen minutes. Minnesota told me he would get to Hollis that night around ten, but that he couldn't chill for long because he was heading out of town.

Minnesota arrived right on time. I headed outside and got inside the passenger; side of his all-white CLK Mercedes Benz.

"*Muah!*" I leaned over and gave him a kiss on his cheek, overexaggerating with the sound effects.

"What's up, ma? You still looking sexy as a muthafucka."

"You know how I do." I laughed. "I gotta keep shit thorough."

Minnesota was dark-skinned and had the look of a muscular bodyguard or club bouncer. And with his bald head and zero facial hair, in some ways, he reminded me a lot of the actor Ving Rhames.

"Minnesota, now you know I ain't never asked you for shit, right?"

Minnesota nodded his head and looked at me, so I could

keep talking and get to the point. When I hesitated, he reached into his pocket and pulled out a bankroll of hundred-dollar bills.

"How much you need, GG?"

"No. Nah, nah, I ain't trying to hit you up for no cash," I said, reaching into my sweat pants and pulling out my own wad of money.

Minnesota smirked and looked at me. "So what's up? Speak to me."

"Okay, look, here's the thing. I wanna get in the game, but I don't have a connect. And I'm not asking you to give up your connect. All I'm asking you is for you to be my connect, but . . . I need you to give me the same prices that you getting from your connect."

Minnesota didn't say anything. He looked at me then turned his head and looked out of his passenger window and then into his rearview mirror.

"GG, what the fuck is the deal? Be straight up with me."

"I *am* being straight up with you."

"This game ain't for you, that's number one. And who the fuck put you up to ask me this shit?"

I sucked my teeth and gave Minnesota a look to kill. "Minnesota, come on now, you know I wouldn't snake you."

"I don't know shit. All I know is, I don't hear from your ass for a minute, and then you call me and have my ass drive out to Queens, and now you talking crazy. I mean, just think about what the fuck you just asked me. And you tell me why the fuck should I do what the fuck you asking me? I mean, you got a mean head game and the whole nine, but come on, ma."

"I one hundred percent feel you, and I know where you coming from. You saying, why the fuck should you do this for me? Like, what the fuck is in it for you?"

Minnseota didn't say shit. He just looked at me.

"This is what's in it for you." I reached into my pocket and pulled out the badge that I had. "You hit me off on a regular basis with what I want, and when you need me to make a run for you, then I'm there to do it. And, yes, this shit is real." I gave it to him for him to examine it.

"I got my own get-out-of-jail-free card right there, my if-the-cops-stop-me-don't-fuck-with-me card. You gotta fucking feel me on this."

Minnesota squinted his eyes and looked at me in a piercing way, as if he was trying to look right through me.

"Baby, I just wanna get in the game and get this money. That's it. No more, no less."

Minnesota handed the badge back to me. "Reach your hand around that seat right there and slide that shit all the way back and recline it as far as it can go," he told me.

He then put the car in drive and drove off, making a series of left turns and right turns. He kept looking in his mirrors, I guess to see if anybody was following us. Then he finally pulled over on a real secluded block and put the car in park.

"Take off all your shit."

I looked at him sort of confused.

"GG, take off your fucking clothes. Strip down butt-ass naked."

I instantly knew where Minnesota was going with this, so I complied with his wishes and.began squirming out of my clothes, which wasn't easy, considering the tight, confined space I was in.

"Gotdamn! I ain't think it was possible for you to get any thicker than you already was." Minnesota took my sweat pants and T-shirt and balled them up and sort of patted them down. Then he put them on the dashboard of his car.

"Can you please turn out that dome light? I really don't need all of Hollis seeing my goods."

Minnesota stared at me and smiled before reaching for the switch that controlled the interior dome light and turning it off.

"Sooo, what are you waiting on?" I asked. I mean, I knew he wanted to fuck, and I wanted to hurry up and get the shit over with.

"Here. Put your shit back on." He tossed me my clothes and put the car in drive. "You caught me off guard and shit, and I just had to make sure that your ass wasn't wearing no fucking tape recorder or some shit."

"Nigga, that shit is so fucked up. I mean, come on now. What the fuck?"

"GG, just put your shit on and shut the fuck up. I gotta protect my shit, and I can't have no trick-ass bitch fucking up my shit."

Just as I was about to respond to Minnesota and get all up in his ass for calling me a trick-ass bitch, the fucking cops pulled up behind us and flashed their lights, signaling for us to pull over.

"Muthafucka! You got me butt-ass naked up in this car, and for no fucking reason, and now the cops is pulling us over."

"GG, word is bond—Watch your fucking mouth! I'll smack the shit outta you!"

I was outta line with Minnesota, but at the same time it was all part of my game, to show that I was a real chick who was 'bout it-'bout it.

After Minnesota pulled over, the three plainclothes cops got out of their car and approached our car.

"Fuck!" I screamed out loud 'cause I wasn't fully dressed yet.

Minnesota's windows were tinted, and it was late night, so the cops had their flashlights shining into the car.

"Don't roll the window down yet. Let me just get these clothes on first."

"GG, just chill. It ain't like they caught us fucking or anything. I ain't riding dirty, but with yo' ass fidgeting and shit, they'll light this car up with bullets."

Minnesota was right, so I just sat still and waited. He cracked the window very slightly.

"Sir, can you turn off the engine and step out of the car?" The cop on the driver's side pulled on the driver's side door handle, which was locked.

"Officer, can you just give us a second while she puts on her clothes?"

"Muthafucka, I need you and your naked black bitch to put your fucking hands where I can see them and open the fucking door. You got two seconds!" The cop drew his hand-gun and aimed at us. At that point, all of the officers had their guns drawn.

Minnesota knew they weren't bullshitting, so he unlocked the doors, and instantly the cops ripped open both doors and dragged us out of the car and threw us onto the dark, dirty street.

"Officer, I'm on the job," I blurted out, not knowing where I had got the balls to say it. But I had to, because if they had looked through my shit and found the badge, they would have wondered why I hadn't said shit. "My identification is in the car."

Two cops kept their guns drawn on us while we were face down on the pavement, and the third rummaged through the car, looking for shit. Within a minute he emerged from the car with my badge.

"What the fuck are y'all doing?" he asked. His tone was now changed. "She a C.O.," he said to his two partners.

"Oh my God, I am soooo embarrassed!"

"Get up and get dressed," the cop ordered.

"We got a call of suspicious activity in the area. Get dressed. Stop walking with so much cash on you. This is Hollis," the cop said then headed back to his unmarked car with the other two cops.

In a flash they were ghost.

"Yo, that shit was crazy!" Minnesota said.

"Now do you see what the fuck I'm talking about?"

"Yo, I gotta head outta town, but I'll be back in two days, and we'll do business. Just keep your fucking mouth shut and don't utter my motherfucking name to nobody. Ya heard me?"

I nodded my head and kept a serious look on my face, but I was beaming on the inside. I had cemented a deal with a "semi-connect," which to me was gonna work out just as good as a deal with a direct connect.

I had no idea just what the fuck I had sparked that night. But I would soon find out how careful I needed to be, and how quickly the streets could devour a bitch.

Chapter 5

Two days had passed, and Minnesota was coming back in town. We were gonna square shit away and get shit on and poppin'. But first I had to deal with some typical female bullshit.

As soon as I walked into our apartment, Monya approached me and said to my face, "So I see you on that snake shit, GG! Can a bitch ever live? Like, just one time in my fucking life, can I live?"

"What the fuck are you talking about? And can you please back up outta my face?" I brushed past her.

"Don't be pushing into me like that!" Monya grabbed me by my hair and pulled me to the ground and began punching and kicking on me.

Monya wasn't that big, so she wasn't as strong as I was. I was able to get to my feet and fight back with no problem. I rushed her and pushed her backwards into the kitchen table that we had, breaking it in the process.

"Uggghh!" Monya grunted in pain.

I knew I had knocked the wind outta her, and proceeded to punch her in the face. Then I grabbed an extension cord that was plugged into the wall and wrapped it around her neck and began pulling on it as tight as I could, choking her.

"I'll kill you, bitch! You hear me? I'll fucking kill you!"

Saleeta emerged from her room and came running to Money's aid. "GG, what the hell is going on? Get off of her."

"I don't know! Ask this bitch!" I screamed. "She's the one that came for my neck as soon as I walked in the door." I decided to loosen my grip of the cord around Money's neck. She looked as if she was about to pass out.

Money got to her feet and was holding her neck and gasping for air. Then she stormed toward the utensil drawer and was reaching for a knife, until Saleeta and I both grabbed her.

"Money, what the hell is wrong with you? What the fuck are you so hot about?" I screamed.

"You know what the fuck I'm hot about!"

"No, I don't! I know you're crazy. That's about it."

"Yeah, I'm crazy, but you a trifling-ass bitch. Why the fuck I go to answer the door today and I see Pete at the door with some fly-ass drop-top shit he was driving? But was he coming to check for me? No. He was checking for GG, and acted like he didn't even know my ass."

"Oh my fucking God!"

"Don't be calling on God's name now after you swore up and down how corny the nigga was. But fast-forward, and the nigga is banging your back out, and you can't even tell me? What the fuck is that but some snake shit?"

"Money, what the fuck! This is some bullshit, so get over it. I already told both you and Saleeta that it has to be about money over niggas. And this is exactly what the fuck I'm talking about. The only reason the nigga come to check me is about some get-money shit, that's it. Fuck what the nigga driving! That's old and tired. Chicks is always pushing up on a nigga because of what he got, but we ain't never trying to get our own money."

Money blew air outta her lungs. She made her way to her room, blurting out under her breath, "Yeah, whatever."

A part of me did feel bad and felt real whorish for having

fucked Pete, but I knew what I was after, so to me, it was like something that I was doing as part of my job. Nothing more, nothing less.

I spoke to Saleeta for a little while, and I explained my position. She understood and said that she would speak to Money for me and help patch shit up.

I had moves to make and a drug run to go on that night, so truth be told, I could care less what Money was thinking. We was about to start getting this paper, so for her sake, Monya needed to get over shit quick, or else her ass was about to be tossed up outta the Cartel.

Chapter 6

The Art of Deception

GG had a plan that was tighter than your average hustler's plan to get money, but the one thing that she didn't have going for her was the ability to know a snitch when she saw one. Minnesota was a snitch, straight up and down. He wasn't your average criminal informant. He was basically a big-time snitch drug dealer who ruled and made money with immunity simply because he had so many New York City cops down with his illegal activity.

He basically would give the NYPD the information that they needed in order to help them arrest certain people. In return he gave cash to certain corrupt NYPD cops, the same cops who he could call on to murder rivals, or get information out of that could help him run his empire.

Minnesota had way too much information that could have sent cops away to federal prison for years if he ever turned state's evidence, so he was always under surveillance by the same crooked cops he worked with. They just wanted to make sure he was staying on the up-and-up with them.

As soon as Minnesota made it back to his sprawling New Jersey home just hours after having visited GG in Queens, an off-duty cop kicked in his door and aimed a 9 mm to his head. "Minnesota! Who the fuck was the bitch?"

"She ain't nobody but some young trick bitch."

"So what the fuck is she doing with a badge?"

"Yo, Mike, word is bond—I got no idea what she's doing with that shit or where the fuck she got it from, but the bitch ain't even old enough to be a fucking C.O."

"Tell me something better than that, Minnesota. I don't like anxiety or shit that gives me anxiety."

"A'ight, a'ight, listen. Here's the deal. We just gotta find out what the fuck is going on. You talk to who you gotta talk to, and we'll set that bitch up. She was coming to me to supply her with some work, so all I gotta do is pass her ass off to one of my people in my crew. But check it—it won't really be somebody from my crew. It'll be somebody from your internal affairs department. They'll just be undercover. Then they can pump her for as much information as they can get outta that bitch."

Mike, the white off-duty cop, lowered his gun and looked at Minnesota. He looked as if he was chewing on his right cheek and then he nodded his head.

"Mike, you need to know what the fuck is up, and so do I. This chick calls me out the blue. I ain't speak to her in six fucking months, and she up and calls and tells me that she wants to buy some work—and the bitch is walking with a badge. How the fuck do I trust that shit? And how the fuck do you trust it?"

Mike nodded his head and said that they both couldn't trust no shit like that. Mike left, but not before assuring Minnesota that he was gonna have someone from NYPD get on shit ASAP, so that everybody could know just what the fuck was going on.

Chapter 7

GG was excited when Minnesota called her and told her that she would be hearing from a chick uptown in Harlem named Cynthia, and that Cynthia would be the one she would deal with from that point forward, as far as making drug purchases.

"I'm always on the go, in and out of town and shit, so it would be better if you just dealt with Cynthia. She'll hold you down with whatever you need," Minnesota explained.

"Okay, cool. So you gave her my number? You want me to call her or what?"

"Yeah, I gave her your digits. Just chill, and she'll get up with you. She's about that money, so you'll hear from her."

It had been about two weeks or so since GG and Minnesota had first spoken about her plan. Confident that everything would go as planned, she went ahead and began banging out plans with Pete as to exactly how they were gonna get the drugs into the prisons.

"Pete, I don't know about bringing all these extra muthafuckas into the mix. I mean, the more people involved, then the more chances we got of slipping up or of some niggas snitching and shit."

Pete understood GG's concerns, but being a C.O., he knew firsthand just how the jails worked. So he knew what could work and what couldn't work. "GG, just get me the work, and I got the rest."

Pete had already worked things out with C.O.'s he knew and could trust at the three jails that they were going to initially target. And he also was cool with some members of the Bloods, who he insisted they use to help them get the drugs in and then distributed, once the drugs got in.

"I don't know, Pete. I mean, I really don't wanna fuck with them Blood niggas right off the bat. We don't really need them niggas anyway. Me and my girls can get the shit in. All we need is to know when to bring the shit. Get the shit set up where, when we arrive on visits, there will be cool C.O.'s that'll look the other way and let us do our thing."

Pete and GG went back and forth until they finally agreed on a plan they were both comfortable with.

So, from that point, GG just sat back and waited to hear from Cynthia.

GG knew right away that her and Cynthia were gonna click simply because the first time that they spoke on the phone Cynthia invited GG to hang out and party with her.

"Yeah, I don't really like talking on the phone too crazy about shit, but Minnesota put me up on what you was looking for. So tonight we'll handle all that shit, get drunk as hell, and really do it up big at this party. You feel me?"

GG smiled a big Kool-Aid smile and told her that she loved to party and that she would definitely be there.

"Listen, who are you gonna roll with?" Cynthia asked.

"Probably just me and my girl Saleeta. I'm not sure."

"I'm asking because we going in a stretch Navigator limo, so you and your girl can ride with us if you want."

"Say *word*?"

"GG, this is how we do. So if y'all wanna go, just meet me

at Ninety-Sixth Street and Third Avenue, right on the corner. Be there by, like, ten, but no later than ten thirty, and just ask the driver for me."

"Okay, no doubt. That's what's up," GG said before hanging up the phone.

Chapter 8

Cynthia

Undercover Queen

One of the good things about being asked to be the lead undercover investigator into Minnesota's possible involvement with a corrupt undercover cop was that at times I got to sort of be my own boss. For the most part I made my own hours, in that I started and ended my day when I wanted. But sometimes the investigation took me to a point where I didn't have that control, where it dictated if and when I'll be able to start or finish my day, or even do normal things like call home and speak to my family and my boyfriend. But that rarely happened, and I was usually free to roam as I please.

Speaking to my boyfriend was becoming increasingly difficult. I was getting obsessed with my work, and building this wedge between me and my man. Subconsciously, I think that was because of what I was contemplating doing, if "it" became necessary. And in my line of deep undercover work, "it" sometimes did become necessary.

Tuesday, September 10th, 1997 marked the night of the anniversary party for *The Source* magazine, and as I had promised GG and her friend, I had a white stretch Navigator limo waiting to take a crew of us to the party in Newark, New Jersey.

GG and her friend Saleeta were the last to get into the limo. As the limo driver held open the door for them to get inside, they both seemed a little hesitant about getting into the twenty-two-seater, which was just about filled to capacity.

Everyone inside the limo got deathly quiet as GG and Saleeta piled into the weed-smoke-filled limo. There was a good mixture of guys and girls. And, of course, most of the girls were scantily clad. A drug dealer named Cheeks and another guy were both sitting next to two very attractive Asian-looking girls. I didn't know who they were, but I wanted to do something to break the tension that GG and Saleeta had created. Not to mention, I had yet to even introduce myself to GG.

"GG?" I asked really loud.

"Hey, Cynthia," GG responded.

That's what I thought. I wanted to go sit next to GG, so I got up and moved over to where they were. As I scooted past Cheeks, I stopped and leaned over and gave him a kiss that wasn't exactly on his lips, but it was right in between the corner of his lips and the start of his cheek. I was wearing a pair of tight jeans, and when I bent over to kiss Cheeks, my red thong was fully exposed, as was the tattoo on my lower back.

"Hey, GG," I said, so everyone could hear me, which was easy, because the music had been lowered.

"You're not gonna introduce us to everybody?" Cheeks asked.

The Asian girl Cheeks was with cut her eyes at me.

"Everybody up in here already knows me, and for those that don't, I'm Cynthia, Li'l Cynthia, Li'l Cent, Ms. Minnesota, or whatever the hell y'all wanna call my sexy ass." I laughed. I was drunk as hell, and the night hadn't even started yet. "And this is my girl GG from Queens, and her friend—I'm sorry, sweetie. What's your name?"

"Saleeta," Saleeta responded with a smile.

"That's GG and Saleeta. Saleeta and GG, that's everybody. Shit, we all grown. Y'all know how to mingle and get to know each other. Turn that fucking music up and let's get this shit poppin'." I really couldn't believe how drunk I was, and I definitely couldn't believe how fucking fun my job was.

GG and Saleeta both were dressed like a million dollars, and they both were attractive as hell. They said hello to everyone in the car and exchanged smiles, and when everyone was done saying what's up, the driver, almost on cue, took off and maneuvered us to the party.

Someone yelled, "Turn that fucking music up!"

Suddenly Jay-Z's music blared through the speaker system.

I was determined to fit in with Cheeks, one of Minnesota's top lieutenants. I immediately lit a cigarette.

As I nodded my head, reciting the hook to one of the songs from his *Reasonable Doubt* album, I noticed Mike Jackson, a petty criminal from Queens, in the limo. I had locked him up years ago, before I went deep undercover. He was looking at me with a deathly "ice grill," like he was trying to figure out who the hell I was, or what exactly I was about. But I didn't pay him any attention, and there was no way I was gonna let him rattle me.

Mike had gotten knocked for a small amount of drugs, like two ounces of coke, but under New York's Rockefeller drug laws, he got hit with a nice bid. Sitting right across from him, I also noticed Chino, a Puerto Rican drug dealer from Spanish Harlem.

"Y'all want some Henny?" Cheeks asked, referring to the big bottle in the bar.

In a matter of seconds, everyone had a glass of Henny on the rocks. Before I knew what was up, the tension in the limo was broken, and a blunt was being passed around. GG and Saleeta took a hit of it, and so did I.

As I drank the Hennessy, I had to remind myself I was working. Since I knew there stood a good chance that I would get really, really, really high that night, I wanted to have all of my important conversations with GG before I was too wasted.

Cheeks held the blunt out to me in a manner that asked if I wanted some more. Without saying anything, I simply reached out and took it, and sucked on it for dear life. I passed it back to him and then began to drink from my glass. In no time, the combination of weed and Hennessy loosened me up and had me feeling very good.

"GG, let me introduce you to Cheeks. Cheeks, this is GG. GG, this is Cheeks."

GG stuck out her hand. "Nice to meet you."

"Yeah, you too," he replied as he gently shook her hand. "Minnesota told me a little about you."

"Really?" GG responded.

"No doubt. We got them thangs for you." Cheeks then took a drink of his liquor.

GG nodded and smiled and then looked away toward my direction. At that point, Biggie's hit song, "Who Shot Ya?" came blasting through the speakers, and even though everybody was just about drunk or high out their minds, they all began to recite some of the lyrics in unison.

All of the guys shouted and exclaimed how that song was "their shit."

Mike Jackson was still looking at me like he had a serious problem with me, but again I had to dismiss it and not let it rattle me. I would be lying, though, if I said I wasn't worried about him saying something stupid and blowing my cover, like questioning if I was a cop or not. Unfortunately, that was just the rough and risky side of operating undercover.

I took a swig from my glass, finishing off the liquor that was inside of it, and then I reached over and got the bottle and poured some more Hennessy into the glass. I knew I was taking a big chance by drinking and smoking, because it could impair my judgment, and also later on down the road, if I had to testify in court about my investigation, my credibility would be in serious question. But the truth of the matter was, I was allowed to drink on the job, but getting drunk . . . well, that was not allowed. Neither was the weed-smoking or cocaine-sniffing. But, hey, it was a stressful job, and I had to do what I had to do.

The alcohol and Hennessy were definitely making me so good, it had given me the confidence to look at Cheeks and pucker up my lips and throw a kiss his way. I was totally disrespecting the Asian chick that was playing him so close, but my impaired state of mind made me not give a fuck. Cheeks smiled, and I smiled back at him. Right then, I knew, with me smoking weed and drinking Henny and flirting with him, there was no way in the world that anybody would think I was a cop. Not even Mike Jackson, who just wouldn't quit ice-grilling me. Although Cheeks was a convicted criminal helping to run one of the most profitable drug organizations in New York, he was still attractive, or at least that's what the liquor was telling me. I mean, Cheeks was cool, and he looked good too, and he had this lighter shade of dark skin. I don't know what it was, but it was just something about his complexion, and dark-skin guys in general, that I liked. A DMX song came blasting through the speaker, and I rocked my body in rhythm with the music and continued to flirt.

GG and Saleeta had both loosened up and were having a good time drinking, talking, and laughing. By the time we arrived at the party, which was being held at a hotel near Newark Airport, both GG and I had had way too much to drink. But we were also primed and ready to enjoy ourselves that night.

We arrived at the entrance of the hotel at about one in the

morning, and there were people and expensive cars every-where, and there was also a strong police presence. Nor-mally there would have been some type of VIP entrance, but seeing that it was at a hotel, the only way into the party was through the front entrance. As we congregated in front of the building, I remember feeling drunk as hell. I didn't know how I was going to hold up throughout the night.

As I stood in front of the hotel and waited for everyone to enter, GG walked up to me. "Girl, I am sooo fucking twisted right now. Thank you for letting us roll with you," she said to me.

"Yeah, yeah, no doubt. The party ain't even get started yet."

GG pulled me to the side and told me she had the money for me and asked if we could knock everything out before we went inside.

"And what was Cheeks talking about? I thought I was fuck-ing witchu?"

"Yeah, I mean, you are. It's just . . . we all family. You know what I mean?" I grabbed GG's hand and led her back to our limo, after I told Saleeta to chill in the hotel lobby, and to give us a minute.

When we got to the limo, I asked the driver to pop the trunk for me. When he did, I moved a shirt and a pair of pants that covered a brown paper bag, which I opened for GG to look inside.

"That's what the fuck I'm talking about!" GG gave me a pound.

I then told her to just give Cheeks the money at the end of the night, and she could take the weed when the limo dropped her off. After I closed the trunk, GG and I then started walking back toward the party.

"GG," I said in a whispering tone. I guided her to come closer to me, so I could talk directly into her ear.

"What's up?"

"I got a hundred stacks for you, but I need one of those shields you got."

GG looked at me and did a double take, and a slight frown came across her face. "What the fuck you talking about?"

I didn't respond verbally. I just looked at her as if to say, *Come on now. You know what the fuck I'm talking about.* "You know I'm drunk as a muthafucka." I burst out laughing, trying to play shit off and break the tension. "Don't pay my ass no mind. Come on, let's get up in here and party. There's a bunch of people I want you to meet."

I didn't look GG in her eyes, but I could feel her looking at me from the corner of her eyes as we walked into the lobby of the hotel and prepared to party until the early morning hours.

Chapter 9

GG

On and Poppin'

Within three months Connie's Cartel had shit on and poppin' in three of the biggest jails in the New York City metropolitan area. The situation with Pete was working out really good. He had a network of five corrupt correction officers he could trust, and they were helping him to move our product into the jails smoother and better than any of us had ever imagined.

As far as cash was concerned, the Cartel was making dough hand over fist. I had been consistently re-upping with Minnesota by way of either Cheeks or Cynthia. We had progressed from purchasing just weed to now purchasing two kilos of cocaine or more every time we re-upped.

Me, Money, and GG were all on perfect terms, and we were really living and doing it up big in the clubs. There was no jealousy or major beefs among us, and that was because everybody in our crew was eating real well.

The only real issue I had was with Cynthia. The chick was cool and the whole nine, but at the same time, she was making me claustrophobic with the way she was always in my face every time I turned around. But ever since the night of *The Source* magazine party when she tried to be slick and ask me about the badge that I had, I knew I had to play her real careful and not trust her.

I never let anyone know about my suspicions, but what I did do in the interim was stay on the lookout for a new connect, so I could totally stop fucking with Minnesota and start getting my product from a less clingy connect.

What's funny is when you start to move in certain circles, you start meeting the right people, the people who can take you to where you wanna go, and then, sort of like by default, you start being around faces that become familiar to you. Like with me, for example, I constantly kept seeing this Spanish dude who looked mad familiar, but I just could never figure out where I knew him. Wherever I went, I would run into him, and we would always say what's up to each other, and that would be about it. One night when I was at the Shark Bar with Money, somebody came up behind both of us and asked us if he could buy us a drink.

I turned around and immediately smiled when I saw it was the same Spanish dude I had been running into. Although I didn't know his name, I stretched out my arms and gave him a slight hug. "Hey, what's up? What is your name again? 'Cause I see you everywhere. I be killing myself trying to figure out where I know you from."

The dude gave me this weird look, as if I was supposed to know who the hell he was, or as if we had fucked or something.

"Chino, ma. My name is Chino. Come on now, don't play me like that."

"Chino! That's right. From the limo that night, right?"

Chino nodded his head. You could tell that his ego was back. Money and I told him what we were drinking, and he ordered a round of drinks for us as we sat at the bar and he stood behind us.

"So what's up for the rest of the night? What else y'all getting into?" he asked.

"We bouncing after we get outta here. I gotta bring my ass back to Queens and get some fucking sleep. Word is bond, I'm tired like a muthafucka!" I replied.

"We partied our ass off last night at that Fat Joe party. We fucking threw up drunk and the whole nine. It was crazy," Money added.

Chino chuckled.

As soon as our drinks arrived and I had taken a sip, he asked me to walk with him for a minute. We took about ten steps or so away from the bar before he started talking.

"So, m what's good?"

"You tell me. I mean, there gotta be a reason that we keep bumping into each other."

"Yo, I'ma keep it straight one hundred with you, but I want you to be straight up with me as well. A'ight?"

"That's all I know how to do."

"This strictly between me and you, but stop fucking with the niggas and let me beat whatever price they giving you." Chino paused.

I knew what Chino was referring to, but I didn't exactly know how to respond. On one hand, I wanted to hear him out and see exactly what kind of numbers he was talking, but on the other hand, I didn't know if he was real close with Minnesota and was just testing my loyalty or what.

"Chino, Minnesota basically put a bitch on. You know what I'm saying? So you know his prices ain't dirt-ass cheap, but at the same time, I know how to respect the game. You know?"

"Listen, this is the deal. Minnesota and Cheeks and that whole crew, them niggas is snake-ass muthafuckas. Like what I'm saying is this: you ain't gotta see me for no work. I'll be good. You see me shining, and the whole nine. And I won't front. A nigga feeling you a little something, you know? But, regardless of all the bullshit, you seem like real good people, and I'm telling you to watch your back. Do you and do the loyalty thing—I respect that—but don't ever be loyal to a snake."

I kept my mouth shut, so Chino could keep doing all the talking.

"Check it. That night we was in the limo, my man Mike Jackson was up in there with us, right. So the nigga just finished doing ten joints upstate, right. But when a muthafucka gets locked up, they don't forget the cop's face who locked them up. You can't forget that shit."

"True indeed," I said.

"So fucking Cynthia is up in the truck smoking and drinking and shit, right, and Mike is looking at her like, I know that bitch Cynthia, but he can't remember where he knows her from. And she was acting real shifty and shit whenever she looked at the nigga, and he didn't stress it, but he could sense something was up. Yo, when we got back to the crib after the party, Mike looked in this scrapbook photo album shit that he keeps that had old newspaper articles from when he got arrested and bam! The bitch Cynthia is up in that muthafucka, with all her blue NYPD uniform shit on."

"Get the fuck outta here!"

"GG, I ain't got no reason to lie to you. I know you trying to come up. You got that 'eye-of-the-tiger' look in you, like you just want it all, and that's good. All I'm saying is, watch yourself, baby girl. And you need to fuck with me and get these good prices that I'm fucking with—thirty percent lower than that garbage they selling you."

Chino handed me a hundred-dollar bill to pay for our drinks and started walking me back toward the bar, where Money was sitting at. Then he wrote down his phone number and handed it to me.

"Ms., what's your name?"

"Everybody calls me Money."

"Ahhh . . . I like that. That's what's up. Money, make sure your girl calls me."

After Chino said that, he kissed me on the cheek, and then him and his boy made their way to the restaurant area of the Shark Bar.

Wow! I thought to myself.

"What's up with that nigga?" Money asked.

"It ain't nothing. That nigga bullshitting. He trying to play games, chasing pussy and shit, and I'm trying to get this paper," I said, not wanting to reveal what he'd told me. I knew I had a fucking problem on my hands. I just didn't have a clue as to how to fix it. I ordered a double shot of Jack Daniel's and took that shit straight to the head.

"Pass this money to the bartender, and let's get the fuck up outta here," I said to Money before we left and headed back to Queens.

Chapter 10

Pete

Snake Bitches

As soon as I left work, I jumped in my car and sped off doing about 90 miles an hour. I was pissed the fuck off and couldn't get to Bayside quick enough. Bayside was the all-white section of Queens that GG had moved to as soon as she started seeing some real paper from our hustle.

A ride that would normally take fifteen or twenty minutes, I did it in five minutes during the heart of rush-hour traffic. That's just how vexed and heated I was.

When I pulled up to GG's house, my car skidded as I slammed on the brakes and jumped out of the car and headed toward her front door. My car was parked crooked as hell, and a lot of it was still sitting in the street, partially blocking the flow of traffic.

I knew GG was home because her new Land Cruiser was parked in the driveway. So I charged toward her front door and tried to open it, but it was locked. I rang the bell and banged on the door like a madman. "GG, open the fucking door!" I paused for a minute. When I got no answer, I continued banging. "GG, I said open this fucking door right the fuck now!"

Thirty seconds later, GG came to the door dressed in a pair of shorts and a T-shirt. It was November and getting darker earlier, and also getting cold outside, so I was a little surprised to see her wearing shorts and a T-shirt.

"Nigga, what the fuck is wrong witchu?"

"Bitch, shut the fuck up!" I yelled as I stepped into GG's house and slammed the door behind me. I immediately grabbed her by the throat, lifting her up off the ground, and rammed her into the wall. I could tell that I'd knocked the wind out of her by the way she grunted, doubled over, and fell to the ground.

I pulled my gun out and stepped on her throat, and pointed the gun at her head. "GG, tell me the fucking truth! Are you talking to the fucking cops?"

GG looked at me real wide-eyed, still trying to catch her breath.

"Bitch, yes or no?"

GG tried her hardest to move my foot from her throat, and fight me off. "Get off of me!" she screamed.

"Answer my fucking question and don't lie to me!" I eased my foot from GG's throat but still held my gun on her.

GG shook her head and looked at me with the scowl of a lion. "I swear to God, you better murder me right now . . . 'cause your fucking ass will die tonight!"

I cocked my gun, my eyes burning a hole through her. From my experience in dealing with criminals, I could tell with fairly good accuracy when someone was lying to me. "GG, yes or fucking no?"

"No, muthafucka! What the fuck are you talking about?"

Common sense finally popped into my head. GG was telling me the truth. I sighed and lowered my gun, gritting my teeth and shaking my head. Stress and anxiety were getting the better of me.

"Yo, my boss and his fucking boss had me hemmed the fuck up in this interrogation room at work today, grilling my ass and asking a million fucking questions about the cars I drive and the amount of cash people been seeing me with. I knew they were just trying to feel me out and see if I would fucking just open up and tell on myself or some shit."

"So what the fuck? And that's why you come up in here tripping?"

"Nah. So then they say, 'So how was that sixteen-year-old pussy? That shit had to be tight as hell, right?' "

"Get the fuck outta here! They asked you that?"

"I swear to God. And then my supervisor was like, well, actually she's seventeen now."

"No way. And my birthday was last week. Ahh shit! So what did you say?"

"I ain't say shit."

"Pete, you got my word. I ain't say shit to nobody."

I started pacing GG's living room, thinking about my options. I blurted out, "Yo, we gotta shut shit down for a minute. Shit is too fucking hot."

GG shook her head. "Fuck! Pete, not now."

"Fuck you mean, not now? I just told you how hot shit is right now."

We brainstormed for a minute, but with every angle we looked at, the only conclusion I could come up with was to shut shit down until I felt the time was right to resume shit.

I did end up apologizing to her for the way I showed up at her crib and disrespected her. Not only did she accept my apology, but we also ended up fucking on her living room couch.

For some reason I felt the need to fuck her, just so I could really prove to myself that she hadn't snitched me out. From the way GG fucked me and responded to my dick, she hadn't snaked me. I just didn't know who to trust or what the hell was going on, but I was determined to find out.

Chapter 11

GG

New Connects

One thing was certain—Cynthia's ass had to be dealt with, and taken out. She was disrupting shit. And now that Pete had decided to shut shit down for a minute, I had to prepare for my first drought, which couldn't have come at a worse time.

Up until this point I had been doing my job very honorably. Everyone who was down with the Cartel was getting their money exactly the way they were supposed to. I was also doing a good job at making sure money was set aside to re-up. I had managed to set aside close to fifty grand for us to make another big drug purchase, but now I was having second thoughts, and was thinking about holding on to the cash instead.

I desperately wanted to keep Money and Saleeta in the dark, in terms of my connects and the overall business side of the Cartel, but with all of the drama of late, I switched up and started telling them the ins and outs of how I moved. I did that so I could get insight from them about our options.

Money and Saleeta suggested that we stop dealing with Minnesota. To my surprise, Saleeta and Money had met two Colombian drug dealers from the Bronx, who supposedly had ties to some Colombian cartel. They had promised

Money and Saleeta much more drugs for our money, way more than what Minnesota could give us, and from the sound of it, way more than what Chino was talking.

Besides, I had already had shit on consignment from Chino and was trying to figure out just how I was going to get his money up with the new drought I was in. So if what Saleeta and Money were talking was true, then it would have been like food sent from heaven. But with anything, when something sounds too good to be true, then it probably is.

The Colombians even promised Saleeta and Money heroin at a very good price. None of us knew anything about these Colombians, nor did we personally know anyone who knew them, so we were all skeptical about dealing with them. Why should we travel all the way to the Bronx to buy drugs and run the risk of getting robbed or busted by the cops? For all we knew the two Colombians could have been feds, so why run all the risks when we had a good drug connection in Spanish Harlem and another one in Harlem? From that standpoint, I was hesitant and not really big on the idea.

But with Saleeta and Money's persistence, and their constant pleading, badgering, and urging, I gave in and decided to go along with their newfound Colombian connection.

"So are y'all wit' it?" Money asked.

Reluctantly, I agreed.

"Well, we have to go up to the Bronx today then," Money said. "GG, you just said our inventory is running real low. Even if there is a drought, we just gotta find another way to move our shit."

Money and Saleeta decided to make the drug run to the Bronx, and I stayed behind. Saleeta thought it was best that I stay behind, since none of the Colombians knew me.

Actually, it was kind of funny to me. Saleeta and Money were basically doing the same thing to me that I had done to them, in terms of not letting me meet their connect. Regardless, the two of them armed with close to fifty thousand dollars in hand left for the Bronx. I chilled at my house and watched videos until I fell asleep.

It felt like I had been sleeping for hours when I was woken by the sound of the telephone, which scared the shit out of me.

Money was on the other end of the phone. She told me that her and Saleeta had returned from the Bronx with an enormous amount of dope and she couldn't tell me all of the details.

"A'ight. I'll be there in about a half," I informed her before ending the call.

Like me, Money and Saleeta had also moved out of the basement apartment we had shared, and they both moved into their own apartments in different parts of Queens. Money lived in Rego Park, and Saleeta lived in Rosedale.

"Holy shit!" I shouted as soon as I walked into the apartment and saw all of the work that Money and Saleeta had purchased. "What the fuck!"

"Stop standing over there gawking, and sit your fly ass down and help us get this shit ready," Saleeta said.

As we worked on our drugs, Saleeta told me exactly what they'd purchased and how much they'd paid for it. After hearing her report, I was able to soundly say that our new Colombian connection was definitely a smart business move. We definitely weren't gonna deal with Minnesota anymore. And Chino neither, for that matter. The deal we struck with the Colombians was way too enticing.

Supposedly, from rumors that Saleeta and Money had heard, the Colombians were dealing directly with a DEA agent who was getting drugs that had been placed onto planes that landed in New York's Kennedy Airport. It probably was true, because there really was no other way to explain just how the Colombians were able to give us the drugs at such dirt-cheap prices.

While we were working to bag up our shit, I decided to get back to Cheeks, since he had been blowing up my phone and leaving messages like crazy.

"What's up, Cheeks? This is GG."

"Hey, GG. What's up, girl? Where the fuck you been at?"

"Shit just been crazy for me. I been going through a little drought and shit."

"Yeah, I feel you, ma. Everybody's been going through it lately. You'll be a'ight, though. Yo, hold on for a second."

A female voice came on the line. It was Cynthia. "GG, what's up, girl? I know you coming through to the spot tonight, right?"

Before I could get a chance to answer, she added, "Yeah, we gonna be drinking and hanging out for Cheeks' birthday and shit. Minnesota got some strippers coming through and all that. So just come through, because if you don't, it's gonna look real disrespectful and shit."

Cynthia needed to knock it off. I knew the real reason she wanted to see my ass was because she wanted me to re-up with her, and hit her off with that side dough she was getting from me by hitting me off with some extra work that Minnesota didn't know about. But, as far as I was concerned, it was time to cut to the chase and be straight up with Cynthia, so her and Cheeks could stop blowing up my phone.

"Cynthia, listen, I gotta be straight up with you—and you can tell Cheeks and Minnesota what the deal is—but I'm about to get out the game. This shit ain't for me. I mean, already we got ourselves into a little jam that's gonna be hard to recover from, so I ain't gonna be fucking with y'all no more on the re-ups."

Cynthia was quiet for a minute. Then she quietly responded,

"Wow. Okay, I mean, I wasn't exactly expecting you to say that, but I guess it is what it is."

"Cynthia, I'll definitely come through tonight and represent for Cheeks. And, listen, even though my cash and shit ain't straight, I'll still get an ounce off of you for five hundred. But keep that between me and you."

"Yeah, that's cool with me. GG, you already know that y'all can come by and kick it whenever y'all get ready, regardless if y'all copping or not. "

"A'ight, Cynthia, so that's what's up. I'll see you tonight. Tell Cheeks' crazy ass I'll see him later."

Later that night, Saleeta, Money, myself, and two of our stripper homegirl friends, Xtasy and Jenny, decided to head uptown. We piled into my Land Cruiser and made our way to Harlem. When we reached Cheeks' building on East 110th Street, I saw Cynthia already standing outside, chilling with some of her people.

I parked the truck and got out and walked over to her.

Cynthia, in a hurried type of way, quickly pulled me to the side. "GG, did you bring money with you?" she asked.

"Yeah," I said. "I told you, I got you. Don't worry about it. I'ma lace you."

"No, it's not that," she said, sounding kind of annoyed. "Minnesota was on my ass and shit, bugging me, asking me why y'all aren't dealing with him anymore. I didn't tell him about them cats, whoever it was you said y'all were messing with. Matter of fact, I forgot their names and shit. But, I mean, he was really stressing me, and I don't wanna have to keep hearing this nigga's mouth every time I'm in the street."

I shook my head. "Cynthia, first of all, I never told you we was fucking with somebody else, so what the fuck is that about? I got money on me, but not that kind of cake. I only got about four G's in my pocket."

"Yeah, okay, that's good," Cynthia said, sounding kind of desperate. "He told me that the next time y'all re-upped, he would hit me off with some weed for myself for free. I guess he's gonna try to spit game to y'all and give y'all a good deal on some more work. You know, he's probably gonna try to gas y'all and lure y'all back as customers, especially if he finds out that y'all are going somewhere else."

"Fuck! Cynthia, I'm really not trying to be stressed like this. I never told you I was fucking with nobody else, so why the hell you keep saying that shit? And Minnesota know me. Why the fuck he acting like gotdamn John Gotti and shit? If he got a issue, tell him to call me. Matter of fact, is he coming through tonight?"

"Yeah, he's already upstairs chillin'. You know, GG, just fuck it. You right. Don't even stress yourself. Just come up-stairs and let's chill and have a good night." Cynthia walked me back over to the crew I had come with.

Being as street-smart as I was, I thought to myself, *Nah, GG. Something ain't right.* I couldn't figure out what it was, but I was starting to smell some kind of a rat. *Is Cynthia and her jake ass trying to set us up?* I wondered. *Why am I bugging?* There was no way in hell that she would ever do that and blow her cover wide the fuck open, but I was still feeling a bit suspicious. Why, all of a sudden, did it seem like Minnesota was fiendin' for us to buy some work from him? I was sure he was supplying many other dealers and crews throughout the city.

"A'ight, listen," I said after quickly pondering the situation, "I'll buy something from Minnesota, but I'm just doing it so that you can get this weed that he promised you. You sure he wasn't just frontin' when he told you that he was gonna hit you off?"

"GG, I doubt it. But, to be honest, it's not even about the free weed. I want you to talk to this nigga and let him know where y'all are at, so that he won't be stressing me."

Since I definitely was not one to be frontin', I wanted to make moves to see Minnesota. Even though I hadn't figured out what was up, I knew I had to handle the Cartel's "binis" with Minnesota. "Okay," I told her. "Then let's hurry and go see that nigga."

"A'ight, good. 'Cause I already told him we would be there."

Saleeta, Xtasy, Money, and Jenny wanted to know where Cynthia and I were off to.

"We'll be right back," I told them. "Y'all just chill here for a minute and wait for us. We'll be right back."

I was praying they wouldn't follow us upstairs, but they did, except for Money, who was chilling in the lobby, talking to some dude she knew from Queens.

Damn! I thought to myself. I didn't care too much if Saleeta and Money came along. In fact, it was probably better if they both were with me, just in case drama jumped off. But I didn't want Xtasy and Jenny to know what was up.

"Where y'all going?" Xtasy asked.

"Up to my friend's apartment," Cynthia answered. "It won't take long. I just have to tell him something real quick. We'll be in and out."

Unfortunately, Xtasy and Jenny were too dull to take the hint that Cynthia and I didn't want to be accompanied by them. So, of course, seeing that Saleeta had followed us, Xtasy and Jenny were also right on our coattails.

When we reached the entrance to the apartment we were going to, a guy frisked us at the door, and took a "biscuit" from me, and one from Saleeta.

"Yo, what's up with this?" Xtasy and Jenny both asked, rightfully alarmed.

"Don't worry about it, X," I said in an effort to calm her down. "I'll explain it to y'all later. Just chill."

"Yo, GG, what the hell are y'all doing with guns? Yo, whose apartment is this? GG, how long are we gonna be here?"

"I'll tell you later, X. Now just chill! Damn!" The bitch was getting on my nerves, acting as if she was a goody two-shoes and shit, and had never seen a gun or been frisked. The bitch took off her clothes for a living. It wasn't like she was a preacher or some upright and wholesome shit, so she needed to calm the fuck down.

That was the last thing I needed, to have Xtasy nagging me like some soft-ass pussy. I was trying my hardest to figure out what, if anything, was about to go down, what moves I was gonna make. And, at the same time, I felt somewhat like a parent because I knew that if anything jumped off that I would have to make sure that Xtasy, Jenny, and Saleeta were all right.

I and Saleeta knew that we were about to enter a drug apartment, or should I say a drug warehouse. Xtasy and Jenny didn't know that, which explains why they'd gotten so alarmed when we were all frisked. Xtasy wasn't the only alarmed one in our clique, 'cause I could sense that Saleeta also wasn't too big on the idea of stepping into that apartment, especially without our burners.

We all entered the apartment to the sound of loud rap music. From what I remember, it sounded like a Ron G mixtape.

Apart from the big, diesel, sweaty-looking guy who had frisked us, there were four guys already in the apartment, and a sexy young lady that we didn't know.

We all were very cordially invited inside, in a street kind of way, to sit down on a leather couch in the living room. As we sat, we were all nervously looking at each other, and no one was talking. A blunt was quickly rolled, sparked, and handed to Xtasy. Xtasy took a pull and then proceeded to pass the blunt around for all of us to smoke. No one was really taking deep pulls on the blunt 'cause we were all feeling very uncomfortable. Then someone passed around a tray with lines of coke on it. Jenny did one line and then passed it along, but everyone else passed on the coke.

Cheeks then called me over to him and Minnesota.

Out of everyone's earshot, Minnesota said to me, "Yo, GG, what's up? You got no love for me?" He gave me a pound and a quick ghetto hug.

"What's up, kid? You or your girls want something to drink? Some Henny? Some Cristal?"

"Oh, nah. We straight. Good lookin'-out, though."

"Yo, GG, so, on the business tip, what can I lace y'all with?"

"You talking in terms of work?" I asked.

Minnesota and Cheeks looked at me as if I was stupid.

"Yeah," Minnesota said, "I'm talking in terms of work. What the hell else did y'all niggas come here for? Especially with burners on y'all waists?"

At that point I began to think that I should have told Minnesota to get us a drink. That way we wouldn't have come across as so nervous and edgy. 'Cause I know I can definitely say that the gangster records and movies never tell about that nervous side that thugs have, but I for one was getting extremely nervous.

"Oh, nah. See, I didn't come to buy nothing. We came through to rep for Cheeks' birthday party. I only got like four G's on me. Didn't Cynthia tell you?"

Minnesota slowly raised his drink to his mouth and took a sip, revealing the gold, diamond-studded pinky ring on his right hand. "Nah, *potna*, Cynthia didn't tell me shit." He sucked air into his nose. "So what about your girls, they got loot on them or what?"

"Yeah, they got loot, but they didn't come to buy anything either. We just came to chill, you knaaimean?" I chuckled nervously. "Shit dried up for us just as fast as it started to pick up."

"What's up, GG? You trying to play us or what?" Minnesota asked, sounding truly ticked off.

At that point I was feeling mad shook. "Nah, man, it ain't even like that."

Sensing my fear, Minnesota knew he was in control and remained quiet.

Trying harder to ease the tension, I added, "Yeah, like I said . . . see, it's not even like that, you know. I mean, you hooked us up, and we ain't gonna ever forget how you hit us off lovely. I know *I* ain't gonna forget that shit. You hit me off and put me into the game when I had absolutely nothing going on, you knaaimean? So, I'm sayin', I would never snake you."

"A'ight, I hear what you sayin', kid. But, yo, listen—I'll give you a kilo for four G's right now, and y'all can come back next week, and I'll give y'all the same price. What's up?" Minnesota said, calling my bluff.

Like I said, I was shook and Minnesota could sense it, but I knew that I couldn't just let him totally play me like a bitch.

"Yo, Minnesota, I'll be straight up with you. I'll buy the kilo for four G's tonight, but that's all I'm buying. And, yo, I ain't gonna stand here and lie in your face and tell you that we'll be back next week, 'cause I doubt that's gonna happen."

Cheeks said, "What's up? Your money ain't right or something like that?"

"Nah, it's tight right now. My shit got fucked up. That's what I was trying to tell Cynthia."

Four G's for a kilo was a dynamite deal, but the Colombians could either match or beat that price. My knowledge of what they could do for us and for just about any other drug dealer in the city was what led me to know for sure that Minnesota had somehow got wind of the fact that we had purchased drugs from them. That had to be why he brought his figure so low. He had to have heard they were selling kilos for as low as four G's, and probably lost mad customers to them.

Yeah, Minnesota wanted to test me and see how I would react when he offered me the "ki" for four G's. And, yeah, I could have fronted and acted all excited about the price, and even made real plans to continue to buy from them if they'd promised us that price from now on. But I knew that they didn't have that kind of juice to consistently supply work at those prices, and that eventually they would balk on the four-thousand-dollar deal.

To get Minnesota out of Cynthia's hair, I had to hold my ground and just straight up tell him what was up. I mean, hell, if he was gonna lose us as a customer, and if his distribution racket was hurting because of the Colombians, then all he had to do was start taking over other cats' retail operations and he'd be fine. Actually that was probably his only option, because I doubt the Colombians would have even sold work to him, because he was their competition.

"Nah, our money is on point for those prices. I'm just sayin', since shit dried up for me, I was just stacking my paper and wasn't trying to spend no money until shit picked up again."

"Oh, word," he said, as if he could read my mind. "A'ight. So your money is right, if the price is right, and all you want is that one kilo? You don't want nothing else, and you won't be back for nothing else? Come on, GG, you know you can't get that price anywhere else on the entire East Coast. GG, don't get on that 'woman shit.' You know we hit y'all off with like, what, a free half-pound of weed, and we basically gave y'all a kilo when y'all couldn't even afford to buy a full one like a month back. And this is how y'all bitches from Queens turn around and front in a nigga's face? We the hand that fed y'all, and you gonna straight try to play us like that?"

Some of my fears were starting to subside, and I was beginning to get a bit annoyed. I mean, the nigga was talking to me like he'd handed everything to us in the past, like we came crawling on our knees begging for a handout. Man, I took risks, and was smart as hell doing what I had to do to get us to where we were, and the truth of the matter was, we had never *asked* them for a gotdamn thing for free.

"Like I already said, good looking-out with that work in the past, but that's it, kid. I'm sayin', we'll see y'all, but I ain't gonna promise you that we'll be back this week. Now come on, homie. Stop stressing me, word!"

Minnesota immediately reached into his waistband and pulled out a silver .22 long—with the seven-inch barrel—and started firing at me. "What!" He hollered, looking as if he had demons inside of him. "You clown-ass ho!"

I'll tell you, and believe me when I do, that having the barrel of a hostile gun cocked and looking you in the face is one of the most frightening experiences in the world. As soon as I saw him reaching for the gun, I started sweating razorblades.

"AHHH!" I screamed as I put my hands up to shield off the bullet, which struck me in my left forearm. While I was trying to shield myself, I'd violently made a 180-degree turn and fell very hard face down on the floor.

As I lay motionless on the floor, I was earnestly praying to God to stop the madness. I was literally terrified and about to shit my pants, but I made sure not to move.

"Yo, what's up?" Saleeta yelled as she heard the shots. "What's going on!?"

Cynthia was screaming. Xtasy was screaming like a fucking lunatic, and I don't remember if I heard Jenny.

Then I heard someone who sounded like that big bodyguard-looking guy who had frisked us tell Saleeta, "Bitch, shut the hell up! I want all y'all bitches to shut the hell up and be quiet!"

Cheeks yelled, "Everybody, face down on the floor! Get on the floor right now! And turn over! Cynthia, you too!"

"Cheeks, what's up?" Cynthia asked in a frantic plea. "Baby, what are you doing? Why are y'all doing this?"

"Cynthia, get on the gotdamn floor!" he insanely screamed. "All y'all bitches is dying right gotdamn now! That's what's up! We should fucking take pussy from all these bitches!"

At that point I was in a state beyond total fear. I knew then that Cynthia hadn't actually set us up, and if she did, then it meant Minnesota was a real snake-ass dude.

The only thing that I could seriously think about was not dying. And for some reason my homegirl Money kept popping into my head. I no longer felt the pain from the gunshot wound to my forearm.

I would have given anything to wake up from that nightmare. I could personally testify to the phrase, "He scared the shit out of me." I didn't want to check, but I thought I had just violated my underwear.

"Yo, turn the stereo up as loud as it'll go," Minnesota angrily instructed.

After the volume was raised, I heard *Plunk! Plunk!* Then there was a pause, which was followed by *Plunk! Plunk! Plunk!* Then I heard a single *Plunk!* After that, I barely heard Cynthia's voice over the music as she screamed in terror. I then heard *Plunk! Plunk!* And I no longer heard Cynthia screaming.

"Yo, check their pockets!" Cheeks barked. "I know all of them got loot. Make sure y'all get all of it. These hoes still owe us dough, and they tryin' to get over."

"Minnesota, what's up with this bitch? You want me to pop a cap in her too?" someone asked.

"Oh, hell yeah! Especially her ass. Murder all these hoes!" After Minnesota had barked the orders of execution, he started chanting, "Mo' money, mo' homicide, mo' murder!"

Bang! Bang! Bang!

Now, along with a burning pain, there were two gaping holes in my back.

I, along with everyone else in the room, had just been shot execution-style.

God, please, please, please, let me live, I remember begging. One bullet went into my shoulder blade. The other felt as if it was in my skull, but actually, it had entered the back of the lower part of my neck. The third shot must have missed, or I just was in too much pain to feel it. My forearm and my back felt as though they were on fire. I was in extreme pain, but yet I refused to scream.

My eyes closed and in shock, instinctively, I wanted to fight back. I was ready to grab hold of the person now rummaging through my pockets. I wanted that four G's they were stealing from me, but my life was much more important. I remember thinking, *GG, if you flinch, you're dead! Just chill.*

I wouldn't let myself breathe 'cause I was too scared that they would see that and kill me. *Never say die, GG. Never say die. GG, don't let yourself die.* I desperately wanted to open my eyes to see what was going on.

Being left in the dark was torture in and of itself. I was silently panicking. I felt like I was drowning and choking on my own blood. I wanted to cough up the blood, but then I knew I would be standing face to face with either God or the devil, so I continued to fake dead.

Then Minnesota said, "Yo, make sure all of those cats are dead, a'ight."

BANG! BANG! BANG! BANG! BANG!

"Yo, you got everything outta the kitchen and the bedroom, right? Well, come on. Let's get up outta this piece," Minnesota calmly said to the rest of his boys.

The stereo was lowered, and a very loud silence quickly filled the room.

I was still afraid to open my eyes. I thought the gunmen might still be in the apartment. I felt blood all over my body.

Why didn't they shoot me again? I wondered. They must

have thought that they'd shot me in the head and killed me. The shot came extremely close to my head, but fortunately it wasn't a direct hit. If anyone else in that apartment was gonna live, I had to do something immediately. But I had to be sure that Minnesota and his crew had totally left the building.

After about five more minutes of waiting I said to myself, "Now or never. Get help. GG, get outta this apartment." As I staggered to my feet, my vision was very blurry. I scanned the room. Pools and pools of blood were everywhere. One by one, I managed to see Saleeta, Jenny, Xtasy, Cynthia, and another guy and a young lady sprawled out on the floor, all lying in their own pools of blood. Ironically, even though everyone's eyes were open, it didn't look promising, since none of them attempted to move. I wondered if they'd all died with their eyes open.

I tried to yell, but all that came out of my mouth was a painful and vague gurgling yell as I threw up blood.

"Saleeta! Answer me! Gotdamn it! Come on, y'all, let's get outta here. We gotta hurry up. Come on!" I pleaded. No way on earth did I want to believe they were all dead. "Saleeta, get up! Come on, y'all, let's go before they come back!"

I was feeling very, very weak and dizzy. I was so weak that I dropped to my knees. Miraculously, with my blurry vision, I was still able to crawl to the telephone and dial 9-1-1. "Hello," I said.

"This is nine-one-one. What's your emergency?"

"I've been shot," I mumbled.

"Excuse me," the operator said.

"I've . . . we got killed. I've been shot. They're dead."

"Miss, did you say you've been shot?"

"Yes. I-I've been shot," I mumbled.

"Miss, what's your address? I'll send the police and an ambulance right away. Hello? Miss, are you still there?"

"Yeah."

"Miss, we need your address so that we can help you."

"Uhm, East One Hundred and Tenth Street in Harlem," I whispered. With that, I had no more energy to even hold the phone. I was beyond weak. My hands were ice-cold. I remember thinking about Pete and about Money. I wondered if I would ever see them again. *Don't die, GG! Hold on!* At that point I blacked out.

Chapter 12
Money

I was pissed like a muthafucka that Saleeta, GG, Xtasy, and Jenny had just disappeared on my ass and hadn't said shit, leaving me standing in front of the building talking to my people. It had to have been more than a half an hour since they'd told me they would be right back.

I didn't think anything was that out of the ordinary, until I saw Cheeks and a bunch of his people leaving the building and hopping into their cars and trucks, and bouncing. I mean, we were supposed to be going to chill with him and celebrate his birthday, so I was confused as to why they was leaving. I wanted to kick myself for just chilling there as long as I did, instead of following up on my instincts.

Ten minutes or so after Cheeks and his boys left, a swarm of NYPD cops filled up the block and had everybody up against the wall and lying face down on the ground to be frisked. Nobody knew what the fuck was going on, until people started piling out of the building, saying that a whole bunch of people had been shot and killed inside one of the apartments.

Immediately my heart started pounding, and I was hit with the obvious. Something was awfully wrong. The cops finally let us up off the ground when they realized we weren't armed, but they quickly made us get behind yellow tape.

Soon there were police helicopters hovering over, police dogs, news reporters, and an army of cops that literally filled the entire block. I had never seen so many cops before in my life. There had to have been at least five hundred of them on the block.

Somebody in the crowd yelled, "Yo, a undercover cop got killed upstairs!"

"This shit is fucking crazy!" someone else yelled. "It's like Viet-*fucking*-nam up in here!"

"It was like ten muthafuckas shot up execution-style in that crib," someone else yelled.

Oh shit! I thought to myself. Right then and there, I knew exactly why GG and Saleeta had me waiting in vain for so long.

The crowd behind the police tape in front of the building grew larger and larger as time passed. Everyone started murmuring amongst themselves when the paramedics wheeled out one person and quickly whisked them into a waiting ambulance.

With the frantic manner in which the paramedics were performing CPR on the person, I couldn't get a good look, so I was still in the dark, as far as trying to confirm who it was.

Chapter 13

GG

The Trauma Unit

I vaguely remember being wheeled into the trauma unit. I remember opening my eyes and seeing doctors all around me frantically trying to save me. I had all kinds of tubes and bags attached to me, and needles stuck into my veins. I was lying face down on some type of table or stretcher. I kept my eyes closed and just lay there.

The next thing I remember was waking up butt naked in a hospital room, except for a flimsy gown, with bandages all over my body. I didn't know what was going on.

No more than ten minutes later, detectives were asking me all kinds of questions. Other than Money, I didn't recognize anyone else in the room.

"Leave me alone! Money, what happened? What's going on?"

"GG, you got shot up last night," she explained. "But just chill and try to relax."

She then instructed the detectives to get away from me so that I could have a few minutes just to gather my thoughts. As my room began to clear out, I started to remember what had transpired. A gruesome picture popped into my head. It depicted Saleeta, Xtasy, and the rest of them sprawled out dead on the floor.

"Money, what the fuck?"

Money came close to me, hugged me, and began crying and thanking God that I was okay. "Don't worry, girl. You gonna be good. You made it. You survived."

"Money, please tell me I'm just hallucinating. I keep seeing this image of Saleeta, Xtasy, and Jenny, and it don't look good for them."

Money looked at me, and then she looked away. Then she again looked in my direction and just started to bawl, tears streaming down her face. "They didn't make it."

"What?" I said in total disbelief. I grimaced in pain from my wounds as I tried to sit up a little to address what Money had said.

Before Money could say anything, three people burst into my room.

"Oh my God! Baby, tell me you okay."

I was shocked as hell that my mother had actually showed up to see me. And to my surprise, she even looked good. Me and my mom rarely spoke, and in fact, I always called her by her first name, Brenda, not out of disrespect, but simply because I didn't really know her to be my mother, since she was in my life so sporadically.

"Brenda, I'm okay. But what are y'all doing here?"

"What are we doing here? You're all over the news. Just tell me who the fuck did this to you!" My mother vented as her two friends looked on.

The detectives who had stepped outta the room came back in and reintroduced themselves.

Money screamed on the detectives, "She ain't ready to fucking talk to y'all muthafuckas yet, so leave her ass the hell alone!"

"Ms., I understand you're real emotional right now, but you're really going to have to curb your hostile tone," one of the detectives calmly said.

I tried to bring some calm to the situation, explaining to the cop that I wasn't yet ready to talk.

The tall white detective who hadn't spoken up until that point walked over to my bed and motioned to the other two detectives and the uniformed cops. He nodded and then reached into the backpocket area of the suit he was wearing and pulled out a pair of handcuffs. While placing one of the cuffs on my right wrist and the other cuff onto the metal railing of the bed, he said, "You're under arrest," and began to read me my rights.

"What the fuck are you talking about? I almost get my head blown off, and you're placing me under arrest?"

"Yo, this is some bullshit!" my mother yelled.

A mini riot almost ensued in my room as the cops began to force all of my visitors to leave.

"GG, I'm gonna handle this!" Money yelled to me as she was escorted out of the room. "I got this. Don't worry."

At that point I felt weak and dizzy like I was about to pass out. I also wanted to throw up.

Once the cops cleared the room, they came back in and began asking me questions about the badge the paramedics found when they were looking for my identification.

"Ahh shit," I said to myself. I blew out some air and then I closed my eyes. I told the cops that they could keep me under arrest and question me for as long as they wanted to, but I wasn't gonna talk until I had spoken to a lawyer.

"A fucking New York City cop is dead! You're gonna open your fucking mouth and talk!" The detective who had placed the handcuffs on me grabbed hold of my chin and my cheeks and began squeezing.

"Urrgggh!" I grunted. With my free hand, I tried my hardest to loosen the grip the cop had on me. He was applying so much pressure, it was really starting to hurt.

The cop relented and mushed my face backward, causing me to ram my head into the bed.

A doctor and a nurse started to chastise the police officers. The officers cursed them and then stormed outta my hospital room.

I simply closed my eyes and blocked out whatever the doctors were trying to say to me, and simply lay there trying to figure out just how in the hell I had gotten myself into the situation I was in and, more importantly, how in the hell was I going to get out of it.

In what seemed like an instant, my lucrative Cartel was totally unraveling. Our sales had dried up, members had been murdered, and now I, the mastermind of Connie's Cartel, was shot the fuck up and under arrest. Yeah, shit was looking really, really bleak for my ass.

Chapter 14

GG

Can't Stop, Won't Stop

It was now about ten minutes to six, and we were just pulling up to the funeral home. As we parked and prepared to walk through the rain and into the funeral home, I could see television news reporters, along with tons of people both young and old, some crying, others hugging. Most of the people formed little huddles as they jammed close together under umbrellas. There was also a large police presence at the wake. Although I mostly saw uniformed police officers, I was sure that, inside and outside, the wake was littered with undercovers posing as mourners.

As we walked toward the funeral home, I felt as though all eyes were glued on me, but I didn't care. I put my dark shades on and proceeded with my sexy walk into the funeral home. Money and a bunch of my friends surrounded me as we walked inside. It was as if I was the president or a celebrity and they were the Secret Service assigned to protect me.

As I made it into the funeral home, I heard someone say, "Yeah, that's her. She was with them when they got shot."

I turned and glanced at the person but didn't comment.

"Who?" I heard another lady ask.

Someone pointed a finger toward me. "Her, right there. The one with her arm in a sling."

Once inside the funeral home, I signed my name and address to an attendance book and then took a seat on the aisle alongside Money. As I sat and looked toward the front of the room, I saw the three coffins but wasn't able to see the faces of those inside.

Out of nowhere I had a quick flashback of the gruesome murder scene. Very clearly I saw everything. Saleeta, Xtasy, and Jenny were lying dead on the apartment floor in Harlem with their eyes wide open.

There was a short, quick memorial service, which was followed by tons of people making comments about what they remembered about the deceased. But mostly everyone came just to view the bodies and talk about how the senseless killings in New York had to stop. Many people stressed that when senseless killings start affecting young women, then that speaks to just how serious a plight there is.

The funerals were scheduled for the following morning at ten o'clock.

As we sat in the funeral home, I felt like bursting out into laughter. I guess I was feeling that way because I was so scared of looking at my close friends and my associates in caskets. Or maybe I was afraid of what my future held. But my internal laughs were really those of insanity, insecurity, and fear all wrapped up into one.

As I continued to sit, I kept asking myself, *When are people gonna stop turning around and staring at me?* I was surprised that I hadn't truly been mentally affected by shit such as this, not to mention the other traumatic shit I'd been through in my life at such a young age. I guess I was becoming numb to such experiences. Maybe I was mentally ill and just didn't know it. Who knows? But I did know that I was strong as hell, and that if shit didn't kill me, it was only gonna make me stronger.

As we all prepared to get out of our seats to view the bodies, I remember thinking to myself, *Just walk as confi-*

dently as you can, hold your head up, and don't pass the fuck out.

We walked past the three coffins, which were set up one in front of the other. I stopped at the head of each casket. I shook my head as, one by one, I stared at three potentially great human beings.

"Man!" I said. "Damn!" With as much affection as I could muster up, I kissed each of my deceased friends on the forehead. "Peace," I softly whispered to each one of them, making the peace sign. Although my back was to the rest of the mourners, I knew for a fact that every eye in that place was glued to my every move.

Very calmly I turned around, stepped away from the caskets, and walked out of the funeral home. I didn't want to sit back down. I had paid my respects and had already seen enough to prove to myself that this was no dream. They were truly dead.

I decided to just wait outside in the rain until the wake was over. I waited all alone with my thoughts, while the media snapped pictures of me. Thankfully, they were respectful enough to not rush me and ask me a million questions.

GG, this is the game you chose, and you knew the risks. You either gotta get used to this, or just get the fuck outta the game. This is probably the worst it can get.

I smiled insecurely on the steps of the funeral home. Yeah, I had to smile. Who was I fooling? I mean, I knew it could get worse, because next time it might be my corpse that everyone was coming to look at. A dead me—that was a concept I didn't think I'd ever be able to get used to. But I kinda knew death would be inevitable if I stayed in this drug game.

Yeah, I know, I answered the voice inside of me that told me I should have been lying stiff as a board in one of those caskets. *Yeah, I definitely know.* Tears ran down my face as I stared into the sky, which was full of misty rain, and I proceeded to nod my head up and down, confirming my intuition. My turn was lurking around the corner, yet I still couldn't muster up the courage to live right. Hustling and the streets was all I knew. Despite losing my girls to the streets, I knew it was my ticket to enable me to live the lifestyle I wanted to live.

Later that night, well after the wake was over, me, Money, and a few of our other close friends gathered for our own little ghetto memorial service at the intersection of Hollis Avenue and 205th Street, right near Hollis Park, which was where we all knew each other from. I would say there was easily close to twenty of us huddled together in a little semicircle as we reminisced about the fun times we all had with Saleeta, Xtasy, and Jenny. We were all getting sloppy drunk, trying to ease the pain, and must have drank close to ten gallons of Hennessy and smoked about a pound of weed.

While everyone was talking, I pulled Money to the side and we began to kick it.

I said to her, "So what's the deal? Whatchu wanna do? I mean, we got this work that we just purchased, and most of the cash we had went to the lawyer you got for me, and to my bail."

"What do I wanna do? You mean, as far as the game is concerned?" Money said in a somewhat somber tone.

"Yeah."

"GG, this shit can't stop, and it won't stop. I mean, I know these past days was straight crazy, but we still gotta get this paper. This is Connie's Cartel, baby!" Money stuck out her hand and gave me a pound, and then she drank some more of her Hennessy.

I took a real long pull on the weed I was smoking. "Shit is fucked up for me, though. My lawyer already told me that my ass should expect to get indicted within the next couple of months."

"See you still on that shit about Cynthia being a cop and shit, but the thing is, she ain't fucking here no more, GG!"

"Yeah, but what the fuck did she say to the cops already? That's the shit that I don't know, and that's the shit that's making me nervous."

"GG, this is the thing: your lawyer is gonna talk that fucking lawyer shit where they looking at shit from every angle and all of that. But what he ain't doing is looking at shit from a street point of view. Okay, a fucking undercover cop is murdered, right, you get shot the fuck up too, and you live and shit, and then your ass automatically becomes the suspect? You know, I know, and they know that is some bullshit. And we both know that if they had strong enough shit on you that Cynthia already gave them, then your ass would be locked the fuck up right now. But they charged you with some bullshit, hoping yo' ass would get scared and start ratting muthafuckas out. But that shit didn't work. GG, you good. Fuck them!"

I looked at Money and nodded my head. She was making sense.

"But I will tell you this: You said Cheeks, Minnesota, and all them niggas was up in that apartment, right?"

"Yeah, they was all there."

"And as far as we know, ain't one of them niggas locked up right now, right?"

"Nah, I doubt it."

"See, this ain't nothing but some corrupt-cop shit. I mean, think about it. You know Cynthia's ass was corrupt. But I guarantee you there's some other dirty cops that Minnesota is running with, and Cynthia must of did something that probably spooked they asses and they had to take her out. So what they did was set the shit up to murder your ass and then, in the process, murder Cynthia, which is who they really wanted dead. The shit was just gonna look like an undercover cop got caught up in a dangerous world and got popped and killed. And by you living, it actually helped them be able to deflect attention away from Minnesota and his boys, and put the attention on you, which is just what they want at this point, because they want Minnesota to keep bringing them that loot."

"Wow!"

"Am I lying?"

"Nah, your ass ain't lying. You dropping knowledge and jewels." I laughed. "When the fuck you get so smart?"

"I guarantee you that them fucking cops wanted Cynthia dead, and they wanted Minnesota to do it, just so they could have something major like a cop murder always hanging over his head."

"Right. So they could really pimp and control his ass."

"Exactly!"

I had finished smoking my weed and was hungry as hell. So me and Money told everyone we would be right back. We hopped into Money's Lexus GS 300 and headed to New York Fried Chicken to get some food.

While Money was driving, I turned down the volume on the music. "You heard from Pete?"

"Nah," she replied.

I thought for a moment. "Yo, that dude ain't come check for me not once, and this shit been all over the news."

"They probably watching his ass like he had told you, so he probably wanna stay off the radar."

"True, but you know how Cynthia ain't a threat anymore because her ass is up outta here?"

Money nodded her head yes.

"If we wanna be smart and one step ahead of shit, then we gotta get this nigga Pete the fuck up outta here. You feel me?"

"You talking about murking his ass?"

"You damn right!"

"Whoa!"

"Money, the dude knows too much. And for all I know Cynthia could have been hip to his connection to us, and if my lawyer is right and I end up getting indicted, then his ass could be the one to bring me down. I don't know what the fuck the nigga is capable of, and I hate that dude has been ghost all these days. Who knows what the fuck is going on?" I said, feeling stressed out.

We made it to New York Fried Chicken on Farmers and Merrick Boulevards, and we headed in to get our food.

"You the boss lady," Money said with a smile.

I looked at her and nodded. That meant she was with it.

"Just tell me how you wanna do this, and we'll light his ass up," she added.

"Did I ever tell you that you was my fucking nigga?" With a huge smile, I stuck out my hand and gave her a pound.

"It can't stop, and it won't stop."

And Money was absolutely right.

Chapter 15

Money

Diva's Lounge, December 1997

GG and I got dressed in her house in Bayside. We jumped in her Jeep, headed to carry out our planned hit on Pete.

We wanted to bring a new chick into the Cartel. Misty was real cool. A little older than us and in college and the whole nine, she was definitely smart and had what it took to help us do this drug shit.

I was dressed like a diva, to disguise for the hit. We had simply told Pete that we'd all be going out to a club in Manhattan called Diva's Lounge, to party and take our minds off everything that had been going on recently.

As GG drove, I sat in the passenger's seat with a .45-caliber handgun in my Louis Vuitton handbag.

"You ready to do this?" GG asked.

I didn't even look at her. I just nodded my head up and down a few times.

"Remember, when Misty gets in the car, just play everything cool."

I didn't respond because I already knew all of what GG was telling me.

We reached Misty's block and let the Jeep sit idle in front

of her crib, while GG called her on the truck's cell phone, letting her know we were there.

Misty hopped in the back seat. "What's up?" She reached forward and kissed me on the cheek. "GG, what up, fam?" She squeezed GG on the shoulder.

GG adjusted the radio station, and just at that moment, DJ Funkmaster Flex's voice came on, promoting a party he was deejaying at that night at a Manhattan club.

I turned and told Misty, "Yo, that's where we're going."

Misty just quietly nodded her head to the music that followed Flex's promotional message.

It was quiet for a moment, and then Misty asked, "GG, you got a burner?"

I was wondering why she had asked that question.

"Yeah, it's inside the door paneling. Why?"

"I ain't bring no heat, so just in case something jumps off at the club I wanna know what's what."

Misty's question about me having a burner had thrown me off, but I guess that she knew about what happened, so she probably wanted to make sure that we were prepared for anything. It was good to know that Misty was not strapped 'cause it eliminated the chances of her reacting the wrong way to the hit that was about to go down.

Misty didn't live too far from Pete, so before I knew it, we were rolling up to his crib.

GG spoke into her cell phone. "Yo, Pete, we outside."

After about five minutes Pete appeared. My heart had been racing and thumping from the moments after Misty had got in the car, and when I saw Pete, my heart rate really picked up. I calmly blew out a little bit of air from my lungs. Pete was just about at the car. I couldn't front on the hit. Even though I had gone over the plot again and again in my head, I had never been able to predict, and prepare for, how nervous I would be.

I opened my door and got out. "Hey, baby." I reached for Pete's hand and stood on my tippy-toes to give him a kiss on the cheek.

"Gotdamn, Money! Why are your hands so cold and clammy?" Pete asked.

I immediately got even more nervous. I wanted to crawl underneath the car. Pete had to know what was about to go down. I quickly replied, "Oh, it's just from the heat blowing through the vents, that's all." Right after I said that, I realized how stupid I must have sounded, since the heat should have had the opposite effect on my hands.

Pete laughed. "You looking like a diva and all that, you can't be walking around with no clammy hands."

GG blew the horn and yelled at the same time for us to both get in the car.

"Pete, you can sit in the front so that your legs won't be all cramped up."

"Nah, I'll be a'ight." Pete reached toward the rear passenger door.

My heart dropped to my feet. I had to act quickly. "Pete, just let me sit in the back and you sit in the front. I got this thong on and it's cutting the crack of my ass. I need to take this bad boy off right now!"

Pete and I both laughed, his laughter genuine, mine nervous. He complied with my wishes and sat in the front passenger's seat.

"Yeah, and our girl Misty is back there, and I don't need you back there trying to hit on her with your corny-ass game."

Pete just chuckled, nodded his head, and then got in the truck.

Whew! As I got in the back seat, I was thinking in my head, *I'm definitely not built to be a hit woman. Maybe Pete wanted to sit in the back so he could kill me. Is GG tricking me, and is this whole plot really designed to take me out?* I was starting to bug out. I wanted to jump out of the car and just bounce.

Pete said what's up to everybody, introduced himself to Misty, and we drove off. There was this eerie feeling in the car as we drove. No one spoke. I was feeling lightheaded. If you ever stood upside down on your head and then stood up straight, you'd understand the flush-like headrush I was feeling.

Misty tapped me on my leg and then pointed to Pete. She quietly smiled and mouthed the words, "He's cute! I think I wanna fuck him."

I knew she was just joking, or at least I hoped so. And I playfully punched her on her leg and did a gagging motion with my finger and my tongue.

Finally Pete broke the silence and started talking about some wild street brawl that had broken out in Kings Plaza Shopping Center the other day. Pete was known for always overdramatizing things when he spoke. It got to the point where it was a bit annoying. You always wanted to smack the nigga and yell, "Enough already! Gotdamn!"

GG rudely interrupted him. "Yo, y'all gotta hear this ill freestyle by this kid. This DJ Clue mixtape. It's some cat named Drama. Yo, this nigga is real. Word is bond!"

To be in this game, you had to be cold-blooded, and I thought I was. I just could not understand what cold-blooded really meant until I was in that position getting ready to murder somebody for the first time. I mean, the nigga was talking about music and talking about everyday shit, just as normal as anything, all the while not knowing a hit was about to go down.

As GG turned up the music, I almost forgot that that was my cue. *Now or never,* I said to myself. I slipped my hand into my bag, and my sweaty palms gripped the handgun. I remember looking out of the car window and looking at all of the streetlights and traffic lights. There were cars all around us as we drove and navigated through the dark streets.

As Pete listened to Drama spit his rhymes, he became his usual overanimated self and began excitedly proclaiming, "Yo, this nigga can spit! Word!"

Pete was about to say something else.

I had to just do it. *Come on, Money!* I urged myself.

I quickly pulled the gun and placed it just to the side of Pete's headrest and fired, immediately silencing his non-stop yapping with a powerful blast from the .45. Even with the loud music, the sound was deafening, and my ears were ringing. I was sure that GG and Misty both had ringing in their ears.

Pete's body sat quiet and slumped over, and his brains were literally all over the dashboard and the windshield. I had just caught my first body.

Chapter 16

GG

No Body, No Charges

"Ahhhh shit!" Misty screamed. "Money, what the fuck? What the fuck did you just do? Oh my fucking God!"

"Misty, shut the fuck up and calm down!" I hollered from the front seat.

I mean, I knew Misty had no idea what the fuck was going on and what the fuck had just went down, but as my heart raced, the last thing I wanted to do was deal with a hysterically screaming bitch.

"Money, you good?" I asked.

"Yeah, yeah, I'm good. The nigga is dead, right?"

"Yeah, he is definitely up outta here."

"GG, pull this fucking car over right now!" Misty barked from the back seat.

I was driving about sixty miles an hour on the Long Island Expressway, so there was no way I was going to pull over.

"GG, pull over and let me out! I ain't trying to go to jail, fucking around with y'all up in here."

"Misty, ain't nobody going to jail," Money yelled.

As Misty continued to talk shit under her breath, I almost wanted to kick myself for bringing her ass along. I knew that if me and Money got rid of the body and no one ever found it, there would be no way they could ever trace the body back to us. But now that Misty had witnessed shit, there was always a chance that her testimony would take us down, if she got questioned or if she ratted.

So I thought real quick. There was only one way to bind Misty in with us. I took a big chance and pulled over to the side of the busy expressway. I was on the shoulder of the road while cars whizzed by us. Before turning around to face the back of the truck, I reached into my glove compartment and took out my gun and pointed it at her.

"You said you wanted to get this money with the Cartel. So, just like the Bloods, baby, it's blood in and blood out. Money, hand her that gun."

Money handed Misty her gun, and Misty knew what time it was. She looked angry and pissed off, but I didn't give a shit.

"Pump one shot into this nigga right here, or else I gotta murder you." I was dead-ass serious.

Misty looked at me and shook her head.

I turned up the volume on the radio and nodded my head, indicating for her to fire the gun. Misty closed her eyes and fired one shot into Pete's already lifeless body.

Money took the gun from her, and I calmly turned my ass around and put the car in drive and continued to maneuver my way along the Long Island Expressway.

After I turned down the music, inside the car was eerily quiet. I guess that's what happens when you murder someone and are driving around with the body and brains on the dash and windshield.

We traveled all the way to the Bronx, not too far from Co-op City. It was a real swampy area and mad secluded. It was cold as hell outside, and the swamps smelled worse than the city dump.

I had already had two concrete cinderblocks with rope attached to them in the back of my truck. We dragged Pete's lifeless body out of the car and placed it right on the edge of the swamp. Then we tied one end of the string around each of his ankles and pushed his body into the water. It took the physical strength of all three of us to move Pete's body and the bricks as well. At that point I was glad Misty was helping us to dump the body, which further roped her in to the murder. If she was to ever rat on us, then she would be ratting on herself.

Pete's lifeless body was now stuck at the bottom of a swamp in the Bronx. And the chances of anyone finding him anytime soon was gonna be slim to none. With no body, we could never be charged with murder.

So with Pete out of the equation, I felt a lot more relieved. I could now focus on getting my Cartel hustle on and popping. I no longer had Minnesota as my connect, but that was all right, because we had Chino and we had the Colombians.

The cops had taken my badge the night I was rushed to the hospital, but I now had a new ace in the hole. Before we'd dumped Pete's body in the swamp, I'd made sure to go in his pockets and take his badge from him. With that badge I would always be able to make money by moving weight out of New York, which was just what I was planning on doing. And with the dirt-cheap prices we were getting from the Colombians, I knew we'd easily be able to make dough in states like Virginia, Ohio, Maryland, and Georgia.

Chapter 17

GG

Hotter than Fish Grease

Since Misty was the college girl and the book-smart one, she had certain nerdy habits, one of which was reading all three of New York's daily newspapers every day. So it didn't shock me that she was calling me at seven o'clock in the morning to ask me if I'd seen the newspaper.

"Bitch, I just got in the fucking house about two hours ago. Hell no, I didn't read the *Daily News*. Shit, I'm 'sleep. The fuck?"

"Well, guess whose picture they have plastered on the front cover with the caption, 'Is This New York City's New Drug Queen?' "

"What are you talking about? Misty, you losing me. It's too early for this shit."

"GG, they have a picture of your ass plastered on the front page of the fucking *Daily News* saying that, at seventeen, you might be New York's next drug queen."

Misty's words made me sit up. And all I knew was that she better not be joking because I would have come to her house and beat her ass. "Come again?"

"Look, this shit is a problem. I'm coming over to your crib, so you can see what I'm saying. Get your ass up outta the bed."

I didn't know what was up, but instinctively my heart started to race. I did get up and started to get dressed, so I could be alert when Misty got there. I called Money and asked her if she knew what the fuck Misty was talking about, and she said that she had no idea. Then she cursed me out for calling her so early in the morning and hung up on me.

When Misty arrived at my house, it took only two seconds, and no words out of her mouth, for me to realize just what the hell she had been talking about. She handed me the *Daily News* and she didn't say anything. I looked at the front page, and sure enough, there I was, decked the fuck out, and looking good as hell. The picture they had was a picture of me that had been taken the night of *The Source* magazine party.

"Is This New York City's New Drug Queen?" I said out loud, a confused tone to my voice. I never read the newspaper, so Misty had to explain to me that I needed to turn to page three for the full story.

My mouth fell open as I read the story. What shocked me the most was how accurate it was. They knew my age, they knew I had fucked with Minnesota, and they'd chronicled all of the little petty arrests I had for gambling, shoplifting, and public indecency. The article went on to say that I was the suspected mastermind flooding the local prisons with cocaine, marijuana, and heroin.

The article also explained that I had been the only survivor in an execution-style killing that took the lives of seven persons, including an undercover cop who was investigating my drug activities and my suspected link to corrupt law enforcement officials, who had gone as far as to issue me a badge, which was found on my person on the night I was gunned down.

"Yo, this shit is fucking crazy! Misty, look at this shit. They got pictures of me and LL Cool J, me and Fat Joe, me and Allen Iverson. What the fuck is this? And look what they say:

'*GG is a rising star amongst the hip-hop industry's elite, but her star isn't rising from her ability to rhyme. Rather, it appears that her star is rising because of her ability to supply a party with what it needs.*' "

"Now you see why the hell I came over here so damn quick."

"Oh shit! Yo, if niggas see this shit and start talking about it, then I am so fucking screwed."

"GG, this shit is gonna have your ass hotter than fucking fish grease."

"Gee, thanks! That makes me feel a whole lot better, Misty! I ALREADY KNOW THAT SHIT! FUCK!"

Misty didn't say anything as I paced back and forth in my living room trying to figure out just what the fuck I should do. "I need a fucking drink!"

It was barely eight o'clock in the morning, but I was so stressed out, I poured me about ten shots of Patrón and drank all ten shots one after another.

Misty was trying to get me to relax. She went into the kitchen and started cooking some breakfast.

And no sooner than the liquor started to kick in and my head started to feel nice and I was beginning to relax, Money called me.

After I answered the phone, she said, "Holy shit! What the fuck?"

"You read that shit too, right?"

"Yesss. Where did that shit come from?"

"That's Minnesota and his crew of corrupt cops feeding that shit to the media so they can keep the market locked up to themselves," I reasoned.

"Well, you ain't said nothing but a word. Two people already called me about this shit, and as soon as I got off the phone from them, I get a call from this low-level dude that fucks with the Colombians, and guess who ain't fucking with us no more?"

"Ahhh fuck!"

Money told me she was hanging up and was on her way over to me.

"Okay."

I took another shot of Patrón to the head. I thought about the Colombians shying away from us. I reasoned to myself that it didn't really matter, because I still had Chino as a connect. I knew he would fuck with me on some consignment shit. Regardless of the bullshit, Chino was a real street dude, and real always recognized real.

But at the rate I was going, I really just had to hope that Chino would still fuck with me, because it was starting to seem like the Cartel had this huge dark cloud hanging over it, and we were getting hit by one storm after another.

Money finally got to my crib, and the three of us began to brainstorm about just how we should handle this, wanting to be on the same page and making sure all three of us said the same thing to anyone who asked what was up. This way people would look at us as trustworthy and not like some reckless wannabe drug "queenpin" chicks just saying and doing anything. Niggas hated recklessness and wouldn't fuck with you if you were reckless, which usually meant that your ass would end up sending someone to jail, or getting someone killed.

Shit wasn't looking good and was getting worse as the hours ticked by. Even my lawyer called me after he had read the article and added more doom and gloom to my already bleak picture.

But the thing that concerned me the most was, I was trying to reach out to Chino, calling him on all the numbers I had for him, and yet he wasn't picking up for me or returning my calls. That was the thing that almost sent me over the edge.

The only silver lining to the really dark cloud was that Misty, Money, and me still had a bunch of product that we had purchased from the Colombians a few weeks back. So we could still double up on our dough and keep doubling. All we had to do was hustle harder and move the work.

But the dark cloud hanging over us was about to get darker and open up and pour down on us in a way we didn't expect, and that we definitely weren't ready for.

Chapter 18

GG

Gimme the Loot

With things being so bad of late, just to get our minds off things, Me, Money, and Misty decided to go to a strip club and hang out and drink and just relax. Strip clubs was one of the favorite things we all liked to do because at times we got tired of always having niggas up in our faces, trying to talk to us and get with us. Not that we had anything against dick. I mean, I could speak for myself and say that, without a shadow of a doubt, I was definitely "strictly dickly." But the guys in the strip clubs would usually be focused on the naked and half-naked bitches and didn't have time for fully clothed bitches.

We ended up going to this strip club in Queens called Day Dreams, which was packed wall to wall with people when we got there. Heather Honey, the porn star, was making an appearance there.

"Yo, I love that chick," Misty said, sounding more excited than a man. "She keeps it thorough."

Misty was openly bisexual, but she knew I didn't get down like that, so she never disrespected. Money, on the other hand, wasn't exactly bisexual, but she'd had a few lesbian experiences in her lifetime.

"Yo, we just gonna get drunk as hell and live it up in here.

Don't even talk about no drug shit. Let's just get it off of our minds for at least one night," I told them.

The three of us got seats at the bar, where we had a good view of everything going on inside the club. I ordered the first round of drinks for us, and Money took care of the second round. Then Misty decided to just buy a bottle of Absolut, and that got us fucked up.

Then Money and her crazy ass ordered a whole bucket of hot wings, and when they arrived, she asked us if we wanted some. Misty dug right in, and the two of them ate like they hadn't eaten in weeks.

"Yo, y'all bitches is crazy, and y'all bitches is fucking nasty as hell."

"What the fuck did we do?" Money asked.

"Y'all are eating food from a fucking strip club? Don't you know that you don't ever eat shit from a strip club? I used to dance in a strip club. I know about all the nasty germs and shit that's up in here."

"Fuck that bullshit!" Money said. "It ain't like they got pussy juices in the food and shit."

Misty and Money both started laughing.

"It taste good to me," Misty added.

"A'ight, now tomorrow when y'all asses are rushing to the fucking emergency room to get y'all fucking stomachs pumped for food poisoning, I don't wanna hear shit, because I warned y'all!"

Money poured me some more Absolut and cranberry juice and told me, "You must not be drunk or something, 'cause you is really talking crazy right now. Just shut the fuck up and let's drink and have a good time."

Money was right. I was still acting stressed out and too up-tight, so I downed the liquor really quickly and then poured some more, hoping to get drunk really fast. The truth of the matter was, my tolerance level for drinking was so high because I had been used to consuming so much liquor. So it really took a whole lot of liquor for me to get drunk.

After about ten minutes or so, I could feel the liquor kicking in. I reached forward and grabbed a hot wing and wolfed it down.

"Oh yeah. See, now that's what the fuck I'm talking about," Money said, and her and Misty started laughing.

"Yo, I don't know what the fuck I was talking about. These shits are good as hell." I grabbed another wing and ate it just as fast as I had eaten the first.

Misty and Money continued to laugh at me. We were experiencing the looseness I was seeking when I'd suggested that we go out and just have a real carefree, relaxed time.

Before I knew it, I was mad drunk and up in a VIP room getting a lap dance that Misty had sponsored for me. Normally I would have been real blasé about the whole thing, because I had been there and done that so many times before, but this time I made sure to really get into it and have fun with it.

I also had to admit, all of the dancers in the club were really looking good that night. It was another sign that I was drunk because, when I was sober, I stayed hating on the strippers and criticizing their bodies and how stank they looked. But that night everyone and everything looked good to me.

After we left the VIP area, as we walked back downstairs to the first floor of the club, some dude tapped me on my arm. "GG, right?"

I looked at the dude and squinted, really trying to figure out who he was. I was usually really good at remembering faces, even if I didn't remember somebody's name. But I was sure that I hadn't ever seen or met this dude before. I nodded my head and kept it moving.

"Who was that?" Misty asked.

"I don't even know."

"I seen that nigga before. He's a Blood from Queensbridge.

Leave that nigga the hell alone," Money stressed as if she had firsthand knowledge about his past.

"Yeah, I ain't trying to fuck with the nigga, but I know the only reason dude shouted me out was because he saw my fucking picture on the cover of the newspaper."

Misty and Money quickly reminded me that I had agreed to not talk about no drug shit that night. And they were absolutely right.

What took the cake and made me wanna immediately leave the spot was when one of the bouncers walked up to me and said, "GG, one of the bartenders told me you was up in here, and word got to Heather Honey, and she asked if you would come to the back for a second before she bounced."

I paused. I had to admit, I was flattered and felt like a huge ghetto celebrity, but then another part of me was tight as hell, because I didn't wanna be infamous for this drug shit until I'd made enough dough. At this point, being in the spotlight was a fucking hindrance way more than it was a help, and I resented that.

"Okay, sure. Take me to where she's at."

We followed the bouncer and went back to the dressing room, where Heather Honey was standing around butt-ass naked, talking on her cell phone.

Misty was so happy to see and meet Heather Honey, she looked like she was ready to straight nut on herself.

Heather Honey quickly got off the phone. She explained that she'd heard a lot about me and that she just wanted to introduce herself to me and say what's up.

"Heather, I so love all your work and all your videos!" Misty said, not even giving me a chance to respond, and sounding like a straight groupie.

"Heather, this is my girl Misty, and this is my girl Money."

Heather said what's up to both of them and held out her hand and softly shook both of their hands. I couldn't believe how small of a woman she was. She was very tiny and petite, but when I'd seen her on TV and in her videos, she always looked a lot taller and a lot heavier.

"Nice to meet y'all," she replied.

Then she asked me where we were hanging out after we left the club.

I told her, "Well, we about to get up outta here, and I'm gonna head to the crib and go to sleep. I been dealing with too much shit lately."

"Okay, that's what's up. Well, listen"—Heather then scribbled her cell phone number on the back of the card—"here, take my card."

"I'm supposed to be moving back to New York pretty soon, but I'll be in Los Angeles for the next year and a half. Hopefully, it won't even be for that long. So if y'all are out in LA, definitely hit me up and we can hang out and I can show y'all around."

"Okay, no doubt." I held out my hand to shake hers, since I didn't want her giving me a hug and have her sweaty titties pressing up against me.

When we left the club and jumped in my truck, I decided to let Misty drive. I was way too drunk. We decided to go to Misty's house, since she wasn't as hot as I was, and we had also decided to use her crib as the stash house until we could move the work we had.

Misty lived in a real cool two-bedroom apartment in Rochdale Village, in the Jamaica section of Queens. The only thing I didn't like about it was, even with the personal parking space she had in the parking lot, you had to walk forever to get to her building. With Christmas fast approaching, the weather was real brick outside on almost a daily basis. She dropped off me and Money in front of her building, so we wouldn't have to walk so far in the cold. Then she parked the car and came to the building and led us upstairs about ten minutes later.

"Oh, this heat feels so fucking good up in here," I said as soon as we were in the lobby of her building.

We took the elevator to the thirteenth floor. When we reached her floor, we got out and walked to her apartment. There were about six other apartments on her floor. The floor was really quiet during the day, so now at like four in the morning it was extra quiet.

Misty finally got hold of her keys and unlocked the door, and the three of us piled in to her apartment. But before she could close her apartment door and lock it, someone had sprang up from outta nowhere and jammed his foot in the door, preventing her from closing it.

"Oh shit! Money, help me! This nigga is trying to come up in here!"

Me and Money turned around and immediately went to Misty's aid. The three of us pushed on the door, trying to close it, but the dude was too strong for us, and the door wasn't budging. Then Misty ran off, saying she was going to get her gun, taking her muscle with her, and left me and Money struggling to close the door.

The dude quickly overpowered us and got the door open. Without hesitation, he whacked both me and Money upside the head with his gun, sending both of us to the ground. I was woozy as shit and literally seeing stars.

Then the dude, who was wearing a ski mask, ran toward Misty, who was in her room, and all I heard him say was, "Bitch, you fucking move and I will fucking murder your ass right up this crib!"

Apparently Misty froze in her tracks, because next thing we saw was him dragging her back into the living room. Me and Money were still in the foyer area, which was connected to the living room, and I was on the ground, trying to maintain consciousness. Money, bleeding from her mouth, had managed to get to her feet and was trying to get out of the door, but the dude got to her and grabbed a fistful of her hair and yanked her to the ground.

"Where the fuck you going, bitch?" The muscle-bound six-foot three-inch dude whacked Money upside the head again with the gun, knocking her out.

Misty ran to the kitchen, but the dude grabbed her and threw her to the ground like a rag doll and whacked her upside the head too.

After checking to make sure the door was locked, the dude then went in the pocket of the oversized coat he was wearing and pulled out duct tape. After our mouths were duct taped, he then duct taped our wrists and our ankles, and kept us in the living room lying face down on the ground.

"Bitches! Making my ass work! Got me breathing all hard and shit. The fuck is wrong with y'all?" Then he kicked all three of us in the ribs, for good measure.

As I lay on the floor doubled over in pain and the wind knocked outta me, I watched as the dude retrieved a large paper bag from his other pocket and then proceeded to rummage through each room in the apartment, until he found the two bricks of cocaine and the two bricks of weed stashed inside of Misty's linen closet.

The dude could have just left at that point, but that would have been way too easy. Instead of just leaving, he came over to Misty and started barking on her that her ass is gonna have to pay for making him chase after her and work so damn hard when he'd first barged in.

"You like making muthafuckas work for shit, bitch?"

Misty couldn't say anything.

"Yeah, I see your ass is fucking quiet now. But, let me guess, you gonna make me work for this fucking pussy too, right?" the dude said in a sinister tone. Then he reached into his pocket and took out a Rambo-looking knife and cut off Misty's winter coat. He also cut her shirt and then ripped it off as well. He grabbed her by the back of her jeans and took the knife and cut her jeans right down the middle and ripped them off as well.

"Damn! I see you making me work for this shit too! But

you know what, I don't work for shit! I take what the fuck I want—just like I'm getting ready to take this muthafuckin' pussy of yours!" The dude then started to unbuckle his pants and pulled them down to his ankles, exposing his big-ass dick. He started stroking his dick to get it hard

Misty squirmed all she could, to prevent the inevitable. I was helpless, and so was Money, who at that point just started to come back to consciousness.

"Bring your fucking ass over here!" the dude said to Misty. Then he whacked her upside the head again with the butt of the gun, making her woozy. The dude had to pick her up, and sort of propped her ass up to face his crotch. He hawked up a big glob of spit and aimed it right at her pussy and then proceeded to ram his dick into her.

Misty tried to move, but she was in a hopeless battle. The dude pumped his dick as deep into her and as hard into her as he could for about five minutes straight, and then he pulled his dick out and shot his cum all over me and Money, some of his hot-ass semen landing right on my face.

"Whooooooo! That shot was good! One of the best nuts I had in a while!"

After laughing, the dude pulled up his pants, buckled them and gathered up the drugs he had taken from us. Just before exiting the apartment, he said, "Nice doing business with you ladies." He paused and then made his way to the door, but before the door closed, he chuckled and said, "Gimme the loot, gimme the loot."

With that, the terrorizing ordeal was finally over. From the looks of things, it appeared that the dude had violated Misty in the worst way. Not to mention, he had also put an end to the Cartel. With no more product and hardly any money left in our stash, I had no idea how we were gonna rebound from this.

Chapter 19

GG

More Drama

The day after Misty had been raped and we had been robbed, Misty sort of retreated into this emotional shell, complaining about being scared of possibly having contracted "the monster" from the nigga that raped her. She was also bitching about how emotionally and mentally debilitated she felt. She explained that she was now afraid to do anything, and that she was just gonna have to stay in her house and stay to herself until she felt she was over the terrorizing effects of what had happened, and could trust people again.

"Money, that bitch is bullshitting," I said. "I don't know, and I can't put my finger on it just yet, but I smell a mutha-fuckin' rat."

Money didn't one hundred percent agree with me, but she did understand where I was coming from.

"Money, the drugs hadn't even been at her crib for a full twenty-four hours and shit, and then she just up and gets robbed at four o'clock in the morning? Get the fuck outta here! And then the nigga just happens to rape her, out of the three of us?"

"You complaining about that?"

"No, no, not that I'm complaining, but the thing is, what

nigga in this day and age would rape a chick and run up in her raw-dog? Niggas ain't doing that, are they?"

"Some niggas, yeah. They don't give a fuck."

"Well, all I'm saying is, I think it was a nigga that she been getting dick from, and the nigga just fucked her to make shit look convincing. She knows that nigga, Money, I'm telling you. Now I gots to sit here and figure shit the fuck out, while this bitch and her man go and get rich, and her ass is complaining about she needs to see a fucking psychotherapist and shit."

I wound up spending that night at Money's house. I tried my best to go to sleep in Money's bed, but I had a pounding headache that just would not quit and was keeping me awake. I knew that the headache was a direct result of having been clocked so hard upside the head when the dude pistol-whipped me at Misty's house. I think it was maybe, like, three or four o'clock in the morning when I managed to finally fall asleep, tossing and turning.

Suddenly I heard this loud noise. I didn't know what the hell it was, but the noise was so loud, it woke me up.

"Money! Money! Wake up!" I started to shake her. The noise got even louder.

Money, in a daze, asked, "What's wrong?"

"I heard this loud noise. It sounded like someone was trying to break in," I whispered in a nervous tone. I noticed that the clock radio said 4:30.

As Money and I sat up in her bed, I'll never forget what I heard next.

"NYPD! Get on the ground! Put your hands out and get on the ground! I wanna see your hands!" NYPD cops in full riot gear ripped Money and me out of the bed and slammed us onto the floor.

With flashlights blinding me, I found myself sprawled out on Money's bedroom floor with just my bra and panties on.

My hands were stretched out in front of me, but then they were quickly repositioned above my head and a cop had his knee on my back. Money was in a similar position on the other side of the room.

Money screamed, "What are y'all doing in my house?"

"Are there any weapons in here?" one of the cops asked in an aggressive tone.

"No, we ain't got any weapons. And y'all still ain't tell me what are y'all doing in my crib!"

The cops, who at that point had our hands handcuffed behind our backs, helped Money and I up to our feet. The lights were now on in the bedroom, and my half-naked body was fully exposed. Money had on long flannel pajamas, which did a good job of covering up her body.

I knew my time was up, and that my card had finally been pulled after my short stint of doing dirt and trying to be a queenpin. My career as head of Connie's Cartel was coming to a definitive halt.

Money continued to ramble, as one of the cops began to read us our rights.

"You arresting us for what?"

The burly cop ignored her and continued to read us our rights.

Money looked at me. "Can you believe this?"

Two plainclothes cops in bulletproof vests took us into the living room, and the other cops continued to thoroughly search Money's crib.

"Can I at least put on some clothes or something?" I asked.

The cops looked at me. I know those white boys just loved looking at my half-naked seventeen-year-old body. One of the cops got the attention of a female undercover cop, who came and escorted me back to Money's bedroom, where she assisted me in covering up my body.

"My jeans are right over there. Can you help me put those on?"

The cop seemed reluctant and stated that she couldn't take the handcuffs off me, but that she would help me.

"Okay. Whateva. I just don't wanna be walking around Central Booking with my panties on." I laughed. Yeah, I was nervous and scared as shit, but as the saying goes, it is what it is, and that was just what I was thinking. There was no sense in bitching up at that point and worrying and crying about shit.

Thankfully the jeans I had were not that tight, and I was able to wiggle my way into them with the assistance of the female cop, who also helped me put on one of Money's throwback jerseys. Then she escorted me back to Money's living room. I looked as if I had no arms, since my arms were behind my back and underneath the shirt, and not through the sleeves of the shirt.

Before long, Money and I were both escorted to cop cars and whisked away to Manhattan with about five other unmarked cop cars following us. I was surprised that we hadn't gone to Central Booking on Queens Boulevard since we'd been arrested in Queens.

I was also shocked and surprised that Money was actually in the car with me. I was sure they had only come for me, so as we drove in the car, I tried to calm Money and reassure her that everything would be okay. "Money, don't worry about nothing. As soon as I get a chance, I'm calling that lawyer you had got for me, Mr. Rubenstein, and he'll take care of us."

Money said, "All I know is, they better have a warrant, just coming up in my crib the way they did."

The sun was starting to come up, and the traffic was beginning to build on the streets when we arrived at One Police Plaza, NYPD headquarters in downtown Manhattan. There they separated us for interrogation. They had yet to tell me what they were formally charging me with, but they still asked me numerous questions, which I refused to answer. I was no dummy. I needed my lawyer to speak for me.

The first chance I got, I called Mr. Rubenstein, who had helped me when the cops arrested me in the hospital the day after I was shot. My lawyer knew I was into illegal activity, and that's because I was always straight up with him. But the last time we spoke, he told me I could continue to do whatever it is that I do, so long as I knew the risks and the potential downfalls. He had also told me that his job as my lawyer was to make the authorities prove my guilt and that if they couldn't, this great country that we live in gives us a get-out-of-jail-free card, and his job was to make them always cough up that card.

I got Mr. Rubenstein on the phone. He told me not to worry about a thing and that he would be there by my side as soon as he could.

As I sat detained for a few hours, I decided to just sit with my eyes closed, and as I sat, many thoughts ran through my head. I wondered what Misty was doing at that moment. Was she planning a trip to the Caribbean with my money?

I wondered what Saleeta, Xtasy, and Jenny were doing at that moment. Like, were their souls with God or with the devil?

How did the cops know I was at Money's crib? Would I actually do jail time, and if so, how much time would I get?

I thought about the first time I'd spoken to Pete. About that phone call I'd made to Minnesota to get reunited with him. About the time Saleeta's man had whupped her ass in our basement apartment. The fight I had with Money. The numerous tricks I had turned back in the day when I was letting this nigga pimp me. The night of *The Source* magazine party.

I thought about the time I cleaned up blood in my truck after Pete's murder. I thought about the cocaine and the weed that was illegally smuggled into and sold at the prisons. I thought about Saleeta and Money making that great connect with the Colombians. I thought about Chino. I thought about how my moms had done me so wrong over the years.

I thought about everything that I had ever been through. And while I thought about all of those things, I came to one resounding conclusion—I was well on my way to becoming a millionaire, had I not run into a few roadblocks. I was going to learn from these few roadblocks, get back on my grind, and hustle ten times smarter, if my lawyer was able to get me out of this jam.

If I could turn back the hands of time, I wouldn't, because everything happens for a reason, and if something didn't kill me, then it was only going to make me stronger. I couldn't undo the past, and I had to be held accountable for any wrong that I had done. But before I could be held accountable, I knew, like my lawyer had said, that the powers that be first had to prove me guilty.

My lawyer showed up at about eleven a.m., accompanied by his partner, David Upstein, another high-profile criminal lawyer. After breaking the ice and going through the introduction of his partner, the three of us sat in a room for a couple of hours, and we spoke at length.

"Did you guys get stuck in traffic?" I asked.

"No, nothing like that. Sorry it took us so long, but we were speaking to the Manhattan D.A., so we could sort everything out and get a handle on what was going on," David Upstein explained.

"So, what am I looking at?" I eagerly asked. "Be completely honest with me, and don't hold any punches."

David responded, "Well, first off, GG, let me explain something. I'm a straight shooter, and I never hold any punches. I tell you how it is, so you won't have any surprises."

"Now, what is going on is this: There is a law called the

RICO Act. RICO is an acronym, which stands for Racketeer Influenced and Corrupt Organizations."

I nodded my head to show that I understood.

David went on. "The RICO law gives prosecutors wide-ranging and sweeping authority, and one of the favorite uses of the RICO law is to go after and take down what they called organized crime syndicates such as the Mafia and things of that nature. The law defines racketeering activity as any act or threat involving murder, kidnapping, gambling, arson, bribery, extortion, dealing in obscene matter, or dealing in a controlled substance or listed chemical. You follow?"

I was soaking up everything like a sponge. "Yeah, I follow you."

"Now, the indictment is a multiple-count indictment and it is charging that you are the head of a newly formed criminal enterprise called Connie's Cartel, which has engaged in murder, narcotics distribution, and conspiracy. It's also stating that your street name is GG, and that you are right at the top of the organization."

"Well, am I the only one being charged?"

"Oh no!" David replied, "See, let me explain how this works. It wasn't just the NYPD who came after you. It was a joint NYPD/FBI task force that came after you. But since you had recently had the previous arrest for impersonating a C.O. and you've now, according to them, gotten into trouble again within a six-month time period, the NYPD took jurisdiction over your arrest. They did that just for the lights and cameras and for media purposes. But these charges they are hitting you with are mainly federal charges, and in a matter of days or weeks, your case will be totally moved to a federal venue. And, see, the feds, they don't go after just one fish. They try to go after a whole school of fish that swim together, and by doing so, they feel that they can totally eradicate whatever organization they are going after. In this case they did not just go after you, but they rounded up about ten other people. With the RICO law, you're looking at anywhere from twenty years to life behind bars."

At those words my heart sank, but I still had enough in me to ask another question. "So am I correct in assuming that someone like myself who they consider to be at the top of the organization would be looking at more time than those at the bottom of the organization?"

Marvin replied, "Well, in general terms, yes, but not always. Because, see, a guy at the bottom of the organization could be responsible for thirty murders. You understand?"

I nodded. Then I made sure to remind my lawyers that I wanted them to definitely see what they could do to find out why Money had been arrested and to also make sure that she was released and able to go back home. But, to my surprise, the attorneys told me some awful news.

"Well, GG, things don't work that easy. Now while we will represent Money, she's not going home anytime soon, and neither are you. She's one of the ten people being charged under this indictment."

"What?" I yelled in total shock and disbelief.

"Okay, GG, listen. We will get to Money, but let us work this one step at a time."

I shut up and listened, but I felt absolutely horrible because Money, all her life, had followed behind me and followed my lead. She was perfectly contented with boosting and doing her petty shit to get bread. I was the one who had convinced her to do this Cartel shit with me, and now she was paying the price for having stuck by me.

The lawyers went on to explain that the RICO law gave the government the right, as we spoke, to seize all of my assets, like my cars and anything in my crib.

I also found out that Chino and some more of his boys and members of the Colombian connection that Saleeta had found had all been picked up during the pre-dawn raid. And my lawyer went on to give me some options. He explained the evidence that was stacked up against me—the wiretap evidence, the video surveillance, and a host of other evidence that went back from the night the cops had ran up on me and Minnesota in the car that night in Hollis, and included everything up until the present. He also explained that there were a number of criminal informants prepared to testify against the Cartel. I knew right away that he had to be talking about Minnesota and his snitch ass.

I jumped in and asked, "Marvin, I don't know for sure, but I think they may have told you about an undercover cop who goes by the name of Cynthia. But even if they didn't tell you about her, I'm sure she was the one that helped get a lot of the evidence and videotapes and all of that. But my thing is this: Isn't there a line that the police can't cross while they are investigating? I mean, I went as far as smoking weed with the bitch and doing lines of coke with her ass. There has to be something illegal about that, or some kind of conflict of interest," I said in a slightly bitter manner.

Marvin explained that the district attorney had told him that Cynthia was indeed an undercover cop and that she had compiled a lot of the evidence, and that after she'd been killed, their investigation went into overdrive, leading to my arrest and indictment so quickly. He explained that normally they wait years before wrapping up investigations like this one. And regardless of what anyone said, Cynthia isn't here to be cross-examined or have her credibility brought into question, so all, if not most, of her evidence would stick, especially since now it carried a sentimental value with it.

"You see," Marvin said, "you're right about what you're getting at, in that informants, cops, and undercovers cannot do anything illegal while they're investigating. But in this case, like I said, Cynthia is dead, so any jury is gonna look at her as a martyr."

"As a what?"

"As a *martyr*, or a hero. Like someone who sacrifices their life doing a good deed."

I sank in my seat. I finally understood why the cops had set up Cynthia to be killed. I knew this was a dirty game, but I never had any idea just how dirty it was.

I sat back up in my seat and explained to Marvin that I was guilty of a whole lot and that I wasn't gonna try to hold no punches and that I just wanted him to do the best he could. But I felt like I wanted to still tell the truth and rat on those cops, even if it meant jail time to me. I felt that way simply because criminals, we do what we do to people in our world and we know the risks, but it ain't right when cops materially benefit from our criminal world with no real risks on their end.

Marvin cautioned me, "GG, I understand where you are coming from, and that is noble and the right thing to want to do. But, see, right now, while my job is to have you tell the truth, the bigger scope of my job is to get the government to prove their case against you. They have to prove to the jury beyond a shadow of a doubt that you should be held accountable, and if so, to what extent you should be held accountable for the charges that you face."

As Marvin spoke, one of the assistant district attorneys came into the room and asked my lawyers if she could speak with them. The lawyers excused themselves for about ten minutes, and then all three of them came back to speak to me.

The assistant district attorney spoke first. She basically told me the same things about the RICO law that my lawyer had explained to me. She also went on to tell me how I could possibly be facing life in prison if I was convicted for what I had been charged. After she was done talking, she asked me if I would listen to a tape recording. I agreed, and she whipped out her tape recorder and pressed play on the tape.

With all four of us closely listening to the tape, she asked me, "Do you recognize those voices on the tape?"

"Yeah," I replied as I listened in disgust.

On the tape was Chino, Saleeta, Pete, some of the Colombian drug dealers, and even Misty, who had not been arrested, all talking greasy about me. The only person they didn't have on tape talking greasy about me was my girl Money, who I loved to death. Especially after hearing that tape, I loved her because she had opportunities to talk greasy about me, and she always defended me instead, which to me was the ultimate sign of true loyalty, because she did it when no one was watching.

When the tape stopped, the assistant district attorney said, "GG, you heard for yourself how your so-called homies were talking about you. You should clearly be able to see for yourself that the people you associate with are only out for themselves and could care less about you and your well-being. Now, what I'm prepared to do is grant you and Money full immunity from all of these charges if you would agree to testify against Chino, the Colombians, and the rest of the members and associates of their crews.

"And Minnesota and Cheeks just skate and get a free ride in all of this shit, right?" I said under my breath.

The D.A. asked me, "What was that?"

"Nothing," I replied. "It was nothing."

I closed my eyes and blew air out of my lungs. As I closed my eyes, I saw an image of me coming to Saleeta's rescue when her man was whupping that ass. I also saw the time that Chino bumped into me at the Shark Bar and was talking so much shit and making like he was the fucking man and shit. Come to find out, the nigga was straight pussy, just like the rest of these so-called gangstas.

I was burning with anger after hearing Misty on the tape. I now knew for a fact that she'd set up that fucking rape and robbery to make her own damn come-up. I continued to just sit there with my eyes closed. I blew more air out of my lungs.

At that moment, I was holding all of the cards. All I had to do was play those cards, and in doing so, I would be able to spring myself and get off scot-free.

The assistant district attorney then reminded me that I was gonna be tried for murder, and she ran down all of the other charges, trying to reinforce what I was up against, to give me the notion that testifying against everyone else was a no-brainer.

Honestly as I sat there, the only thing that was making me lean toward turning against everybody was the fact that I could help spring Money. Personally, I was willing to do whatever time in the joint I was facing, but I would not have been able to live with myself if Money had to be sent to prison.

"Can you just give me some time alone with my lawyers?" I asked.

"Sure. No problem," the lady replied as she prepared to leave the room.

With her gone, Marvin said, "GG, it's a sweetheart deal."

"I know," I replied. I thought to myself that no matter how bad people had spoken about me, I couldn't let any resentment or bitterness cloud my thinking. I couldn't turn into a rat. It just wasn't right. Not one of the other defendants had ever forced me to do anything, so I couldn't now turn the tables on everybody. But I do definitely know one thing: If I could have spoken up and sent that bitch Misty to jail, then maybe I might have. But her bitch ass hadn't gotten caught in the sling, which made me wonder if she was down with Minnesota and his corrupt undercover cop crew.

"Marvin, I just can't do it," I said. "I'm gonna have to roll the dice and go to trial."

"GG, just think about what you're doing. You're risking jail time for yourself and for Money. And not only that, you can bet that if you don't go through with this deal, well, you can bet that the same assistant district attorney will be talking to Chino in a minute and trying to get him to turn against you and the Cartel. The government is willing to sacrifice one, if they can guarantee themselves that they will get the majority," Marvin explained.

"Marvin, look, no one knows this, not even Money, but I secretly stashed a whole lot of cash. I did that in the event of something like this happening. Now, the stash ain't that crazy, and I'm gonna tell you where it is. I need you to take that cash and use it as your fee. I know the government doesn't know about that money, so they can't freeze it. It ain't in no bank account, and it ain't in my crib. I want you to take your fees out of that money and use it to represent both me and Money, and do the best job you can do, because I just can't go through with testifying against nobody and forever being called a fucking rat. That's just not me. I know I'm rolling the dice, but I gotta do what I gotta do. Find another way to help me . . . please."

Marvin took off his glasses and rubbed his eyes. "Okay."

For myself, I had to believe that the government had a weak case against me in particular. Even with all of their bugs, wiretaps, videotapes, and witnesses, why were they offering me such a sweet deal so soon? Because they didn't have a rock-solid case.

I would be lying, though, if I said I wasn't nervous and thinking maybe I was cutting my own throat, placing all of my chips on the table and letting everything ride by going to trial.

Was I stupid? True street niggas would say no. Everyone else would have said that I was stupid as hell for not taking the government's deal. Only time would tell if I'd played my cards right.

One thing I did know, and no one would ever be able to take from me, was, I had honor. True honor. And by going to trial at seventeen years old, unlike muthafuckas twice my age, I really knew what death before dishonor meant. I never wanted to be considered a snitch or a fucking rat. And I never would or could be.

Again, was I stupid? Only time would tell if I had played my cards right.

To be continued in "Connie's Cartel, Part II."

THE FAVOR

By Rahsaan Ali

Chapter 1

Black Bastard

I was ten years old when my mother passed away. She liked to run the streets at night, partying and drinking. I can recall the days when it was just she and I against the world. Then there were those other days when she'd leave and not return until the next day. I didn't care though. I'd just stay up all night watching TV. Shit, every once in a while I'd put my feet up and sip on one of her half-filled cans of Miller beer.

I remember stroking her long black hair. It was dark and silky, and would glisten whenever the light hit it. She was pretty, nothing at all like myself. I was bony and unusually tall for a female, awkwardly shaped and more attracted to my own gender than them pussy-hungry boys. I later learned that was all they wanted from a woman.

Nevertheless, men chased behind my mother as if her ass was going out of style. Having that knowledge played a major role in my decision to alternate what was deemed a natural and morally correct lifestyle into that of a gender-bender. I liked women. From a young girl to pre-teen to young adult, certain things about me just physically dictated *butch*.

My mother never once shunned me for being who I was. My wonderful mother, she never once was ashamed of me. She's no longer here anymore because of her wild ways. So it was no shock when life's third rail spit on her soul, beating her down in the street until her tragic death.

> *Ohhhh, baby, gotta get you home*
> *Gotta get you home with me tonight*
> *Oooooh, baby, Ohhhh*
> *Gotta get you home with me tonight*

The Foxy Brown/Blackstreet joint vibrated against our tenth-floor apartment door as I stepped out of the elevator from school. I turned the knob and pushed. It was latched at the top from the inside. I had to pee, and the music was playing so loud my knocks went unheard. I began pounding it until the latch detached and the door flung open inwardly.

"Girl, what's the matter with you? You running from the police or something?" My mother smiled as the door opened.

I ran off into the bathroom. I hopped in place, trying to pull my pants down before I pissed myself, but it didn't work. By the time I finally got them down, a homemade Jacuzzi equipped with a heating system had formed a pool of shame in the bottom of my panties. I quickly kicked the soiled panties off and tossed them in the cabinet under the sink.

I scrubbed the piss off the floor with ammonia. Hey, I didn't know any better then. The strong fumes burned my nostrils, eyes, and lungs. I dropped to my knees and struggled to breathe. The constant-running ventilation up above couldn't expel the poisonous toxins in the air that was overwhelming me.

"Quiana," Ma said, knocking on the door, "you wanna hurry out of there so you can eat this sandwich? I'm having company tonight. I already called Grandma. She said it's all right to come over. I already laid you out an outfit on your bed to wear to church tonight. Quiana." Ma knocked again. "Don't play with me, girl. You better open this door."

I wanted to cry out, but my voice had become just as heavy as my limbs. My eyes started to close, and vomit ejected from my mouth and splattered on my face.

"You gonna make me beat your ass," she said, turning the knob and walking in. "Quiana!" she screamed and immediately dragged my naked body out of the bathroom by the arm. She pulled me all the way into the living room and out onto the balcony. "Breathe, baby," she said, fanning my face. "Breathe." She held up my head under her arm. She shouted, "Breathe!" and shook me by the chin.

I coughed up more vomit before involuntarily inhaling a long stuttered breath from deep down. I'd have to say, looking back on it all, it was the only time I can recall seeing death around the corner. No, more like meeting death on my own front porch.

Going to church with Grandma Thomasina was like hell. My mother loved leaving me with her on Friday nights. That was church night. Grandma would get all dressed up in her fancy clothing and her favorite feathered hat. Those were the most boring days of my young life, sitting up in church listening to some crazy nigga whooping and hollering about a highway to heaven. I think it was called First Truth Baptist Church. Quite often I'd nod off to sleep.

Grandma would pinch the hell out of my leg every time. "Pay attention. He's talking to you."

Pastor Charles King sipped a glass of water. "God spoke to me today." His curly salt-and-pepper hair offset any color coordination with his brown pinstriped suit. And the white collar around his neck seemed to tighten each time he turned his head from left to right.

"Go 'head and preach," someone shouted from the congregation.

Two black six-foot metal fans blowing from opposite sides

of the room did little to suppress heat rising from the bodies of the overly dressed religious fanatics. Notes from the organ up above played a melodic tit for tat each time the pastor said something pivotally motivational.

"I was on my way here to give you the Word, as I do every Friday and Sunday. And I was stopped by a police officer for speeding on the I-95. I pulled over, and he arrogantly walked to my window and told me to roll it down. I kindly obliged and smiled. He stood stern and asked if I knew I was exceeding the state speed limit. I said, 'I honestly wasn't paying attention, officer, but as you can see on my license plate, I am a pastor and I'm running behind schedule. I'm not making any excuses, but I'm sure you can understand the concept of being on time for the Lord.' "

"We're listening. Go 'head," another crazed freak shouted out.

"Now how many of you have licenses?"

The majority of the congregants raised their hands.

"Yeah. But how many of you are legally registered? You don't have to confess anything to me, if you don't want to. I'm not the DMV."

A young lady seated beside my grandmother sang, "*Well...*"

"Let's just say that the Lord is like our DMV." Pastor King smiled as he removed his glasses. "You listening, brother," he said to the drummer in back of him. "Now I say the *Looooord* is like our DMV. And we are his vehicles. Without him your vehicle, my vehicle, our vehicles cannot legally be driven on the road. Are y'all feeling me yet?" He chuckled. "We are all the Lord's vehicles, and it is our responsibility to get licensed with Jesus. The license is acknowledging that there is none after, before, or in between. The license leads to the registration, and the registration is the Lord, and if you don't go through the tunnel of Jesus, then you do not get registered with the Lord. Your vehicle will be off the road, and you don't want to be off the road with the Lord. So if you're not licensed, or you're driving with a suspended one, please get registered." He wiped the perspiration off his forehead, while the congregation displayed their zeal, clapping their hands, and stomping their feet in the middle of the aisle.

Grandma pinched my already sore thigh. "Pay attention. He's talking to you."

Chapter 2

Tyrone called from our small kitchen, "Quiana!"

Tyrone was one of my mother's latest man friends. I went from sleeping in the bed with her to sleeping on a second-hand leather couch in the living room, once his ass came on the scene. There was a loose spring sticking out of the material because of the midnight rats that chewed on everything in sight when the lights went out. But it didn't matter. It was all my mother could afford, and the only conditions Section 8 would allow black people to live in. I didn't understand it back then. For a while I thought it was normal to see a roach crawl out of a box of "No Frills" corn flakes cereal. I thought it was the prize.

"Yeah." I wiped my sleepy eyes as I walked into the kitchen. I looked up at him groggily in my dingy pink Rainbow Brite nightgown.

Tyrone held up a napkin with thoroughly cleaned bones on them. "You know you left this chicken out last night?"

"No. I ate them all. Mommy saw me."

"I don't care what she seen. You eat the rest of this meat off these bones, or I'ma kick your ass." He dropped the bones on the kitchen table. "You . . . you, you boy thing.

Look at you—talk like a boy, walk like a little boy. I bet if I lift that nightgown, I'll probably see a little boy."

Every morning after Ma left, it was the same ol' shit. If I walked into the kitchen, it was all about what I left on the table. And this nigga wasn't even my father. I didn't know who or where he was, but here this dude was tryin'a be a father. If I walked into the bathroom, it was about me not flushing the toilet. He didn't like me because Ma had to spend some of her money, their money to smoke crack, on me. That morning she had ran out to get me some baloney for school lunch. He called me every name in the book but a child of God. But his favorite name out of them all was "black bastard." BLACK BASTARD! Because, according to him, I was a useless, fatherless burden.

"Why you just standing there like a dummy, boy? You know what a bastard is?" He scratched his balls through the open slit of his dirty green-and-white pinstriped boxers. "You's about to learn something from me today. Come on," he said, stepping barefoot onto the beige carpet of the dining room. The heels of his calloused skin dropped scales as he slowly dragged his feet across the carpet.

He pulled a red Webster's dictionary down from the bookshelf then handed it to me. "Look for the b's." He shoved me over to the couch.

I looked up at him in confusion, the book on my lap.

"I'll do it." He took the book and flipped to the page he wanted me to find. "You see what this shit say, boy? Read this shit," he said, pointing his finger to a word. "Say this word right here."

I looked down at it wondering why he wanted me to say that word. It wasn't that I couldn't sound it out, but it was just that I knew it was a bad word. God would strike me down or run me off the highway to heaven. But I was scared of Tyrone and didn't want that pointy finger to poke me.

"*Bay-stad.*"

"Read it again," he shouted.

"*Bastard,*" I quickly corrected myself.

"Go on." Tyrone frowned, folding his arms.

"*Bastard. I-l-i-lee-le-gi-gitimate. Illegitimate. Parents not married.*" I looked up, still confused.

"That's right, and don't you ever forget it."

I couldn't figure out, for the life of me, why this man was being such a brute to me. I know why now, but at the time, it only sounded like the unadulterated hate of a basehead.

Ma walked through the front door. "What y'all two doing? It is cold out there." She removed her wool hat then shook off the snow.

"Hi, Ma." I ran over to her for a much-needed embrace.

"Hey, Cheri," Tyrone said, placing the dictionary back on the shelf. "I was just teaching Quiana there a couple of new words before she take her ass to school."

"Can you watch your mouth around her? She don't need to be hearing that."

"I'm about to go and see about that job Steve was telling me about. I'ma need ten dollars, baby."

"I need to go food shopping with that, Tyrone."

"What you on welfare for if you not gonna use the stamps? Gimme some money so I can find some work."

"I gave you fifty dollars last week. What happened to that?"

"It cost to get around. You know that. Why you wanna start doing me like this? You go out and party every night with your friends. You spend your money on them. None of y'all work. Shit."

Ma turned to me. "Get yourself ready for school." As she walked to her bedroom, she said to Tyrone, "I don't got no money."

"See, you don't want me to work. You just want me to stay

here and watch that li'l thing out there. She ain't my son, I mean daughter, Cheri. I ain't in the business of babysitting."

"You ain't in the business of shit no way, and I'm tired of it. You gotta find something, Tyrone. You supposed to be a man. I shouldn't even have to be giving you money. You should be giving me your money, but no, you'd rather take mines and use it to get yourself high and drunk. The money I could be getting high with."

"You's about a complaining bitch. You knew I wasn't working when I moved up in here. And don't act like I don't bring shit up in this bitch. I put food in the freezer whenever I can find work."

"Yeah. But who in the hell considers vagrancy a real job, Tyrone? Don't fool yourself."

"No. *You* don't fool yourself into believing that your shit doesn't stink. You a government recipient just like the rest of these muthafuckas in this cage. Nobody in this whole damn complex is employed—yourself included—so don't you tell me about not having a job. Shit."

"Fuck you, Tyrone. At least I got my ass out there to apply for a place to live. You won't even do that. That's why you grubbing up in here off me."

Through the partially closed door, I could see them pointing in each other's faces and screaming at the top of their lungs. Every once in a while, he'd raise his hand to her.

"I wish you would." Ma quickly spat a razorblade from inside her mouth. "Come on, I dare you to. No. I want you to."

This went on at least once a week between Ma and Tyrone. Unwarranted threats on each other's lives, heated discussions about money. Who was right? Who was wrong? There never was a moment of peace in this drug-induced war between two lost souls struggling to maintain a relationship solely based on crack cocaine, but built upon the perception of love.

In the end, Tyrone left Ma grabbing on to his ankle, begging him not to leave her. "Ty, please," she cried. "I'll do anything."

"Let me go, or I'll hurt you," he said, stepping out of her grasp.

"Baby. Come on, let's take a hit right now." Ma stood up. "Come on, daddy, let's get high," she said, all wide-eyed and enthused. "We can use the rent. I'll think of something." She grabbed his hand.

"Get high by your damn self." Tyrone snatched his arm away then rushed out, slamming the door behind him, and the mother I once believed was so strong fell to the floor and banged on the door.

Ma got high that night. Higher than I'd ever seen her. Her eyes bulged, and saliva formed at the corners of her mouth. Entranced by the persuasive influence of the devil's handpicked medium, she spoke in a frantic pattern of unsteady incomprehensibility. Yet again, her soul was momentarily set free to soar above the clouds of genocide, only to free-fall back down to earth thirty seconds later.

"Don't cry, Ma," I said, holding onto her hand.

"I need to get some air." She stood up then rushed into her bedroom.

I could hear her scrambling through her dresser drawers, slamming them in and out then letting them drop to the floor. I ran to the back room and stood in the doorway watching her.

Ma frantically searched under piles of clothes in the closet. "Where is it?" she cried, flinging clothes across her back. "Where's the money?"

Then it hit her. Tyrone had robbed us, and he took the food stamps too.

"Oh no. I ain't going for this no more," she cried, grabbing me by the hand. "Come on, we're going to find that nigga. He not gonna be taking no food out my baby's stomach." She dragged me by the hand.

Ma shuffled her feet in place as we rode the pissy-smelling elevator down into the lobby. The doors opened quickly, and the fluorescent light inside dimmed.

Ma dragged me out and stepped to the complex's local dealer. I always admired him. At that time he just looked like somebody to respect. He was clean. Paid. He dressed like the guys from the videos, and every once in a while he'd say to me in front of my friends, "What's up, li'l man?"

To him, I always looked just like a little boy. Even though he knew I was a girl, my swagger hinted otherwise.

"Where's he at, Sakou?" Ma said, walking up to my hero.

Sakou's mouth was full of gold teeth, and he had his name spelled out in the top row. He wore a huge gold rope chain with an expensive diamond-studded medallion dangling from it. A gold nugget ring on his right index finger displayed a small ruby faceplate. He was on the come-up and had probably seen more money in his young life than half the retired tenants in the whole building.

An eye patch covered his left eye. I thought it made him look cool, until he told me later on in life how he'd gotten the pleasure of sporting it. He'd been stabbed in his eye after a bad drug deal, and there was nothing the doctors could to salvage it. It made him even more attractive to the squares trying to geometrically shape themselves into his tight circle.

Sakou stood smiling in the middle of the lobby, counting his money while music blasted from the huge boom box set before his feet. His dedicated entourage of followers stood by smoking cigarettes, sipping malt liquor, and taking tokes of marijuana out in the open.

"Come on, Cheri," he said. "I ain't your man's caretaker. Word up. You better get a hold on that situation. Know what I'm saying? Go on," he said, waving us off. "Hold up, li'l man," he said to me, "here go some ducats for your pocket."

"*He* is a little girl, man. Stop calling her a *he*."

Sakou handed me a couple of singles then went back to business as usual.

Ma stood staring at him, waiting on a more informative response and wasn't leaving until she got one.

Sakou pointed toward the Puerto Rican bodega at the corner, and once again, Ma dragged me down behind her.

Tyrone was standing in front of a brown garbage bin, talking to himself, trying to peddle a large broken cellular phone to patrons as they entered and exited the store.

Ma yelled in his face, "Tyrone, where's the money?" She released my hand and grabbed him by the shirt. "Where is it?"

A local crowd of amused spectators began encircling them as their circus-like antics ensued and increased in volume. The kind of volume that drags the cops into the mix. Which was bad for Sakou's business.

Sakou ran from across the street with a group of his "b-boy standing" cronies, stopping traffic in the process. Little boys and girls across the street stood excitedly in ankle-deep snow, watching the action through an iron green gate. Wrapped around the cold, rusting iron, their hands had to be frozen. And even though their teeth chattered in the frigid weather, they just couldn't turn away because there was always something about Brooklyn beef that made everybody want to see.

"Yo!" Sakou yelled, slushing his black Timberlands through the snow. "Are y'all crazy or something?" he said, separating them.

Tyrone swung wildly.

Sakou pressed him back against the bin with a thud. "Chill out," he said, holding him in place. "You high muthafucka, what I tell you about being zoned on my spot? Look at you." He shook him by the chin. "You don't even know where you at, muthafucka."

"Come on, man," Tyrone said in a slur, "you know that she be acting all crazy on me too."

"This is my block. You making shit hot for me right now." Sakou looked back at me and Ma. "What he done did, Cheri?"

Ma took a swing at Tyrone. "He done took my food shopping money."

"Chill out!" Sakou pushed her back. "Where her money?"

"I smoked it."

"See? Now you know," Sakou said to Ma. "Problem solved. Y'all better cut this crackhead shit out around here. Get high on your own time, not on mine."

"Well, what I'm supposed to do about food? How I'ma feed my daughter?"

Sakou looked down at me then back at Tyrone. "You're gonna work this off for me, dukes. Wurdupp!" he said, looking into Tyrone's eyes. "How much he took?" Sakou reached down into the deep pocket of his Triple F.A.T. Goose.

"Three hundred and fifty dollars."

"I'm only doing this shit for you because li'l dude there my partna. He gotta eat."

"*She.*" Ma corrected him. "*She.*"

"He's going to work for me one day. Right, boy?" Sakou said, ignoring her correction. "Right, homegirl?" he asked, smiling with his hand out.

"Wurdupp!" I said, emulating his lingo.

Chapter 3

For my tenth birthday Ma threw me a party. Actually it was like both of our parties. Whenever her friends came over and started ringing the bell, it only meant one thing. Everybody was about to get their buzz on. None of my friends had parental restrictions because all of their parents were already here. Yo, man, we had a ball that night. We all danced the night away and really enjoyed ourselves. Back in '87 you could do that, you know. Still party and have a good time without everybody in the joint becoming victims of a circumstance and whatnot.

Us kids drank red Kool-Aid that night and stuck out our tongues at one another, competing to see who had the reddest. Ma and her friends drank until they thought the earth was slanted. A drunken fire set ablaze in all of their eyes. We formed a circle around Ma and her homegirl, Ms. Tarsha. They were the only ones able to drum up enough rhythm to dance on beat to Earth, Wind & Fire's "Let's Groove."

"Awwww sooki-sooki now, y'all. Do it," Byron said from down the hall in apartment 10A.

"Come on over here, birthday girl." Ma grabbed my hand and swung it back and forth to the musical wave of earthly funk.

I twisted, turned, and bumped hips with Ma. Flashes from Polaroid cameras lit up from every direction as we spun around in a circle.

Ma sipped from her glass then released my hand. "All right, birthday girl, time to open your gift," she said, walking toward the back. "Turn off those lights, somebody. Tarsha, come on back here and help me."

We all stood in the living room anticipating what Ma had got for me. I wasn't expecting anything, but Ma made miracles every Thanksgiving. Today was no exception.

Ms. Tarsha emerged from the back carrying a white, blue, and pink decorated birthday cake. Nine burning candles led them through the dark hallway. Behind her was Ma walking a Rottweiler puppy on a leash. All the kids surrounded it and gleefully pulled at its short tail. He playfully retaliated with non-threatening snaps, his teeth razor-sharp.

One of the kids said, "Man, you lucky. My moms won't let me have no dog."

Ma began singing, "*Happy birthday to you*," and everyone else joined in.

"*How old are you now*," they concluded, adding the second half of the traditional song in the way only black people could.

Ma, standing behind me, her hands on my shoulders, said, "Blow out the candles and make a wish, baby."

I inhaled one deep, long breath with my eyes closed then exhaled, blowing out the yellow wicks. Everyone clapped, cheered, and whistled.

Ma hugged me and kissed my cheek. "So what'd you wish for, hon?" she asked out loud.

Before I could respond, a pounding at the door startled me and everyone else. Byron walked to the door and opened it. It was Tyrone, dressed in a ridiculous suit that was dingy and wrinkled. And he reeked of alcohol, which spelled trouble in the making.

"What you doing here, Tyrone?" Ma said.

"What? You think I'd miss the boy's birthday?" he slurred, stumbling past Byron's frail, wiry frame.

"You wasn't invited. Get out!" Ma pointed at the open door.

"I ain't going nowhere, and ain't nobody gonna do nothing about it."

Ma attempted to go at Tyrone, but Ms. Tarsha and some of the other tenants held her back.

Tyrone grabbed a half-empty bottle of Moët and began guzzling it.

"Don't even worry about it, girl," Ms. Tarsha said. "Let his drunken behind have it. Long as he leaves."

Tyrone handed me a five-dollar bill. "Happy birthday, boy."

"She don't need no money from you, and stop calling her a boy." Ma pulled me back. "All you'd be doing is giving back the food you been taking out her mouth. So just take your tired ass on where the fuck you came from. I don't want nothing to do with you no more."

"I don't got nowhere to go, Cheri."

Ms. Tarsha responded, "The shelter right up in Manhattan. Better get there before lights out."

"You stay outta this. You don't got shit to do with this," Tyrone shouted, foam seeping from the corners of his mouth.

"All right, that's enough." Byron approached Tyrone with caution and reached out to touch his shoulder. "Why don't you calm down, man?"

Tyrone grabbed Byron's wrist and pushed it back, dropping him to his knees.

Ms.Tarsha rushed to Byron's side. "What the hell is wrong wit' you?" she screamed. "That crack really got you messed up."

As the others stepped forward, Tyrone could sense that they meant to cause him bodily harm. "You not gonna get away with this, Cheri. You playing me." He backed himself up against the door and turned the knob.

"You playing yourself," Ma said. "Step!"

"I'ma see you again, bitch. Won't be love either." Tyrone opened the door and stepped into the hallway.

Ms. Tarsha slammed the door in his face.

Byron stood rubbing his wrist, a frown on his face. "Man, he lucky I didn't have my gun on me." He poured himself a drink, while everybody patted his back for trying to save the day.

"Turn back on that music," Ms. Tarsha shouted. "It's time to party."

> *"It takes two to make a thing go right.*
> *It takes two*
> *To make it outta sight."*

When the Rob Base and DJ E-Z Rock hit came on, I walked off and stepped onto the balcony, from where I could see the red-white-and-blue tip of the Empire State Building's antenna blinking on and off in the distance.

Moments later, Ma touched my shoulder from behind. "What's the matter, baby? Talk to Mommy. You didn't like your present?"

I nodded yes, but carried on my glossy-eyed stare of catatonic suspension.

"Girl, I'll be right back," Ma said to Ms. Tarsha. "I gotta talk to my baby."

She said to me, "You all right?"

"Are you going to let him come back?" I asked, tears in my eyes.

I was always questioning and challenging everything. At that point in my life, I started noticing something was wrong. I was looking for a father, but he was gone. My only mentor was the street. Ma's choice of men often made me wonder what planet she was really living on. After seeing kids with both parents living at home laughing, hugging, and being a family, it made me cry, and left a bitter taste in my mouth.

"Where's my father?" I asked.

"We had this talk already. I told you before, I don't know. I'm sorry, but I just don't. I know what it is. You see all your friends inside chilling with they daddies. I'm sorry, but that's the only gift I can't get you," Ma said, lightly squeezing my hand. "I love you, Quiana. Nothing's ever gon' change about that. You don't worry about a daddy. I've been that your entire life. Cool?" Ma held up her hand for a high-five.

"Cool," I responded, still not satisfied.

Ms. Tarsha walked out with two red cups of soda. "Is this a private party, or can I get an invitation?"

Chapter 4

It was around three in the morning when the loud thumping on the front door woke me up. I heard Ma scurry to the door in the dark. I crept over to the doorway of my bedroom and stuck out my head.

Ma turned on the table lamp next to the door. "Who?"

Thud! Thud! Thud!

"I said, who the fuck is it?" Ma yelled. She looked out the peephole then unlatched the door, which flew open and knocked her backwards.

Tyrone rushed inside high and drunk. He grabbed her by the neck and slammed the front door closed. She struggled, but his long, skinny fingers had a secure grip around her neck.

"I need some money. I'm not playing wit' you either. You better come out your pocketbook with something. Shit! Throw me out, I'll show you!" He flung her helpless body around by the neck.

"Get off her!" I yelled, charging toward him.

Tyrone jabbed me with one quick punch to my forehead, and I fell to the floor, holding my head, as blood leaked onto the brown tile floor.

All of a sudden, Ma's parental strength erupted out of

nowhere, and she broke free of his lock. She grabbed the lamp off the table and swung the metal stand into his face. "Run, baby!" she said, standing at the doorway.

I darted out the door with her behind me, and she pushed me forward, banging on every apartment door we passed. Doors opened one by one, as our cries of distress echoed off the walls of the once silent corridor.

Our neighbors caught up with Tyrone before he could catch us. Then we heard his pleas for help as he was introduced to some street justice.

Three months had passed, and Tyrone was nothing but a bad memory.

Ma had finally gotten her shit together and landed herself a real job with an official check. Ma was a trooper and wanted nothing more than to get me out of the projects. She wanted me to go to a better school with a more positive environment, but I was starting to like it there. Red Hook was home, and suburban life was no longer a star I was shooting for.

It was late Thursday night, and I'd just finished my homework. Ma was working overtime, and I was trying to wait up for her. When the master lock of the front door turned counterclockwise and slowly opened, I ran to my room because I knew it'd be ass-whupping time if she ever caught me up late again during a school night.

I jumped into my bed and quickly pulled the covers up over my shoulders. The door quietly closed, and the sound of heavy footsteps strode across the hardwood floor. I rolled off the side of the bed and looked under it. I saw Tyrone's feet. He headed straight toward Ma's room and began rummaging through everything.

Then the front door opened again, and I could hear Tyrone's footsteps become more distant.

"What you doing here?" Ma yelled out in shock. "Quiana!" she shouted.

"I told you I'd get you. How you kick a nigga out and forget you gave him the keys to the place?"

"You better get out of here."

I crawled across my bedroom floor and poked my head out the door.

Tyrone reached into his back pocket, simultaneously covering her mouth with his free hand, and produced a long blade with brass knuckles as grips for his fingers. He plunged it into her shoulder.

I stood at the door and screamed, "Ma!"

Blood shot up through her shirt and painted a premonition of death on the wall. She clawed and grabbed at his face, but he was just way too strong for her to overcome the deadly tool being plunged down inside her chest.

Ma held on for as long as she could, but it was the final cut. A film of blood quickly covered her body and was eventually developed into photographs for the newspapers and forensics.

I held on to her even after she drifted off from her fast and furious life, and stayed with her until the EMTs arrived. Ms. Tarsha had to pry me off Ma. I didn't ever want to let her go, but I knew I couldn't hold on to her forever.

Chapter 5

After Ma's funeral, friends and family that I'd never seen a day in my life showed up at Grandma Thomasina's broken-down home in Far Rockaway, Queens. Hardly anyone could afford a suit, so most of them paid their respects wearing jeans, sneakers, and T-shirts. The women wore slacks, blouses, and thirdhand Gucci boots, a half-inch missing from the inch-high heels.

I was sick and tired of all the hugs, kisses, and the "Oh, poor baby, Auntie loves you" bull. Those fake-ass functional crackheads didn't give a shit about Ma. Just there for the food, the greedy muthafuckas ate everything but the furniture.

The only one I trusted was Ms. Tarsha. She was Ma's only true friend. When Ma couldn't afford to feed me and clothe me, she was there. Ms. Tarsha was kind of like Willona from *Good Times*. The nosy, bothersome, know-it-all neighbor who still believed in the African proverb, "It takes a village to raise a child."

Ms. Tarsha said to me in a low voice, "You know you can come by anytime you want. Don't worry, Qui, they'll find him. If they don't, I will. I promise you that, baby."

"What's the matter with her?" Grandma Thomasina asked.

"You better go 'head get yourself something to eat. I'm not for going to no doctors in the middle of the night now. I'm too old for it," she said, forcing the plate onto my lap. "Eat!" She pointed at the pile of steaming barbecue chicken wings sitting on my plate.

"I'll make sure she eats it all, Miss Thomasina," Ms. Tarsha said.

Grandma Thomasina was always taking some member of the family in. She had seven foster kids, ranging from ages six to sixteen, and I had to live with her because no other family member would take me in.

Chapter 6

Seven years later

M y guidance counselor, Mrs. Able, said to me, "Every-thing starts from here. You and I both know that your life is a farce. I've watched you the entire four years you've been here. Consider this a break, you know, giving you the extra push and all."

At that time, that lady just didn't know all of the things I'd been going through. And the amazing thing was, I just sat there and listened while she talked to me as if I was a man. I remember thinking how easy it would've been to snatch up the pair of scissors sitting on her desk and just start poking the bitch in her fat fucking mouth.

But the truth of the matter was, I really didn't earn my diploma. It was given to me. What did it matter, though? I'd never anticipated graduating in the first place.

"Are you listening to me, Miss Shareef?"

Rising from my seat, I kindly responded, "You have a good summer."

"Miss Shareef, do you really think you've accomplished something? Personally, I think that if your mother were alive, she wouldn't be so proud of you."

I guess it was the apathy in her voice that made me react the way I did, but I snapped. She shouldn't have said anything against my mother, so I pounded the bitch out.

The following day I was arrested at Grandma Thomasina's house on a second-degree assault charge, to go along with several other miscellaneous charges I'd accrued in my teen years.

Chapter 7

After serving a year and eight months on Rikers Island, I was released back into society. Being locked up was like living in a community of caged wild animals, a jungle where lions ruled, often splitting off into vicious packs in search of defenseless prey.

I knocked on my grandmother's door wearing nothing but a netted duffle bag over my shoulder, a white T-shirt and baggy blue jeans. My hair was cornrowed and tied into a ponytail. A small cut under my right eye stood out, solidifying my status of past wars. I was about to be nineteen, although it seemed as if I was just eight years old yesterday.

The door opened. "Yes," Grandma said in a tiresome voice, a white crocheted shawl tossed around her shoulders.

"It's me, Grandma. I'm home."

"Well, look at you." Grandma smiled and pushed the screen door open.

Even though I'd only been away for a year and change, the stress of dealing with those smart-ass foster kids to make ends meet seemed to have taken its toll on Grandma, and it showed within each and every patterned wrinkle drawn upon her face.

"Step on in here and let Grandma see you. You know my cataracts be acting up." She tiptoed to hug me. "You've gotten taller."

Dana, the eldest foster child, said, "What's up, Qui?"

Dana was now seventeen, and the one giving my grandmother the most trouble. The teachers from her school would call every day, and boys would call the house and ring the bell all times of the night. That wasn't happening before I left, and it wasn't going to happen now. Not as long as I lived here. Grandma should've thrown her out a long time ago, but she was afraid that Dana would fall into the cracks or become another statistic.

"Hey, Dana," I said, hugging her.

"Shit! Looks like you were up in there bending back them bars." Dana felt the bulk on my right arm. Then she headed toward the front door.

"Where you going?" Grandma asked.

Dana continued forward without responding and closed the door behind her.

Meanwhile, the other kids were running through the house, throwing things at one another, and wrestling near the coffee table in the living room.

"You want me to take care of it?" I asked Grandma. "Listen, y'all, stop all of this and go do some homework. Grandma Thomasina is getting upset."

"Shut up, *man-girl*," Jovan said to me. "You ain't nobody."

Jovan was the youngest of the foster kids. He was just six years old when I left. Now he was talking as if he was fifteen.

"Forget about it." Grandma Thomasina walked toward the kitchen. "I was about to get started with lunch. You hungry?"

I followed her. "Sit down, Grandma." I pulled out a chair.

Going through the pantry, she said, "I can't sit. The kids have to eat."

"They can wait," I said, taking her by the shoulders. "Let

them burn off some more of that energy. Just sit down for a minute."

Grandma sat down and began swiping crumbs off the table.

I clasped her hands. "Grandma, Grandma, Grandma . . . what's the matter? Do you want me to leave? Is that it?"

"Don't be foolish. You're my daughter's only child, my only granddaughter."

"So what is it then?"

"They're taking the house away from me."

"Who's taking the house away from you?"

"The bank. I can't afford to make the payments anymore."

"Even with your social security, pension, and the kids?"

"It's just not enough anymore. These kids are eating more and more, and the prices of food have gone up so high. I've been here for over thirty years, never late on one single payment, and now after almost having this house paid off, they want to take it from me." Grandma complained with a hurt I hadn't heard in her voice since Ma's funeral.

"What can I do?"

Grandma wept with her head down. "I don't know."

"Don't do that." I touched the side of her face. "I'm not used to seeing you cry. I'm used to seeing you strong, Grandma. We'll figure something out. Don't worry."

"I hope you don't plan on getting into no more trouble. I can use your help around here with these kids. I can't control them. I just feel like there's nothing I can do."

"I'm home now, Grandma. You don't have to worry about nothing no more. I'm going to get myself into community college."

"How are you going to pay for it? I don't have any money, and I don't want you out there doing anything foolish."

I cupped her face in my hands. "Grandma, I'll get a full-time job, a part-time job, and whatever other kind of job I could get. Whatever I have to do. But you are not going to lose this house."

Grandma placed her hands on my lap. "You turned out all right," she said. "I may have acted like I didn't care about what was going on with you when you was younger. I had to let your momma be her own woman. I was upset with her for living that life she was living, but I never meant to take it out on you."

"Grandma, the past is the past. I don't live there anymore, okay." I kissed her cheek then stood up.

Chapter 8

Even though a year and change in prison doesn't seem like a long time, to that person putting in his or her bid, it does. The shit doesn't go by fast, and it ain't no walk in the park. Anybody that tells you otherwise is a muthafucking liar. Don't expect no big parties to be thrown for you by your so-called peoples when you come home. Don't even think that your girl is still your girl and that she been keeping her legs locked until your release. What you can expect is for everybody to shit on you, unless you have a supportive family or family member. Otherwise, you're forced to make a choice. The kind of choice only a nigga on his face can make.

Contrary to popular belief, there will come a time in life where you may have to do the wrong thing to make things right. Hustling was out because I never was for nickel-and-diming. Besides, when it came to drugs, the system was throwing the books at niggas left and right. I couldn't fuck with that kind of time. Public defenders? Shit! Black or white, my nigga, their only job is to show up in court on your behalf. They don't give a shit if you did the crime or not because once you're accused of an alleged felony and have been processed through the system, that's it. You'd have to be a dumb-ass fool to think someone is going to represent you for free, especially if you have a long record.

Nevertheless, all that shit gets pushed to the back of your mind when you're living for the city. So I turned to my once-upon-a-time hero/father figure, Sakou, from Brooklyn, whose popularity and income was bigger than when I'd left.

"I'm stuck, yo," I said, sitting in the passenger's seat of Sakou's green Navigator.

"When I wrote to you, what I say? I said I'd put you on when you came home, right?" Sakou was rolling his reefer up in some Bambú paper. "I'll front ya, but that's all I can do."

"Naw, man, the drug game ain't me, yo, you know that. What the fuck, man? I grew up around the shit my whole life. I see what it does to people. I watched what it did to my mother, Tyrone, naw. No." I shook my head. "Fuck that!"

"So what you want me to do?" Sakou was becoming irritated. "Give you free money?"

"That's not what I'm saying."

"Then what are you saying?" he said, exhaling marijuana smoke. "You better talk to me, boy. A lot of people would jump on this opportunity."

"Stop calling me *boy*."

I wasn't one for telling my business, especially something as personal as my grandmother losing her house, but I needed money bad, so I confessed to the god my situation.

"Then you already know what it is. You have to man up. I mean, *girl* up." He passed me the marijuana.

I pushed his hand away. "I don't smoke that."

"Don't be bitch-made. It'll ease your mind. Go on, nigga. It ain't gonna hurt you." Sakou relit the tip.

Much as I'd been through in my lifetime, I'd never once tried smoking weed, but considering my current circumstances, I needed something to relieve the stress. I inhaled deeply and choked on the "chronic smoke." Spit jumped out from the corners of my mouth as I coughed up a lung.

Sakou laughed then snatched the drug away from me. "Li'l man, I told you to smoke it, not die in my truck."

He rolled down my window from his side of the vehicle and patted my back as I continued coughing with such severity, I tossed up nothing but bile from my empty stomach. Adults and children alike laughed as they walked by waving at Mr. Popular.

A female who appeared to be in her late teens smiled through Sakou's window at me. "What's the matter with your man?" she asked him.

"He's a virgin." Sakou passed her the weed through his window as she approached.

"You all right over there, virgin?" She smiled. "Damn, your eyes are mad red."

Sakou reached in his glove compartment for a tissue. "Here, man, clean yourself up."

"Now I know why I ain't never smoked this shit." I hawked a wad of spit out the window. "Yo, pardon me, ma." I dabbed my lips with the napkin.

I pulled out a Newport and began quickly puffing it, to ease the effects of the chronic coughing. I know what you're thinking. How ironic, right? Using cancerous smoke to kill the side effects of another kind of smoke.

"You all right?" Sakou asked.

I wiped the last teardrop falling from my eye. "I'll live."

"He's cute," the girl said. "What's his name?"

"She. You got it? She's sitting right there. Ask her."

"Quiana," I said to her.

"Quiana?" She giggled. "They really fucked you on that name, huh? You look just like a dude with no hair on your face."

Sakou gave her a quick slap in the face. Not to hurt her, but as a reminder not to disrespect his company.

"Why you do that? It is a fucked-up name for him. I mean, to be looking like a he. She still sexy, though." She stared at me with that beautiful smile.

Right then and there I knew I was in love. Sabrina was a dime. A fine-ass redbone with long, brown hair twisted and divided off into pigtails. Her clothing was tight, and she stood five-seven. I loved light-skinned girls to death. Always did.

"What you think my name should've been, ma?"

"I don't know what it shoulda been, but not that shit." Sabrina laughed.

"You funny." I laughed.

Sakou looked back and forth between the both of us then wrapped his arm around my shoulder. "My nigga," he said, smiling, "I just thought of a way you can get that money you need."

Chapter 9

Now that I had Grandma Thomasina's situation covered, I could focus more on getting into a community college. Yeah, right. Little did I know that shit would never come to pass, all because of a desperate attempt to get money. But you saw. Grandma was going to lose her house, man. Can you knock me for stepping up to the plate and trying to make shit right? I'm talking about a lady who took me in when everybody else turned their backs. Naw. I know you can't knock me. That's Grandma. Y'all know what it is.

When I showed Grandma Thomasina the one hundred thousand dollars inside of a Gucci briefcase, she fainted and fell back on the couch. Her eyes fluttered up, and she began immediately crying as she stared at the open briefcase full of money.

"Grandma," I said, shaking her lightly. "See, Grandma, now you don't gotta go nowhere. Nowhere."

"You get that on out of here." Grandma turned her head away from it. "That's murder money."

"What you talking, murder money? You don't even know where this came from." I counted through a stack of hundred-dollar bills. "You really don't."

"I know you ain't earn it. Where'd it come from then?"

"It came from God." I smiled as I rose to my feet. "It's a blessing, Grandma. Why can't you just accept it?"

"Oh Lord," she cried. "This bitch done sold her soul to the devil."

"I'm not going to let you lose this house. You raised me here, and those kids need you. I don't care what you say."

"How'd you get the money?"

"Look, get the kids together so we can go over to your bank. Don't forget your identification and paperwork, please."

After a long day of filling out paperwork and speaking with Joe Shmo and Mr. Charlie at the bank, I couldn't have been more ecstatic as we returned home. Now Grandma could be at ease and not have to worry about that evil-ass government snatching her shit from over her head. And for the first in my life, since the days of pulling Tyrone off my mother's ass back in the day, I did something significant for somebody else. That's the good shit, but now I had to do some felonious shit to make that up.

I was in the basement of Grandma's house lying in my old bedroom, pondering what Sakou had lined up for me to do, when a knock at the door from the top of the stairs startled me.

"Yo!"

"It's Dana. Can I come down?"

Dana was butterscotch-complexioned with long, straight hair. She had the potential to be a model but didn't care to really be one. She liked hanging out with them rowdy bitches that claimed to be 'bout it-'bout it. That's why Grandma was having the issues with her.

"What up, superhero? Heard you saved the house like you was Obama. Girl, come home." She laughed then broke out singing the Jim Jones chorus. "*Balling, we fly high, we stay fly, you know this.* Yeah, baller, Grandma told me you paying for the house and shit. Can I get on?"

"Shut your shit. Fuck you talking about balling? I did what

I had to do. I see you ain't try to get out there and work on nothing."

"I'm a foster child, nigga. I'm too old to be kept and too old to get adopted again, so I gots to makes my own way. You smell me?"

Sometimes you don't realize how stupid shit sounds when people say it, because you might've been the same exact way at one point in your life. But I gotta tell ya, this little girl sounded straight dumb. I'm not being judgmental or nothing like that. Okay, yes I am. But it ain't her fault the way she turned out.

When she was five she watched her pops shoot her moms in the head before turning the gun on himself. That ain't no image you just forget or ever get over. I don't give a fuck who you is, you're lying if you say you could. I think it's, well, not think, but I know that's why she was the way she was.

"No, I don't smell you." I playfully grabbed at her nose. "You don't worry about what I do. Just be happy that, for the time being, you got a place to live."

"You know we all missed you around here while you was doing your bid, right?"

"I know. That's what kept my head up in there, knowing I had y'all to come home to. A lot of niggas up in there don't have nobody to come home to, so they go back in and chill with the other niggas that don't got nobody. See the science behind that? In their hearts, even if they don't admit it, all the family they got is each other. It's just fucked up that instead of it being brothers in arms, it's brothers behind bars."

"Don't tell me you done changed your name while you was up in there? You sounding kind of righteous, my dude."

I huffed and then sucked my teeth.

"So does this mean that you're not going to tell me where you got the money?"

"Is Chelsea Clinton pretty?"

"Hell to the naw."

"There go your answer then, nigga." I laughed.

Chapter 10

I was linking up with Sakou tonight. He wanted to talk about repayment. A promise is a promise, so I had to be ready for whatever.

"Grandma. I'm about to bounce," I said, bending down to kiss her cheek.

"Well, where you going so late?" Grandma looked back at the clock over the oval-shaped entrance of the kitchen. "It's seven o'clock. You know you got that curfew. I don't want you in any trouble out there. Lord knows, I have enough."

Just as she said it, and as if right on cue, a crashing sound of shattering glass exploded from upstairs. Scattering feet of troubled children raced up and down the corridor thumping and bouncing their bodies off the wobbly walls.

Did I just zone out on y'all? My bad. What I mean is, those little niggas was up there fucking it up. And I can see why Grandma didn't want to let them go. Those little muthafuckas had problems. They needed somebody that cared, and don't nobody cared more than Grandma Thomasina. I'd die for her. That's why I took Sakou's offer. Took that shit and didn't even know what in the fuck he wanted of me.

"These kids, my Lord." She sighed. "They lucky I love

'em," she said, picking up a belt and snapping it before walking up the stairs. "And sometimes love can hurt."

"Don't hurt nothing now, Grandma."

I smiled as I walked out of the front door.

Sakou was sitting at the curb of Grandma's house in a white Escalade. Even with the darkening clouds above, I could still see his 32-inch sterling silver rims glimmering. The music inside his truck was set on low, but the bass was strong enough to give the block tremors and set off nearby car alarms that go, "*Protected by Viper*" and *Honk! Honk!*

The truck shook as I stepped inside of it. I grabbed onto the strap above the passenger seat and climbed in, plopping on the seat.

"So everything secure, my man?" Sakou looked at the house through my window, the blue light inside the truck reflecting on his sunglasses.

"Yeah. Everything's everything."

"I like that." He smiled. "I told you I'd take care of you. You my little nigga."

"No doubt, man. So what's goody? Anything you wanna do."

"That's what I like, my nigga, that's what I like." Sakou laughed as he pulled away from the curb. "You done growed up to be an ill bitch . . . thoroughbred, with your ol' gangsta ass."

Sakou was evil. I saw him do a lot of crazy things when I was younger but kept my mouth shut. The nigga committed crimes in front of me, a girl of all people, and trusted me to keep quiet. I didn't even tell my moms. I thought I was being loyal. Can you believe that? I thought I was the shit.

I remember when I'd first met Sakou. He thought I was a boy as I strolled up the street where the new drug dealers had opened up shop. I guess the bop in my shoulders might've suggested disrespect, because everybody knew who Sakou was, and what could happen if things were mistakenly taken out of context, like an imprecise gesture or even a wrong choice of words. At that time, in that particular instance, fear was not the first thing on my mind. Pride was. After seeing my mother get beat up, jerked, and knocked around by Tyrone so many times, it was already in me to defend myself, when it came to a man.

It hurt my pride to see his boys laughing at me, so I picked up the nearest rock I could find and threw it at his face. He roughed me up real good that day, but I kept my mouth shut about it. That's how I gained his respect. In retrospect, if my mindset had been just a little bit different, maybe I'd never have given him the mutual stare that enabled him to enter my life.

Being a child, I thought he was my friend. He made me believe he cared, with all of his bullshit advice and crisp five-dollar bills. He kept money in my pocket and made sure that Tyrone never stole food out of my mouth again. What did it matter, though? All he really was doing was keeping me contented, while he prostituted my moms in the back alleys of Flatbush. I looked up to him like he was some kind of hero because he'd saved my moms and me from a lot of hungry nights. Now in my adulthood, the man that killed my mother with his drugs had saved me yet again from another hungry night.

We pulled into the overcrowded parking lot of Nassau Coliseum on Long Island. All of a sudden here come the crowd. Niggas and bitches were all over the place. High-profile cars with flashing headlights and windows down beeped their horns. Thunderous bottom bass from their surround sound systems bounced off the bodies of the bitches catching new niggas in their life on the rebound.

The man didn't say shit about where we were going or nothing. I owed a debt, so I didn't ask shit. I was loyal like that. "So, what's good, man?" I asked him.

Sakou waved as he slowly drove through an aisle of cars. Even though he was in his forties, he was well known and rarely had any drama. That was back in the days, though.

"My nigga, you home and shit." He patted my lap. "Don't ever go back. That ain't no place for nobody, not even for a bitch."

"You don't gotta tell me. After I do what I gots to do for you, our time is over. I don't even want to know you no more."

"Yeah, yeah." Sakou chuckled. "Stop talking nervous." He pulled into a free parking space. "I don't need you to do nothing tonight. I just wanted to take you out. What? I can save your grandma's shack, but I can't take my homegirl out?"

"I'm not little no more, man."

A burgundy Lexus coupe droptop pulled up beside us, and two females wearing Christian Elijah bikini tops and jeans smiled up into the truck at us.

"What's up, boo?" the driver said to Sakou. "Hello, boo. I'm Tawana, and that's my niece, Sabrina."

Tawana was Sakou's mistress. He had a wife and kid out in Danbury, Connecticut he'd leave all alone for weeks at a time, but whatever that crazy bitch may have been complaining about in his absence changed soon as he returned home and dropped all of that paper in her hand. After the money ran out, the shit started all over again. It took for him to marry her to know she was only, and always, after his money. How the fuck could he not expect that?

So, that's what Tawana was for. In her late twenties and wild, she could be a lady when necessary. Her body was designed in "the shape of thick," and she had a tattoo on her right thigh that read, *The Shit.*

"She knows who I am." Sabrina smiled as she climbed over the door.

We all walked toward the rear of the vehicles we'd arrived in and watched as niggas our age danced, talked shit to chicks, and battled in rhyming, strictly using lyrics.

Suddenly, a shot rang out. And just like a scene out of *Boyz N the Hood*, a retaliatory succession of artillery erupted. When it was all over, another statistic of a friendly hip-hop battle lay dead in the lot. We rose from beside Sakou's truck, only to witness six physical altercations spawning from the previous event.

"Let's get out of here, man." I stood up in the truck. "I'm out, yo."

"You pussy like that?" Sabrina asked, standing under the window.

I spat down into her face and pushed my door open, the blow causing her to stumble back into the Lex. I stepped out. "All right," I said, waiting on Sakou to lead the way. "We supposed to be going inside, right? Then let's get on then."

We were seated in the first row of Mary J. Blige's concert. Her red satin dress and red four-inch high heels lifted her toward heaven with each note she sang. Her strawberry-tinted hair matched her softly applied blush, accentuating her sexy lips every time she smiled, flossing her pearly whites.

"Hold up. Hold." She was breathless after an hour of performing. "Y'all mind if I take a rest?" she asked, leaning on a stool placed on the stage for her. "Whew! Y'all must love me. Shoot, I know if I paid good money to see somebody perform, they better not be resting." She laughed.

What began as small applause grew into a full house of claps, roots, and cries.

Sakou and I sat side by side, while the girls sat opposite one another.

Tawana squeezed Sakou's arm tighter. "Thank you, boo."

I asked Sabrina, "You having a good time?"

"Don't talk to me."

"Yo, shortie, I'm sorry, but you were being disrespectful to me by calling me out my name. I'd never call you out your name. That ain't cool. So can we start all over again?"

She ignored me and continued watching the queen of hip-hop and R&B express herself through mournful riffs and regretful tears.

"Friends?" I asked once more.

"You better not do that again." Sabrina said, pointing in my face.

"Same goes for you," I responded with an apologetic embrace.

"Awwww! Look at y'all," Mary said as Sabrina and I hugged. "Young love. That's what's up. I think I got a song for you two lovebirds." She turned to her band.

We both yelled out loud, "We're not in love!"

She walked to the edge of the stage and began singing,

"I will love you anyway
Even if you cannot stay."

In about five minutes flat, Sabrina and I both fell in love with one another, immersed within the soulful parenthesis of teenage love. A classic romance, if you will.

When I was younger, after my moms passed, I used to think that love was bullshit. Where would I ever find a love like my momma's? But with Brina, which I called her for short, it was something different. Something special. I knew she was the one when I met her the first time, when I was with Sakou. I felt that shit pumping through my heart. I wanted to love her. I liked her spark. It was sexy. I wanted to be dedicated to her high-yellow ass.

Tawana said, "Look at those two fools." She looked over Sakou at Sabrina and me. "Ain't that cute, boo? The lesbians went and fell in love."

Sakou ignored her and continued focusing on the star attraction.

Chapter 11

One month later, Sabrina and I were going "hard body" with our new relationship. She was enrolled in York College and lived with her sister Evelyn out in Brownsville. She was paying her way through school, and half the rent on a nineteen-hundred-dollar apartment. She was getting that paper working for Sakou, and it wasn't from selling drugs either. She didn't tell me what it was that she did for a long time, but when she finally did, I was like, "FUCK!"

But, anyway, a whole entire month had passed, and this fucka still hadn't let me get the favor done and over with. He'd even stopped coming around unannounced. As a matter of fact, dude stopped calling, and stupid me was like, "Maybe he forgot." Wrong. He didn't forget shit. The bitch just wanted to keep me at his disposal.

I sat at the edge of Sabrina's bed and stared off into the darkness.

"You all right?" She pressed her naked body up against my back and rested her head on my shoulder. She then kissed my cheek before resetting her head on my shoulder. "What's the matter, Q?"

"I don't like the way Sakou got me."

"What you mean?"

"I mean, he's got me all fucked up, ma. I got other shit on my mind, and I gots to be thinking about when this nigga gonna holla."

"You need to just chill. If he's not saying nothing, then just keep doing you. You nervous or something?"

"I'm not no fucking nervous." I nudged her off my back with an elbow.

"Well, stop acting like that then. So you figure out if you want to try school?"

"I can't afford that shit, and I'm not working for that nigga to pay for it. I'm not even trying to get down like that. I know he up to no good."

"Quiana, stop acting like you from the suburbs and shit. You right from the fucking hood, just like the rest of us. You be talking the talk, but your walk be sometimes sounding real suspect, babe. Word up, you be acting real unofficial."

"You telling me that you want to be a criminal all your life even though you in school?"

"Don't judge me." Sabrina swung a pillow into my head. "School is to secure my future. What the fuck I'm supposed to do for now? Do that shit you thinking about doing? Ten dollars an hour, bitch. Are you fucking kidding me?"

"I told you about calling me out my name," I said, raising my voice.

"I didn't call you out your name."

I turned around my head to her in the dark. "Yes, you did. You said, 'Ten-dollars-an-hour bitch.' "

"I wasn't saying it to you. I was saying it like, Ten dollars an hour, bitch. Period. You need some *P*-noid pills or something. Stop worrying about that ol' bullshit. Far as me, I'ma keep getting paid, because somebody gots to pay for my education. At least I'm doing shit to better myself. I ain't pregnant with a sob story and a crack addiction. I don't have

AIDS. I'm not gay. A bitch be sending money over to the Christian Children's Fund, so them bitches can feed a hungry child."

"For one, you are gay."

"I'm bisexual."

"You sleep with women. You're gay."

"I like dick *and* pussy. It's just that right now, I feel like it's pussy season." She pushed me backwards.

I leaned back with my legs wide open then stuck my hands under the headboard.

Sabrina reached over to the nightstand and turned on the small lamp. I played with myself, rubbed myself and entered myself, saturating my fingers with nectar so sweet, she'd need an insulin shot to recover.

We then kissed with the tips of our tongues, quickly flicking them around each other, our nipples fully aroused. She sucked on the right nipple then the left, breathing hot and heavy breaths on both before pinching and plucking them with her finger.

Sabrina rushed her face into my deep pool of love, my fat pulsating clit standing out amongst the forest of hairy bush. I arched my back upward as she ran her tongue up and down, and from side to side bombarded every angle of my elastic walls of pinkish caress with savage strokes of sexual madness. An explosion of pleasure ejected from inside the depths of my fetish, wetting her face.

I flipped the situation. Her eyes shut tight, she clenched under the headboard. Her body shook, and her toes turned into fists as I returned the favor.

"You good?" I was ready for round two.

"Hold up." She laughed, her eyes still closed. "Whoa! You made me lose my bearings." She huffed with exhilaration. "Come here."

I crawled up beside her and hugged her. "I'm happy you're in my life." I closed my eyes as I kissed her lips.

* * *

I walked from Sabrina's bedroom into the kitchen. I held my fingers under the faucet and waited until it was cold enough to quench my midnight thirst. As I ventured back toward the bedroom with only the kitchen's nightlight acting as my guide, I took a sip of water from my glass.

Evelyn's door opened. An older version of Sabrina, her face was pretty and she was just a li'l more on the pudgy side, and wasn't like us. "I thought you'd be asleep after all the work you was putting in." She adjusted her headscarf as she walked toward the refrigerator.

"Didn't know you was listening."

"Hell yeah, I was listening. What choice did I have?"

Evelyn had been in and out of jail since her late teens for things like shoplifting, credit fraud, identity theft—federal shit. Somehow, though, according to Sabrina, she always seemed to walk away scot-free. She was another one that stayed with no money and had no job. Her various man friends took care of her every need, whether it'd be late bill fees, or beef. She was 'bout it-'bout it and would rather "ox" your face than talk about insignificant shit. She and Sabrina had a tightknit, kill-for-die-for kind of bond. The type my momma and I used to have.

Sabrina peeked her head out her door. "Why you bothering my company?"

"Oh, shut up, bitch. Earlier y'all were keeping me up with all that fucking. Shit, you don't hear me complaining, so I can bother anybody I want to. This my apartment." She shoved past me into the kitchen.

"Rude ass." I chuckled.

"And I'ma be a rude ass until I'm a dead ass."

"Might as well. Your room already smell like ass." Sabrina laughed.

"You clowning?" Evelyn took a gulp from a half-gallon container of Tropicana orange juice. "You ol' high-yellow, they-killed-Cornbread, banana-pudding-mixing, wannabe golden lady, butter-churning, gender-bending half-breed. That's why your mother's white."

"We got the same mother, *ig'nant*. You wack. Come on back to bed, Qui." Sabrina chuckled. "I'll see you in the morning, bitch."

"And good night to you too, bitch." Evelyn belched. "You too, nigga."

Chapter 12

There was ten thousand dollars left over after saving Grandma's house. I purchased a used blue Jeep Cherokee. Just wanting shit to be basic, I didn't bother looking for anyone to tint my windows or hook me up a system or expensive rims.

I refused to grow up angry at the world because I didn't have a father. Niggas who used that excuse . . . well, you see how the majority of them turned out. So, after thinking about it long and hard, I decided to apply to York College, like Sabrina. Financial aid would take care of the rest.

Only thing was, I couldn't start classes until the following semester, which gave me even more time to look for a job. It wasn't going to be no fast-food joint. Sometimes beggars can't be choosers, but choosers can't be desperate either. Somebody else would be flipping them burgers and dropping them fries, but it wasn't going to be me.

As luck would have it, just when I thought all was lost, a call came in. PC Richard needed a salesperson soon as possible. A girl for the cashier position. A girl. Somebody accepted that I was a girl.

* * *

Lo and behold, after two months of silence, Sakou's ass finally comes out the woodwork.

"Thought I forgot about you, huh?" he asked.

"I didn't forget shit, man," I said, bouncing my basketball around in Grandma's backyard. "I got a car now, so you don't gots to be coming by here to talk to me. We can meet up and talk." I shot a three-pointer while looking at him.

"You right. Let's get out of here then. There are some things I need to talk to you about."

"The last time we talked, I ended up at a Mary J. concert. Is this for real this time? I kinda want the monkey off my back. See what I'm saying?" I ran down the small concrete driveway and did a lay-up with the ball.

"You better get your shit together and come on." Sakou snatched the ball as it bounced above the half-broken garage after hitting the ground.

"Where we going?"

"When you said you needed the money to save this funky ol' broken-down house, did I say shit? That was a lot of money, homegirl. Get your mind right." He bounced the ball at my feet and walked back toward Tawana's droptop Lex.

I began slowly following his lead.

Dana opened the side door of the house. "I heard everything," she said, closing the door.

"That's a damn shame." Sakou turned around. "I know they didn't think you saved this dump by your begging-ass self?"

Just as I suspected, to every favor received, a bigger favor must be returned. But I had no idea it'd be anything of the magnitude Sakou finally divulged to me. Yeah. Sakou was making money, but it wasn't under the circumstances I'd once thought. Whatever. Once I did this, I'd never have to deal with dude again.

"I don't know, Sakou," I said as I sat in the back seat of Tawana's Lex. "I ain't too sure about this."

We had driven out to Mount Vernon without uttering a word to one another. I started to wonder if this nigga was bringing me all the way out here to murk me. Then again, I could've been paranoid from the sour diesel we'd smoked on the way up. We were on the north side of town, where ninety percent of the population was inhabited by those animalistic cave dwellers—in layman's terms, whitey, the man, bo-bo.

"Turn the music down," Sakou said to Tawana as we pulled into a condo parking lot. "The lights." He pushed a button on the dashboard to bring the cover of the car over us.

The digital clock read one a.m., and it was quiet as fuck.

A light on the fifth floor balcony of the condo came on behind the white blinds of a sliding glass door.

"Be cool." Sakou whispered. "Don't move."

"What we doing here, man?" I whispered.

"This is where the favor is."

"What is it?"

"Just be cool." Sakou looked up at the balcony as the light went out.

"You ready to do this, baby?" Tawana pulled a gun out of her glove compartment.

"Whoa! You ain't say nothing about no guns."

"Did I ask you to talk, Qui?" Sakou spun his head around. "Don't say anything. You don't know what's going on, so just chill."

"You scared, boo?" Tawana asked. "Don't worry. I got your back." She smiled and kissed the nose of her gun.

"Shit, nigga. I might even give you a li'l something out of this if it all go down right." Sakou faced forward again then grabbed the keys out of the ignition. "Come on." He got out and lifted the back seat. "Don't forget your gloves, Tawana."

"I ain't new to this, boo," she said, pulling a pair of black leather gloves out the waistband of her black jogging pants.

We all quietly crept up the white wooden steps to the fifth floor of the grey complex.

"Watch for my signal, Tawana." He told me, "You keep lookout."

I stood nervously on the deck of the fifth floor and looked around for passing cars on the road.

"Now watch how niggas get caught slipping," Sakou declared. He pulled the car keys from the back pocket of his black jogging pants and chirped the alarm of the car. Its lights blinked twice before letting loose an ear-deafening alarm.

As we heard the feet of the tenants in the apartments below scrambling toward their windows, including the frantic fuck behind door number one, he yelled to Tawana, "NOW!"

Tawana gave the door one great kick, and it flew open. Sakou deactivated the alarm, and we all quickly scrambled inside, camouflaged by the scrambling feet of the neighbors next door and below.

"Get your shit and let's go, Max."

"You better listen." Tawana cocked her gun.

"Watch the door," he yelled to me as I stood guard, nervous and unarmed.

Max stood in shock, wearing only a pair of boxers that read *McCain* across the waistband.

Sakou shook his head. "What is that supposed to be? Some kind of fucking joke or something?" He waved Max toward the door with his gun. "Matter of fact, let's just go."

"You're going to kill me? I'm busting my balls trying to get your money back, bro."

"Do I look like your fucking bro? Huh?" Sakou walked toward him. "What? You tryin'a be smart, muthafucka?" He slapped Max in his face. "I should shoot you in your head right now, nigga! Get the fuck out the door."

Max began walking toward the door, Tawana right beside him, and Sakou in tow. Doors were partially cracked, and sirens could be heard in the distance.

Sakou helped Max's slow stride along by giving him a hard kick in the ass. "Get on, nigga."

Max fell on his face outside the door.

"Naw, nigga, get up." Sakou pulled him up by the neck. "Let's go," he said, the nose of his .45 plugged into the back of Max's head.

I drove while Tawana and Sakou held Max at bay.

When we pulled into the parking lot of an old church under renovation, Max cried, "Just tell me what you want me to do."

"Too late for that. Everybody knows—you don't have my money, you don't have your life. Give up the routing number to that bank account of yours."

"If you let me live, you can have it all. Even the money I have in the safe at my house in Baltimore. You know that I'm good for it." Max sniffled.

"You know, Max, you sound like a real bitch."

Sakou hollered, "Shut up. Get out a pen and paper."

Max gave both account numbers and felt comfortably relieved thereafter. And, not for nothing, so did I.

"How do I know this is the official shit, Max? You sitting up here telling lies to me?" Sakou stared him down with his one good eye.

"This is my life, man. I wouldn't fucking play around, dude."

"He's lying, babe. I know he is. I can feel it. I say we stick to the original plan and just kill his ass, go back to his spot, and just get the information we need."

"Wait a minute. What type of shit y'all talking?" I opened the door. "Yo, come on, man. Get out," I said to Max.

Soon as Max tried to crawl out, Sakou shot him in the ass

then kicked him out of the car. He got out and stood over a screaming Max, allowing rage to possess his damned soul, and Tawana hopped out on her side and slid over the hood to where we were.

As I prepared to run, Sakou said to me, "Stay right there."

"What you bring me all the way out here for, man?" I contemplated which direction to sprint, but chose to remain motionless.

"I want you to see what happens when debts ain't paid. Nobody cares about no fucking excuses or no shit like that. Not in the streets." Sakou shot Max once in back of the head. "And not in the corporate world neither. Let's get out of here." He hopped in the driver's seat then dropped the top down.

Tawana jumped into the passenger's seat and held tightly on to Sakou's arm.

The car's engine roared as he pushed down on its accelerator. I was mortified, wishing I'd been anywhere but there.

Tawana was evil. How could she smile after a scene like that? Sakou just blew Max's head off, and the bitch was just chilling.

"I'll leave you, nigga. Let's go." Sakou threw the Lex into reverse.

Racing sirens that once screamed off in the distance were now speaking with tinnitus-like clarity as they neared the murder scene.

I was stuck. My feet had grown roots and had me planted to the ground.

"GET IN THE CAR!" Sakou yelled, slowly pulling off.

I hesitantly climbed into the back seat, and Sakou zipped off before my ass could sit.

Chapter 13

Sakou and I had torched the Lex soon as we were back in the city. We dumped it over in the swamp-like waters of the Far Rockaway marshlands. We torched its interior and exterior, but that fucking DNA can find moose genes inside Sarah Palin's chromosomes. And the only thing the detectives, police, National Guard, and Marines had to do was find the killer of this white man found murdered behind a church. Even with the car singed beyond recognition, technology still discovered fingerprints, blood splatter from Max getting shot in the ass, and the footprint from getting kicked in his ass, not to mention Tawana's footprint on his condo door she'd kicked in. We all touched the steering wheel. Only thing we did do right was remove the license plates.

"Oh." Grandma held her face as she sat at the table in the kitchen, watching a live news report on the 12-inch black-and-white television.

"What's the matter?" I asked, walking beside her.

"A ol' white man done got himself killed, and they saying the suspects they looking for is black. That's bullshit. Don't no black people be near that side of Mount Vernon."

"I wouldn't know. I've never been."

"You not missing nothing. So when you supposed to start that job?"

"I got to call them. I missed my first day because something came up."

"Came up like what? Why you gotta be missing your first day at work? I hope it ain't that girl you been seeing. You know I don't approve of that kind of living, but you my granddaughter and I love you anyway, but that girl looks like trouble. How come you ain't never bring her inside so we could meet?"

"You never asked. Besides, I know how you are about strangers in your house. Especially openly gay ones."

"I'm willing to make an exception. Bring her on by this weekend."

"I will, Grandma. I was on my way upstairs to kick it with Dana." I looked back at the live telecast.

"Good evening. I'm Angela Pileggi of Channel Zero News. I'm reporting live from the scene of a horrific murder on Mount Vernon's northern side of town. Max Cogelleti, also from here, was heard struggling earlier this morning, but his neighbors thought it was one of his usual late-night arguments with one of the many women he entertained frequently. The question that everyone is asking is, Why? How could such a savage crime take place in such a quiet community? Investigators say they've tracked down a vehicle that's been burned and dumped that was spotted at the scene. They soon hope to have a break in the case. This is Angela Pileggi reporting live from the northern side of Mount Vernon, New York. Back to you, Jim."

You never think shit can get that deep, until you find yourself knee-deep in it. My world was spinning, and all I could think was, *If they're showing the shit on the news, eventually they'll catch up with us.* Even though I wasn't the shooter, I may as well have been, because I did nothing to stop it.

"Hey, Dana"—I stopped in mid-sentence as she jerked her door open.

Thumping sounds of bass vibrated the frame of her doorway as a young rapper's platinum hit single shook the house.

"What you want? You here to front some more?"

"Shut up." I pushed her into the room and closed the door behind me.

"What's the problem?" I asked, shoving her onto her bed. "Is there an issue you feel you need to get out?"

"Why you owe dude money? He the reason this house got saved, ain't he?"

"Why does it matter to you?"

"You the one walking around acting like you the shit. Turns out, you are. Straight bullshit, if you ask me. What was it all about between you and him? What you done did? Get into debt wit' a loan shark?"

"Mind your business, Dana. You need to be focused on stopping them niggas you be fucking. Stop them from ringing my grandmother's bell all times of the night."

"Look at you, fresh out of jail and tryin'a give orders. You don't get to tell me what to do. My daddy been dead since I was three. You the one that was out in the yard the other day like yours was talking to you. And what?" Dana swirled her neck as she stood up to my chest. "What's the sense in being butch, if you not gonna defend your manhood?"

"This ain't about me, bitch. You don't want me to have to talk to one of them li'l niggas." I pointed down on her forehead as she sat defenselessly on her bed.

"Ain't nobody fazed by you. Get out my room. Just know that your shit stink just like everybody else's." Dana stood then pushed past me toward her door. "Make moves," she said, opening it.

"Hold up." I closed the door. "You can't let Grandma know. It'd break her heart if she thought I got that money up the wrong way. Besides that, if she loses the house, all of y'all will be lost. She'll lose every last one of y'all. And you'd end up in a shelter because you're not a child anymore."

"So you feel you saved the day, right?"

"I feel I spared my grandmother a broken heart."

It was a little after two in the morning when I heard noises on the side of the house. I peeked out of the basement window and saw two sets of feet shuffling back and forth in the driveway, near my truck.

I crept out through the front door with a bat in hand. Slowly walking down the four steps and across the yard's raggedy brown grass, I crept around the side of my truck. It shook and squeaked vehemently as I closed in.

"What the fuck?" I shouted, the bat raised over my head.

There was Dana, bent over the hood of my truck, her plaid skirt lifted up over her ass, getting fucked from the back.

"Oh shit!" She pulled her skirt down.

I swung the bat into dude's leg, and he dropped to the ground, holding his leg and groaning loudly.

"I should cave your fucking head in." I stepped forward with the bat as if to hit him again.

"Stop!" Dana yelled, dropping by dude's side. "You crazy or something?"

"That's what you do—fuck niggas on the side of your house in the late night? Get your ass outta here, man." I kicked dude in his shoulder. "You turn around one time while you getting up out of here, I swear to fucking God, I'll swing this bat into the back of your big fucking head."

"Who do you think you are?" Dana yelled, getting up in my chest.

"Get your ass in the house." I grabbed her by the arm. "You out here disrespecting my grandmother's house. I should slap the shit out of you," I said, releasing my grip on her arm.

Dude slowly rose to his feet and began his painful trail out the driveway.

"Don't come back," I warned.

Dana began following dude.

"Where you think you going?" I asked her.

"You ain't my father, nigga. Remember that." She slapped her ass.

Chapter 14

Sakou and I sat in Crown Fried Chicken on Sutphin Boulevard in Jamaica, Queens. We was all out in the open like we didn't have shit to worry about. And you know what? After a while I began to feel like we didn't.

Suddenly I was feeling strong, stronger than I ever felt, strong enough to tell that nigga Sakou I was done, whether he liked it or not. While he spoke, I stared directly in his eye with a hate I hadn't felt since the days of Tyrone. I was feeling like a man and had forgotten very long ago what it might've been like to act any different.

"Something the matter. Qui?"

"Ain't shit, yo. I'm just listening to you."

"Yeah? Well, you acting as if you not here with me."

"What you want from me, man? Why you fucking with me?"

"I ain't been being straight with you, but I'm about to."

"I don't even care. I just want to be done with you. You got it where I might have to leave town and shit. I'm not fucking with you, man," I said, pointing in his face.

Sakou slapped my hand down, and we both shot up from the table ready for whatever.

The Indians behind the counter of the restaurant began lining up to watch as our angry voices interrupted the patrons trying to peacefully enjoy their lunch. An officer directing traffic happened to look over at us through the window, and the patrons rushing out the store's single door.

"You making a scene," Sakou said through his gritted teeth.

"Yo, I'm telling you, man, this the last time. Tell me what the fuck I got to do."

"I'm not scared of no bitch, Quiana. Don't let those niggas out there fool you."

Sakou hailed a cab down through the store window. The driver stopped at the corner and waited for us to walk out.

The officer began walking toward us as we opened the back and front doors to the cab.

"Everything all right, officer?" Sakou asked, stepping down into the front seat.

"I might want to ask you the same. Miss,"—The officer looked at me with concern in his eyes—"is everything all right?"

I put my head down and turned away.

The officer said to Sakou, "Please step out of the car, sir." Then he called out a sequence of numerical codes through his radio.

"What's the problem, officer?" Sakou stepped out of the car with an attitude. "You just a traffic officer."

"I'll ask you once more, sir. Is there a problem?"

Sakou stepped back inside then slammed the door closed. "Shut up and mind your business."

"Buddy, don't slam door please. It cost very, very much to fix." The Arab cab driver looked in his rearview mirror. "Where to, buddy?"

After being dropped off in Flatbush, Brooklyn, we picked up Sakou's truck from the garage of a mechanic shop that his friend owned then headed out to Danbury, Connecticut, where his wife and a three-year-old son resided.

Sakou ran inside his house and quickly returned. He exchanged his truck for the blue SLK parked in his driveway and headed right back toward the city. He dropped me off at home and was right back to pick me up at the crack of dawn. According to him, there was major business to handle, and he needed me to be there.

We stopped at the homes of well-to-do people with extravagant homes and expensive cars. Doctors, lawyers, real estates agents and drug-dealers all shared their peaceful New Jersey community, living comfortably within the confines of a lower tax bracket.

Sakou and I paid a visit to one of those homes in the extravagant community. He beeped his horn at the green iron gates before us. They soundlessly opened, and we entered. We drove a little way before turning down a winding curve that soon straightened. A brilliant green wall of ivy blocked the surrounding light of the sun as we continued forward in silence. Neither one of us had said a word since the Jamaica Avenue argument.

As we approached the five-car garage of the Sicilian-style home, Sakou said, "This is what I need from you right now. You listening?"

"Go 'head."

"When you get in here, don't say shit."

"I'm not going in until you tell me what's up. Word up. You'll just have to shoot me."

"I ain't got time for this right now. Bring your ass." Sakou opened his door.

"What? You don't understand English, nigga? What I say? I ain't moving until you tell me something."

"All right. If I tell you, you're down for good, and that's that. You really want to know that bad?"

"It can't be no worse than it's already been, with me looking over my shoulder and shit. Spit that shit."

"I kill for a living. And now that you know, so do you. Let's go, bitch." Sakou pointed his gun at me.

After Sakou rang the intercom bell attached near the front door and announced himself, a butler answered the door and led the way through the foyer, the guestroom, the kitchen, the plant room, the bathroom, and the portrait room. We walked outside through glass patio doors into Mikey Sarionni's enormous backyard. He was floating on an inflatable cushion in his Olympic-size swimming pool. Armed guards, associates, and other shady-looking individuals mingled about the yard, keeping a very watchful eye on the man of the hour.

"Stay right here," the butler said. "I'll let Mr. Sarionni know you're here."

Mr. Sarionni looked over at us from the pool and signaled for us to wait. Then three of his men came over and patted us down, and came up with Sakou's gun.

We sat inside in Mr. Sarionni's home office, where four of his guards were staring us hard. Mr Sarionni did the whole Tony Soprano routine. He pulled a cigar from a box sitting on his desk and clipped the butt off with a cigar cutter from Cuba. He dragged it under his nose, sniffing pleasurably. He lit it, inhaled deeply, and let loose chronic coughs. "I gotta quit these things," he stated, red-eyed and breathless.

"I know what you mean," Sakou said. "You just can't find a good cigar anymore, right?"

"This is not a time for jokes, Sakou. I mean, I wouldn't be joking around if I were you. Know what I'm saying?" He looked me up and down. "Who in the fuck are you? What are you, a girl or boy?" Then he said to Sakou, "I hope this isn't what you brought for protection, because, frankly, I'm not impressed."

I looked over to Sakou for a directive.

"What the fuck you looking at me for? The man asked you a question."

I rolled my eyes at Sakou. "Quiana."

"Excuse me?" he said, cupping his ear with his hand. "You'll have to speak up. What'd you say it was?"

"I said *Quiana*."

"What are you, some kind of basketball player or something? Most of yous giants always play that shit. Fucking WNBA. I have something you can dunk—fucking Kobe Bryant, the greatest player to touch a ball since Michael Jordan. Fuck you! They pay Kobe all of that fucking money to rape white women. Get the fuck outta here." He kicked himself away from his swivel chair. "You do know why I called you here, right?" he asked Sakou. "The shit is all over the news. It's just a matter of time."

"Where's the money, Mikey? I'm not here for your bullshit."

"You're not here for my bullshit? YOU FUCKED THE FUCKING JOB UP, COCKSUCKER!" Mikey banged on his desk. "HOW DO YOU GET THE MONEY IF HE'S ALREADY DEAD?"

"You wanted him gone, right? He's gone."

"Not before you got the accounts. You needed to know the accounts. Now what the fuck am I supposed to tell my people?"

"That's your problem. I did my job."

"Hey, you," Mr. Sarionni said to me, "leave your identification here."

I shot up out my chair. "What?"

Sarionni's men surrounded me then fished through my pockets for my wallet while Sakou stood idly by. I struggled with them, but one of the men managed to pull my license out.

"Now I know where you live," Sarionni said. "If any of this

bullshit he got me into falls on me, it falls on you. I already know where you live. That goes for you too, Sakou."

"The money . . . you don't have to worry about giving it to me. You know the fuck who it really belongs to," Sakou responded.

"Yeah. You think you're so smart, don't you? Get them the fuck out of my house. Tony, get that briefcase from behind the bookshelf."

Tony walked over to the shelf and retrieved a brown briefcase. He brought it back over to Mr. Sarionni and placed it into his awaiting hands.

"That's one hundred thousand dollars in there. Do you want to count it, Einstein?" he said, holding it out to Sakou.

"I don't have to," Sakou said, snatching it from him.

"Oh yeah? Why's that?"

"Because if it's not all there, you'll end up like Max. Get your bitches to walk me to the door."

"What makes you think I won't shoot you and your little transvestite over here before you even make it out of this office?" Mikey pulled a gun out from his desk drawer.

"Be sure to tell your bitches to give me back my gun when we get to the front door."

As we exited the office, I caught a glimpse of Mr. Sarionni holding up his gun in the reflection of the portrait-size mirror by the door. He acted as if he was about to take an imaginary shot, and smiled after realizing I saw him.

Chapter 15

"I want to give you something," Sakou said, slowly pulling in front of my grandmother's house at three in the morning.

"Naw, you don't gots shit to give to me."

"We a team now. Shiiiiiiiit, girl. You done made a deal with the devil." He laughed. "What? You don't gots nothing to say? Let me give you a little something, man." He reached toward the back seat for the briefcase. He placed it on his lap and popped open its latches to reveal stacks of crisp, clean hundred-dollar bills perfectly aligned upon one another.

I turned away then slowly looked back.

"It's all right to look, baby. This is our American dream, and there's more where this came from." Sakou pulled two stacks of hundreds out of the case. He held them up and clapped them together before holding it out to me. "This is you. Buy your grandmother a new wardrobe and take her out somewhere nice. It's on me." He smiled.

I stared at the money but didn't reach for it. I knew accepting it would mean that I was drilling my own hole into hell, but suddenly I was curious, greedy, and selfish. I gladly took the money.

Out of nowhere, Sakou quickly turned and kissed my lips.

lesbian shit is starting to get real old. You do know that, right, Quiana?"

"Speak, man," I said, rolling up an L.

"Look at you—got some money, now you think you a boss. Fuck it. You buy yourself a gun yet, big man?"

"Don't need one."

"Yes, you do." Sakou reached down on the side of his seat. "Catch." He tossed me a 9 through his passenger window and mine.

"What the fuck is this?"

"A gun, nigga."

"I mean, what you giving it to me for?"

"It's a gift from me to you . . . killer. Let's go." He laughed and made a U-turn out of the parking lot.

Word had gotten to Sakou that Tawana had been taken in for questioning on the night of Max's murder. She'd been smiling in his face and sucking his dick every night, not once mentioning the interrogation she had from the police. It could only mean one thing—the bitch was talking, and we were going to have to kill her. All I could think was, *How'd they find out she was involved?*

Her Lexus was videotaped coming and going earlier that morning at a local shopping market. Later that night, her car was flashed by one of those red traffic lights by the parkway then twice again when we got to Mount Vernon. When they went to her house in Laurelton to question her about her car, she couldn't explain its whereabouts, and even tried saying it'd been stolen. Still, there wasn't enough proof to hold her, so she was released with a warning not to leave town.

Sakou knocked on the door of Tawana's small house. She opened it and waved at me with a smile.

"Lock the house up and come on." Wasting no time, Sakou walked back toward his truck.

"Where we going, boo?"

"To that comedy club in Far Rockaway."

"Oh word? Nasty Mouth Cartel performing tonight, right?"

"Yeah." Sakou hopped back inside of his truck.

"I'm calling Sabrina, so she can meet us up there."

Sakou yelled out the passenger window, "She's already there."

"I'ma just grab my jacket then." Tawana's porch light flicked on, and she walked out, double-locking the door behind her.

Chapter 16

The crowd roared with laughter as comedian Nasty Mouth Cartel made his way onto the stage of the Laugh In Comedy Café. Nasty Mouth Cartel, who was more offensive than funny, smiled at his many fans as they all impatiently awaited one of his usually critically acclaimed performances.

Sakou, Tawana, Evelyn, Sabrina, and I all sat together at a round table with nothing but drinks on it. Tawana was all leaned up on Sakou, who was looking at her with the greatest of disdain.

"What's wrong, boo?" she asked, feeling on his chest.

"Nothing. I was just thinking about something." Sakou poured himself a drink then one for her.

"Let's watch the show, boo." Tawana turned his face toward the stage.

"What's up, muthafuckas? What's up?" Nasty Mouth Cartel said. "How y'all feeling out there tonight? So how about it, y'all—Obama for president?"

We all cheered along with the racially mixed crowd.

"Is it just me, or are we starting to see less and less white people now that Obama is president? Them muthafuckas are like, 'If that nigga wins, I'm moving to the moon because there is no way I'm listening to the first monkey.' White people, the niggers are coming."

The crowd laughed.

"Man, I'ma tell ya, when Obama won the election, white people lost they minds. Acting like they was in the courtroom with O.J. after the verdict of not guilty came back. The niggers are coming, white folks."

The audience cheered.

"The niggers are coming." He calmly whispered with a smile. "Yeah. It's a crazy time we're living in. Racism is on the rise. You can get shot just for thinking of the color black, much less being black. Obama better be careful with everything he does. They can't wait for him to slip up. They'll send his ass straight back to Hawaii with his ol' purple-lip-having ass."

Nasty Mouth walked back and forth, sipping from his plastic water bottle. "They don't want a black man doing shit. If black people were to be forced into slavery again, you could damn sure bet your last bowl of chitterlings that the white friend you promised to love for life would be the first one in line to pick out your big, black buck." He pointed to the overly enthused Caucasian couple applauding in the front row, too stupid to realize that they were being insulted. "And all of y'all muthafuckas crazy. No disrespect, I love everybody, but tell the truth." He laughed. "You never heard a brother or sister talk no crazy shit about spaceships coming from out of space, or aliens breaking into their home. Not unless you're talking about illegal aliens. Border violators. They come in a ship, but not from out of space.

"Let me ask y'all a question. How it feel to shake your hair the way y'all be doing when you get around a nigger? My peoples, y'all ever notice that? You be talking to a white person then all of a sudden they shake their hair out of their eye? They be like, BOOM!" He stomped his foot on the floor, portraying an imaginary employer. "Here's the difference between you and I, you smelly, rotten nigger you." He shook the hair out of his eyes.

The audience roared in unison, causing the white folk to feel just a wee bit uncomfortable.

"Gay people . . . please . . . keep that shit to yourselves. I'm all for freedom of expression, but y'all is getting ridiculous. I ain't bullshitting. Every day somebody new stepping out of the closet. Teenagers walking around holding hands, kissing in the street, publicly professing their love for one another.

"Two of the greatest child molesters of our time beat rape charges—piss and Jesus juice, oh Lord. I'm bothered, people. Why we didn't see R. Kelly on *To Catch a Predator*? All of that nigga's songs dictate molester. '12 Play'—underage girls. 'Bump 'n Grind'—humping little girls like we did when we was kids. 'I Believe I Can Fly'—every young boy's dream. 'Your Body's Callin''—That shit is simple. It's a song about a young virgin convinced that she's ready for the Pied Piper to influence her path with his beautiful music. And I ask my people, what in the fuck is going on? I can't fuck with it, my people. Give it to me one time." He held the mike out to the crowd.

They all shouted, "OBAMA!"

He dropped the microphone and the entire auditorium stood up with applause as the curtain closed on his outstanding performance.

We all left the show together that night and stopped by a bar called The Devil's Cesspool, a spot where the first drink was on the house and the next was in hell. Only the fittest of criminal minds and street pharmacists called this their home away from home. Motorcycles, hot cars, and loud conversation gave life to the crowded parking lot.

Sabrina and Evelyn rode in my truck with me, while Tawana stuck close to Sakou in his ride. Never once did she realize the danger she was in.

All Sakou was doing was getting more people involved, prolonging the night. In his own sick way, he was showing Tawana one last good time on earth before sneaking up and robbing her of her life.

I really didn't know her that well, so I'm not sure why I even felt a way about it. But if killing her was going to stop me from doing life in prison just for being an accomplice to a murder, then she had to go. Only one thing, though; as usual, Sakou didn't tell me all the details involved in his little diabolical setup.

"Party over here, boo!" Tawana yelled, drunkenly wobbling on the dance floor.

"*Hey to the left. Hey to the right,*" Sabrina and Evelyn sang, drinks in their hands, wildly dancing circles around Tawana.

"See that shit?" Sakou asked me as we sat at the bar watching Tawana. "You never know someone until they cross you. Even if they is the one you fucking. Let this be a lesson to you."

"It is fucked-up, man. But do you really think she'd rat?"

"Only reason me and you not locked up right now is because the camera and video pictures was too blurry."

"So why we doing her then?"

"We can't be taking no chances."

"Ain't she your girl, though?"

"Don't matter. And it shouldn't matter to you either."

After two or three songs, Tawana was drunk enough to sleep with everybody in the spot. She ended up passing out in front of the ladies' bathroom door.

"Come on, girl, get up," Sabrina said, pulling her by the arm, while Evelyn grabbed the other.

Tawana stumbled to her feet. "I need another drink."

"You don't need shit but some air. Let's go." Sakou dragged her out the bar to my truck. "Stand up," he said, slapping her face as her legs went limp. "The girls are going to take you home." He tossed Evelyn the keys.

I looked at Sakou then the girls. "Huh?"

"Just shut up and get in," he said.

"Why are they taking her home?"

Chapter 17

Two weeks later, Sabrina and Evelyn began spending paper out the ass. A week after that, Sakou pulled another one of his famous disappearing acts. Coincidentally, so did Tawana. The police wanted her back for more questioning and became suspicious after repeated knocks on her door and telephone calls went unanswered.

"What's up, baby?" I kissed Sabrina as she stepped into my truck after school let out.

She tossed her textbooks into the back seat. "These classes are busting my ass."

"I want to ask you a question, and I want you to be honest."

"What's that?"

"What happened to Tawana?"

"You want to go to jail?"

"You work for him." I stopped the car in the middle of traffic. "All along you've been working for the muthafucka. Did y'all kill her?"

"You can't hold up traffic." Sabrina looked back at the cars honking their horns behind us.

"Fuck them! Answer the question."

"I do what you do."

"I can't believe this shit." I slapped my hands down on the steering wheel. "When were you going to tell me?"

"What difference would it have made? You gonna point fingers? Think about why you in the mix you in."

"Fuck. It wasn't supposed to go that way. I was going to talk him out of popping her."

"This is life, Quiana. It's all about money and loyalty. We were paid to do a job, and we did it. Which is more than I can say for you."

"I'm not no killer."

"What you sign on for then?"

I'd been asking myself that very same question from the get-go. I had more than enough money in my pocket now. Grandma was straight. My truck was hooked up. I was about to enter school in the next couple of months. I couldn't have done any of that without money. The reality of it all, though, was technically that money belonged to Sakou. Just like we all belonged to him.

Regardless of how hurt I was from Sabrina lying to me, I still loved her.

That evening I took Grandma up on her offer and brought Sabrina over the house for them to meet.

After making our way past the toys scattered all over the floor of the foyer, we entered the kitchen, where Grandma was sipping hot tea at the table and watching *Jeopardy*.

"Grandma!" I called over the loud television.

"What is it?" She turned around. "Oh my goodness! This must be Sabrina, right?"

"Yes." Sabrina hugged Grandma and kissed her cheek. "Nice to finally meet you."

"It is. Sit yourself down. Can I get you something? Coffee, water, juice?"

"No, thank you. I'm fine."

"What about something to eat? I'm not letting you leave

until you taste my famous pork roast. You wouldn't deny an old frail lady, now would you?"

"No, not at all."

"Good. Then it's settled. Y'all go on ahead and get washed up then. Dinner will be ready shortly." Grandma smiled and started pulling plates from the cabinet over the sink.

"She's sweet," Sabrina said as I led her downstairs to my bathroom.

"You wouldn't have thought that when I was younger."

"It's not until you show that you can hold shit down do the old folks start looking at you different."

"Speaking of . . . what's the story with your family? I met your sister already. Is there anyone else?"

"Nope. My moms lives in Arizona, and my father got killed in the streets of Brooklyn trying to hustle a drug dealer back in the early eighties." She closed the bathroom door.

I walked into my room while Sabrina handled her business. I checked on my money in back of my drawer under neatly folded white T-shirts, but it wasn't there.

I thought maybe I was mistaken, so I checked once more. "No!" I said out loud, pulling out all of my clothes from the dresser drawers. "Fuck!" I sat on my bed and thought about where the hell else I could've possibly placed it.

I started speculating. Only person that would come down here looking for shit was Dana. Forgetting all about Sabrina, I ran up the basement steps, through the kitchen and up the stairs toward Dana's room.

"Stop running through the house!" Grandma yelled.

"DANA!" I pounded on her door. When she didn't answer I kicked it open.

"What the fuck you doing?" She covered her bare breasts.

"I'm only asking once. Where it at?" I closed the door behind me. I grabbed a T-shirt off the top of her dresser and tossed it to her, so she could cover herself.

"Why you just busting all up in my room?"

"You want to play stupid? Where's it at?"

"I don't know what you talking about."

"You don't know what I'm talking about?" I grabbed one of her porcelain dolls off her bed and smashed it against the wall.

She attacked me, but I blocked all of her attempted swings. I picked her up off her feet and slammed her into the wall.

"I WANT MY MONEY!" I screamed.

"Let me go." She screamed and kicked as I securely pinned her to the wall.

Just then the bedroom door swung open, and Grandma stood at its entrance holding a broomstick without the bristles.

"What you doing, Quiana? You let her go right now."

"She done stole something of mines."

"Ma, I ain't stole nothing. I don't even be downstairs."

"You better stop lying." I squeezed her bony arms.

"What you think she took?" Grandma asked.

"She knows."

Grandma hit my arm with the broomstick. "No, she doesn't."

"She's lying, Grandma."

"I know what you're looking for. You bringing drug money up in here?" Grandma reached down in the pockets of her apron. "What is this?" she asked, holding out both stacks of hundreds. "You dealing?" She threw the money in my face.

"Oh shit!" Dana looked all wide-eyed at my money.

"I want you out of here. You not going to get nobody hurt up in here with your foolishness. Is this how you saved my house? With drug money?"

"It's not drug money, Grandma."

"Yeah? Where else does this kind of money come from? Don't you remember that this is the same kind of lifestyle that took your mother?"

"You're wrong, Grandma. There are no drugs involved. What was you doing down in my business anyway?"

"I was going to surprise you by cleaning up."

"You were cleaning up in the back of my drawer?"

"I want to know where the money came from, or you'll have to leave."

"It's like that, Grandma?"

Grandma walked over to Dana.

"Are you all right?" she asked, checking the red bruises I'd left from pressing my fingers down into her arms. She then embraced Dana, turning her back to me.

I touched her shoulder. "Grandma?"

She ignored me, and held Dana even tighter.

"All right. I'll be here to collect my things in the morning." I slowly walked back down the steps and into the basement. I put the money into a book bag just as Sabrina walked out of the bathroom.

"Sounds like world war three going on up in here."

"We about to bounce."

"What about dinner?"

"We'll just grab something from The Rib Shack on the way to your spot."

"You don't look too good." Sabrina rubbed my warm hands.

"Don't feel too good either, baby."

When we walked inside The Rib Shack, it was the same old long line as always. Flies buzzed around the kitchen of the soul food restaurant, most of them getting stuck on the fly-paper hanging from the ceiling. After ordering our food, we went to wait in my truck.

"Hey, come here. I wanna holla at you for a minute, you fucking butch." It was dude that I'd smashed with the bat a while back at Grandma's house. Dude walked up with four of his friends.

"Who that, baby?" Sabrina asked.

"Get in the truck. I got this," I said, opening the door for her. I led the group of thugs away from the truck to the corner.

"Remember me, bitch? Wanna be a nigga?" the dude asked, his entourage inching closer.

"You know you was in the wrong. You disrespected the property. Next time go fuck on the side of your own house, nigga."

"You think so?" He lifted his shirt and exposed a gun. "You ain't nothing but a bitch."

"Ay yo, man." I raised my hands. "You going to shoot me in public?"

Even at gunpoint, right out in the open, no one paid any attention to us. Either they were too scared or just plain didn't want to get involved. I started thinking about Max and the way I'd just stood there not wanting to intervene.

"So, what's it going to be?" he asked as all of his boys tugged at their pants.

"Uh-uh, not at all." Sabrina rushed toward the boys with her gun out before they could react. "You're out here beefing with a woman? Nothing's happening." She cocked it and gave no time for excuses. "Now y'all either let us get our food and be on our way, or I'm shooting the first one of y'all closest to me."

"Ha! Look at you," I said to dude. "Scared shitless."

"This ain't over," dude said. "Put it down and let's just shoot 'the five,' since you wanna act like a man. You can get duffed out like a man. Won't nobody jump in. Unless you going to get this bitch to fight your battle for you." He laughed.

"Go on and get the truck, baby," I said, taking the gun from her. Tightly gripping the gun by my side, I said to dude, "Whatever you want to do."

"We outta here, but I'm definitely going to see you again."

Dude calmly walked away backwards with his boys by his side.

When they got to the corner, dude let off one in the air before they all dispersed around the bend.

I took a deep breath and thanked the Lord for sparing my life.

Chapter 18

There was nothing but flashing red lights on top of squad cars in front of Sabrina's building. That was a regular scene in the hood, so no one was ever surprised to see it. We rode the elevator inside Sabrina's building to her floor. When the elevator doors opened, a squadron of police was dragging Evelyn out, and she was cursing, kicking, and fighting with them as they tried to place handcuffs on her wrists.

"I bet I don't got to tell you what that's about," I said, letting the elevator doors close back.

"That's my sister, and I ain't leaving her." Sabrina pushed the button to open the doors up again.

"Hey, you," one of the officers from down the corridor shouted, "hold that elevator."

"We not waiting." I let it close back.

"Take my gun and get Sakou's car and bounce. I'm not leaving my sister behind." Sabrina opened the doors for the final time. "Just go." She kissed my lips and walked out into the corridor.

Just as the doors closed again, I heard another officer shout to Sabrina, "Stay where you're at!"

I got off on the floor below and took the staircase the rest of the way down.

A group of officers parading in the lobby looked as if they were waiting on orders and a description. A group of young kids bouncing a basketball down the hallway playfully played defense and offense toward the lobby.

I acted as if I was waiting on them as they rushed out. "Listen for the whistle," I said, trying to masquerade as their coach. I wrapped my arm around one of the youths.

The kid jerked away. "Get your hands off me."

"I'll give you fifty bucks. Matter of fact, I'll give all y'all fifty bucks a piece just to walk with me until I get to the gate."

I went into my pocket and pulled out four neatly folded fifty-dollar bills.

They all collected, smiled, and brought more realism to the image that I was perpetrating. Even as we neared the gate, other officers were standing by watching the police in the lobby.

After separating from the future Michael Jordans and Kobe Bryants, I headed toward the parking lot to get Sakou's truck. It was too late. Investigators from the K9 unit were already rummaging through it with dogs and everything. They didn't know my truck, but I wouldn't be able to get to it right now, and my money and my damn gun were in there.

I began backing away before turning around and running. I went directly to Port Authority in Manhattan. I was going to catch a bus to Danbury, Connecticut to see Sakou.

From the bus depot in Connecticut, I took an expensive taxi ride to his place of residence. All of his cars were parked in the driveway, and his wife was on the porch playing with their child.

She quickly scooped her child up in her arms as I progressed up the walkway. "Who are you?"

"Quiana. I'm a friend of Sakou's." I extended my hand, only to be left hanging. "What's up, little man?" I asked Sakou's son, ruffling his full head of curly hair with my hand.

"Don't touch him." She jerked him out of reach. "Sakou not here."

I turned around and looked at all of his vehicles posted up in the driveway. "Look, I don't know what's going on, but tell that man that things are real serious and he need to talk to me."

"I already told you, he's not here. But I am his wife, and you can tell me what is so important. Are you fucking him? I don't think you're his type. You're a little too much on the rough side for his taste. So, see ya and come another day."

Sakou walked out the front door of his house with no shirt on and took hold of his son.

"What is the sense in you telling me to tell people that you not here if you're just going to come outside anyway?"

"Go inside." Sakou buried his face inside his son's chubby cheek.

"You make me sick." She sucked her teeth. "Don't be bringing no trouble to my house," she warned me before walking inside. "And give me my baby." She snatched the child from Sakou's embrace then slammed the door shut.

"Stupid ass." Sakou walked to the edge of his neatly manicured lawn. "Why you out here?" He wiped "sleep crud" from his eyes.

"People getting arrested left and right."

"People like who?"

"People like Sabrina and her sister."

"Yeah? For what?" He patted down my shirt.

I jumped back. "What you doing?"

"You don't come out here. Ever! Not unless I tell you to. Now since you done violated my family and me, get the fuck out of here. I already told you before, I'll call you when I need you."

"You listening to me? Sabrina and Evelyn got arrested today, and your truck got impounded."

"This is why you young, schoolgirl. That truck is not in my name. I do crime, nigga. Nothing goes in my name. You better get your mind right, bitch." He looked up at me. "Anything else?" He rubbed his nose, drool leaking from the corners of his mouth.

"This how you treat me? Fuck it! Oh, by the way, thanks for the warning about Evelyn and Sabrina killing Tawana."

"You want to talk out loud?"

"That's not what I'm saying, man." I slammed my fist into my hand. "What type of game you running? I'm out. That's all I came to tell you. You do whatever the fuck it is you need to do, but I'm done. I'll see my own way out." I walked into the street and up the road to God knows where.

Between Tawana being dead, Sabrina and Evelyn locked up for her murder, and me being kicked out of the house I'd saved, I was fucked. Each night I stayed at a different hotel, trying to figure out my next step. I was grown as a mutha-fucka, and no one could save me.

"Hello?" I groggily answered my cell phone at three in the morning.

"Why that girl keep calling here collect from jail?" Grandma shouted into the phone.

"What girl?"

"That girlfriend of yours. What she done did, Quiana?"

"Don't accept the calls."

"I just know you out there in some kind of trouble. Don't you bring none of that foolishness back this way."

"You don't have to worry about it, Grandma. I won't be coming back."

"Well, where you going to be? Where are you at now?"

I began hearing clicks through the telephone, but there was no way in the world Grandma would set me up. "One of the kids picked up the phone?"

"Everybody in here sleeping."

I heard the click again, except this time it was even louder. "Hang up the phone, Grandma."

"Why? What's going on? Quiana? Hello?"

She didn't hang up fast enough, so I disconnected the call on her. I knew that clicking sound all too well from the stories told by various cellmates in the belly of the beast. They'd all ignored the clicking sound.

"Whenever you hear that click," they'd always begin, "you can bet your damn black ass that it's the feds listening in on you while you tell them everything they need to know."

I'd known too many females and men locked up behind unrecognizable clicks over the landlines. This one chick up in that muthafucka, right, she was explaining to me how the feds had knocked her brother. She said that he was using the buttons on the keypad of his phone to send messages by using the different tones in the numbered buttons. He'd sent a message out by tone, admitting to some murder, and the dicks deciphered that. There ain't nothing you can do without them finding out sooner or later. I never thought we'd committed the perfect crime, but I didn't think that all of this shit was about to rain down on me.

I didn't get up until twelve p.m. that next afternoon. I was contemplating taking a trip to Jamaica to lay low. I'd probably fuck around and call that shit home.

I was just stepping into my truck to grab a meal from somewhere when my cell rang. "Yeah," I answered, starting up the truck.

"Miss Quiana," the caller said with an accent.

"Who this?"

"Mikey Sarionni."

"What are you calling me for?"

"You see the news yet?"

"No. Why?"

"Are you near a radio or something?"

"Why? What's going on?"

"I think you'd better turn it on."

It was a fucking wrap. My name was all over the radio. But why wasn't Sakou's? Not one fucking time.

"Do you remember how to get to my house?" he asked.

"Why?" I nervously looked around for five-O.

"Sakou is not who you think he is. You don't got much time, so I'd suggest that you move your ass."

I was out like a bolt of lightning as the adrenaline rushing all throughout my body influenced my actions. I didn't stop for traffic lights or adhere to the speed limit on the parkway. I swerved in and out of traffic, stopping short of a state trooper waiting in the cut, off the side of the parkway.

The frantic honking of my truck's disturbing air horn alerted the guards at the iron green gate to hurriedly grant me access to Mikey Sarionni's wondrous estate.

Two cars waited up ahead as I drove up the curving driveway. A fat Paulie look-alike escorted me on foot to the front door. Once we entered, I was searched for weapons and wires then taken into Mikey Sarionni's office. His brotherhood of "guidos" stood by his side, staring at me with hateful eyes, like I was Betty Shabazz selling bean pies out of Sal's Famous Pizzeria right in the heart of Bensonhurst.

"Quiana, the man-thing. Here." He slid me my ID. "You're gonna need that when they take your black ass in." He laughed.

"Is this what you called me all the way down here for? To make jokes?"

"No, no, I did not." He turned serious. "I might be able to help you get out of your situation, but first you have to do me a favor."

"Mr. Sarionni, I'll have to refuse. I'm good."

I was just going to turn myself in. I mean, I got myself into this shit. After everything my momma taught me, showed me, how the goddamn freak could I ever let it come down to this? Can anybody answer that? I don't think you can.

My mother's death was all in vain because I fucked up. It got me all fucked in the head, man. Everything about me. I knew one thing for certain, though. If as of right now I started taking responsibility for my own actions, I could one day alter my mother's disappointment as she looked down on me from heaven up above.

"Now I'ma walk out of here, and hopefully one of y'all won't shoot me in the head. I don't got no weapon." I slowly turned toward the door.

"Hey, Q, let me ask you a question before you walk out of here. If I told you that I could get you out of the country, all expenses paid, to go anywhere you wanted to go, to live, be lesbian as you want to be, whatever the fuck, I'm just curious, what would you say?"

I stared at this character for a minute and studied the audacity of his dumb ass. He thought I was just another dumb black woman hungry for money, petty promises, and fine bitches. "What is it that Sakou has on you? It can't be just this situation. It's gotta be something so undoable, he's stuck to you. Can you answer that?"

"Why fucking not? You're going to jail anyway. Sakou did something, I swear to freaking God." Mike made a cross with his fingers and kissed it. "That fucking guy shot a three-year-ol' baby in the head that wasn't even in the same house I contracted him to be at."

"I'm not understanding. I thought Italian Americans didn't work with us kind of people."

"Sakou is good at what he does, and business is business. I'll work with anybody who brings me the most revenue. I don't give a shit what you are. I only see green. I gave Sakou an address and he went to the wrong house, a captain's house."

"Fucked up."

"It is."

"So why is he still alive?"

"No one but me knows who did it. I use Sakou for my dirtiest work. The kind of work I wouldn't send my worst enemy out to do. And if he doesn't do what the fuck I ask of him, then guess what?"

"Let me guess. You let the cat out of the bag?"

"Binga-*fucking*-roni!" Mike slammed his fist down on his desk.

"So Sakou not running this shit?"

"Sakou don't got the brains to run water. He sure had you fooled. What'd he do? A favor for you then said you owe him? Then after you did the favor, you never got out of his debt. Dumb broad. What is it with you people? If somebody put a sign up on the side of a departing ship that said *free fried chicken*, all of yous niggers would be right back over in Africa before the first bone is cleaned."

"So what is it you need me to do? I'm tired of being under his thumb." Sakou had been playing me from the very beginning, even when I was a child. Payback was a muthafucka, and it was time to pay that muthafucka back.

"Sakou's about to be in a jam. I can almost bet my bottom fucking dollar that whenever yous two are finally picked up for that girl's murder, he'll try to make a deal. I want you to get him to meet you somewhere, anywhere, and we'll follow you."

"You want me to set him up so that y'all can kill him?"

"How's your grandmother and the little foster kids?"

"How you know about them?"

"If you want them to stay healthy, then you're going to do me this favor. If you really think about it, Quiana, you'd also be doing yourself a favor. On the other hand, I can call the police and hold you until they get here. Or you can take that trip and never come back, because if I ever hear anything about what was discussed here today, your grandmother's little shoebox will go up in smoke."

Chapter 19

Turns out that Max was sleeping with Mikey's wife. That's why he had him killed. His wife disappeared off the face of the earth, never to be heard from again. Mikey had been extorting Max to maintain his life after he found out the news of his wife sleeping with Max. Max had real paper and had played a role in creating the blueprints for the Twin Towers.

Sakou was only supposed to bring Max to Mikey, but instead went for the money inside his bank accounts and killed him. So the police weren't only looking at me, they were also looking at Mikey, because his number showed up twelve times in Max's recovered cell phone.

It was way too much for my mind to contain, but I had no choice. I couldn't go visit Sabrina all disoriented in the heart and mind while she lived her day-to-day behind bars.

Even in her prison uniform, she was still as pretty as the first day we met, fucked-up hairdo and all. We quickly grasped hands as we sat at the long picnic-like table.

"I missed you so much," Sabrina said, tears in her eyes. "I thought they'd have caught you by now. How'd you get past the guards without them noticing?" She looked around.

I smiled. "Grandma must be praying for me." I pulled my

fitted cap down over my eyes. "Mr. Sarionni. He is connected. I don't know who may know in here." I tugged my
cap down even further. "Sabrina, let me ask you something.
Do you think Sakou set you up?"

"Hell yeah. Me and Evelyn do the damn thing, then next
thing you know, two bitches is behind bars."

"Why, though? Why would he set y'all up?"

"I should've known something was wrong when he asked
us to do it."

"You should also know that me and Sakou was supposed
to make that happen that night then he suddenly changed
the format. So we have to think why."

"Have you spoken to him?"

"He on his bullshit. I'm done with him, though. So are you.
I got something in the works where I can end all of this shit."

"What?"

"I said I got some shit in the works where you might be
able to get out, but it'll require you possibly taking the stand
against him."

"Fuck that! I'm not a snitch, Quiana."

"What you talking, snitch? We're talking about you possibly facing a first-degree murder charge. You wanna do life in
prison for this dude? You're going to do his time? I'm not."

"You know what? I did what I did, and if I'm caught then
fuck it, Quiana. I gotta just swallow that shit because I made
that plate. You can't do foul shit then expect not to pay. I can
see if I was lied on, but they got the truck with my fingerprints
all inside of it. Evelyn's too. So, tell me, how in the fuck am I
going to beat that charge?"

"I don't know. They don't have a weapon. Where is it? I
can get it and hold it down."

"I gave it back to Sakou the next day."

"Why didn't you just get rid of it?"

"Nigga said he wanted the shit back."

"That doesn't make sense. Why would he want it back?"

"All I do is follow orders and get paid for my services," Sabrina said, a tear leaking from her left eye. "My time is almost up." She wiped it off her face. "I got to go, baby." She stood up as a C.O. walked over toward her. "You not at your grandmother's house no more, right? How we going to keep in touch if I get sent up?"

"Baby, I'd find you anywhere. Don't worry about it."

We hugged for so long and so tight. I didn't want to let her go, but that C.O. had different ideas on his mind.

"Time's up," he said, grabbing her arm.

We both were able to get in one last quick peck on the lips before she was led away.

I'd decided to take that trip. I just wanted to check on my grandmother and make sure everything was straight with her. I'd try to leave her with some money, but she probably wouldn't accept it.

As I turned on her block that night about nine p.m., there was an immediate orange brightness followed by smoke. A single police car escorted three fire engines racing down the block from the opposite direction.

I parked at the corner and jumped out of my truck, engine still running, disregarding that I had my gun jammed down into the back of my pants. I ran down to my grandmother's burning house as the fire quickly engulfed the old wooden structure of her home.

"GRANDMA!" I screamed out from the front of the house, but my voice was overpowered by the ear-piercing wails of the approaching red saviors. Through the second-floor window of her home, I could see someone waving a white towel outside and choking on thick black smoke.

The fire had obviously been set from the ground up, possibly accelerated by gasoline. Nevertheless, there was no possibility of escape. Jumping from the windows would be fatal.

All I could do was keep circling the house, trying to find a way inside, but there wasn't one. Through the broken windows above in back of the house I could hear the kids inside screaming in pain and coughing. As I ran back around to the front, I tripped over a red plastic can of gasoline and picked it up.

By the time I got around to the front, a hose from one of the fire trucks was already being screwed into the fire hydrant across the street. The neighbors all came out to witness New York's "Brave Hearts" preserve life. The ladder on the fire truck was extended to the second-floor window while the powerful water hose rained on the house, breaking all of its windows in the process.

As more police arrived on the scene, I was helplessly standing off to the side looking on, still holding on to the can. One of the firemen started pointing at the can I was holding to one of the police officers.

"Hey, you," the officer said.

The crowd began pointing and speculating at the potentially incriminating evidence in my hand.

I dropped the can to the ground and began walking back toward my truck. I picked up the pace, as other officers and some firemen joined him. My walking eventually changed into running, but I never made it to my truck. Six officers, two participating crowd members, and three firefighters tackled me to the ground. As I lay on the ground struggling, wanting to prove my innocence, I could still see Grandma's house burning to the ground then the roof eventually caved in.

They flipped me over to lie on my stomach and found the gun, and eventually the money I had in my car.

Chapter 20

"Oh, shit," Detective Shudemall said, as I sat in the interrogation room. "You are in some real fucking trouble there, lady—murders, arson, sex with a minor."

"Sex with a minor? What you talking about?"

"Sabrina Jones. Does that name ring a bell? The one you went to see earlier today. That minor."

"She's nineteen."

"Seventeen. In New York it's considered statutory rape. That's just one of the problems you have. You better talk to me."

"Talk to you about what?"

"Everything. Starting with the day you, Sakou, and Tawana killed that poor schmuck out in Mount Vernon. Let me tell you this right now: Don't start off lying. That gun we found on you is the same gun used in Tawana's murder."

"What? That's bullshit. I didn't kill nobody."

"How are you going to deny that? Unless there's more to the story. Ballistics found a match with the bullet she was shot to death with and the ammunition inside your gun.

I needed a second to think, but his ass kept pressuring me. He left me in the room cuffed to a table for a while by myself, so that gave me time to get my story straight. I thought long and hard about how my prints got on the gun. Was this one of those police tactics to get me to confess to some shit I didn't do? Naw, too far-fetched.

But what wasn't too far-fetched was what I'd just remembered from a while back. The gun Sakou gave to me was the gun used in Tawana's murder. Sabrina said she'd given it back to him the day after. Then it ends up in my hands with my prints all over it. Not to mention the pictures from the traffic lights, indicating our possible involvement in Max's murder.

The cops found out that Grandma's house was paid for by untraceable money. He wanted to know about everything.

Detective Shudemall returned to the room with a bucket of "Sambo's Famous Chicken," two 22-oz. bottles of "Righteous" grape soda, and a smile. "I thought you might be hungry after all the running around you've been doing. I guess I can take the cuffs off so you can eat, right?"

After the cuffs were taken off, I began tearing into the hot and spicy chicken thigh.

"Look at her go." The detective laughed. "Better take your time. They don't make it like that in prison. Or did you forget?"

I put the chicken back down in its carton and wiped my mouth with a napkin that came in the bag.

"You can play the tough act all you want to. The fact of the matter is, I'm not intimidated. I know about you, and I'll let you know something." Detective Shudemall inched closer toward me, closed my box of chicken, then pushed it aside. "Let me tell you something. To me, you mean nothing. To Sakou, you mean nothing. You need to think about that. By the way, while I was out and about fetching you some food, I happened to hear some good news. It wasn't you who burned down the house after all."

"I told you that. Who was it? Mikey Sarionni?"

"No. It was your sister's boyfriend. The one you and Sabrina pulled a gun on right out in public. He was upset and try-ing to get back at you."

"How's my family?"

"No word on that yet. So what are you going to do about this Sakou issue? Snitch or quit?"

I took a sip of my soda. "I don't snitch."

"Wise up. This is the only chance you've got."

"So what you telling me, I have no choice?"

"You have a choice—freedom or life in prison. You decide."

"What you need from me?"

"A favor."

I laughed out loud, long and hard.

"What's so funny?" he angrily asked.

I looked him in the eyes and laughed even harder at the irony of it all. This all began with a favor. "You need a favor from me? That's what got me here in the first place."

"Why'd you make mention of Michael Sarionni's name? I never said anything about him."

"Because I owe him a favor too, and Sakou is working for him."

"Well then, I guess you've come to the right place after all. Start talking."

"First, tell me what's in it for me. Then I need to know for certain that I'ma walk away from this all free and alive. How you gonna guarantee my safety?"

"Witness protection. But . . . only if what you tell me leads to an arrest."

"I can do that."

"I'm sure you can and will."

Chapter 21

As far as the public at large knew, I was still on the run. As for Mikey, the same went for him. Now unless he and Sakou's connections were that great, nobody knew shit about the new favor I was doing. I was wired up and ready for war against the people who tried to fuck me. It was only right that I did them back even dirtier.

"I hear you went up to see Sabrina last week. How come you didn't let me know?" Sakou asked.

I responded, "Remember you said don't contact you, you'd contact me?"

We were inside Sakou's Connecticut home discussing the layout for a new hit he had on his to-do list.

"There's so much money involved in this hit, you won't have to ever worry about me again after this."

It was bugging me out the way this nigga could just sit there and be so ordinary about everything. "I heard that one before. Why you set me up with the murder weapon that killed Tawana?" I blurted out. "Sabrina told me she gave you back your gun. And then you gave it to me."

"I don't know what you're talking about." He turned on the

radio and raised the volume. Then he pulled out his gun. "Stand up and lift your shirt." He pushed the gun into my chest.

"You bugging, man. Why?"

"Just do it." He cocked the gun.

I slowly pulled my shirt over my head, titties hanging and everything. There was nothing, so he turned the radio back down and patted me on the shoulder. "Never can be too sure," he said. "You come up in here talking that crazy shit. Don't you know you can get that head blown off?"

"How I know when we do this last job, you're going to let me be?"

"Bitch, you don't. You're just going to have to take my word."

Take his word? His word? Yeah, right. "Who we hitting?"

Sakou looked down at his watch. "Mikey Sarionni."

"What's the matter?"

"My wife was supposed to be back here an hour ago. She just loves to get out there and spend my money until every last dime is gone."

"Call her."

"I already did. Three damn times."

"And?"

"No answer. She's got five more minutes then I gots to go."

Sakou had no idea he was driving right into a trap constructed by Detective Shudemall.

I could feel the wire I was wearing giving me miniscule shocks in between my thighs, causing me to twitch uncomfortably as I drove to Westbury. "So why exactly are we hitting Mikey? Isn't he how you make your bread and butter?"

"He's going to turn on me. I need to take care of him before he takes care of me."

"And you really think that you can just walk up in his house and start shooting? How you think you're going to pull that off?"

"What's the matter with you?" Sakou asked suspiciously.

"Nothing."

I honked the horn of my truck at Mikey's gate, but no one was there to respond.

Rinngg. Rinngg.

Sakou looked at his cell phone. "Doesn't she have perfect fucking timing? . . . Where you at? I told you I had important business to handle today."

"Sakou," Mikey Sarionni calmly said into the phone.

Sakou pressed *Speaker On.*

"Hello?" he said, not sure who he was speaking with.

"Sakou, this is Mikey. Your wife and son are all right for the time being, but won't be if you don't follow my instructions. Do you have a problem with that?"

Sakou's wife was not supposed to have anything to do with this. I guess she was picked up as insurance, to be certain that Sakou showed up. The only fucked-up thing about that was his three-year-old son was taken as a hostage too.

"No. Just tell me where you at. If anything happens to either one of them, you're a dead man."

"At a time like this, Sakou, I would not be threatening me. Bring me the money you stole from Max's bank accounts. I know you have it."

"I will kill you if anything happens to my family."

"Here is where I want you to meet me at. You bring any police, and the deal is off. You hear that? The deal is off, and your family is fucking dead—*d-e-a-d*, dead."

Mikey had a funny feeling about Sakou, so in exchange for a pardon and a large sum of money, he'd revealed to the mob lieutenant whose son had been accidentally killed who the true shooter was. This was a good look for me because Detective Shudemall would be getting more than he bargained for, everyone would be locked up, and I'd have a chance at beginning life anew, no strings attached.

After Mikey explained to him the location to meet him, Sakou ended the call and looked at me.

"He's got my family. Now he really got to go. He's a fucking memory, man. A fucking memory." Sakou pulled the clip from his gun then stuck it back into place.

Chapter 22

"I'm here," Sakou said as we neared a waste management site in Brooklyn.

The further we drove into the isolated civilization, the darker it became. If not for my high-beam headlights, I'd have gotten lost.

The electronic gate slid open, and I cautiously entered, driving slow as possible, and looking left to right. Garbage trucks were parked side to side on both sides of the yard, some just simply running, others compacting waste in the bottom of their disposal bins. A distant light flickered on and off from a large warehouse about two hundred feet away.

Sakou received another call and was directed to continue forth slow and steady.

"This is it," he said after the lights went off in the warehouse. "Do not turn the engine off in this shit." He stepped out of my truck. "Let's go. What the fuck you just sitting there for?"

"Yeah, a'ight, man." I smirked, feeling mighty secure with my position.

There was a chill in the air and it was very quiet. Then the motorized garage door of the warehouse opened with a disturbing hum.

"What am I supposed to do?" I whispered to Sakou. "I ain't packing."

"Just be easy," he said, aiming his gun at the garage.

The headlights of the trucks aligned on our left and right came on and provided the light we needed to see our destination. We both quickly turned around, wondering how that happened with no one in the trucks. As the garage door went up, twelve finely polished Italian-looking shoes stood side by side impatiently shuffling.

Mikey said, "As you can see, Sakou, you are truly outnumbered. That means you're fucked. Toss me your gun."

His five men all dressed in suits held us both down, their guns cocked and ready. One of us was about to be on a strict iron-only regimen.

But Sakou didn't care about the odds against him and stayed focused. "Where's my family?" he yelled.

"Where's my money?" Mikey yelled back.

"Fuck that! My family first."

As Mikey and Sakou argued back and forth, bright headlights behind us added life to the dismal party. With only one gun between us, it wouldn't be possible for Sakou to watch his front and back. So I watched the approaching car, and Sakou kept an eye on the "Goodfellas."

The luxury vehicle stopped dead on our ass, and four mafia-type individuals exited and stood silently staring at Sakou.

"Is this the fuck?" the driver of the luxury vehicle asked Mikey.

"That's him."

"Drop the gun." The driver pulled out some protection of his own before Sakou could turn around. "I said to drop your gun," the man repeated.

Not only were we being held at gunpoint by five guys on the inside, we were being pointed at on the outside. Sakou had no choice but to drop his shit.

I started to feel bad that I set him up like this, but what goes around comes around. I'm sure I'd be getting it back one day. Just not today.

"Mikey, man, what the fuck? I thought we was cool," Sakou said, observing his soon-to-be killers.

"You know what? Funny thing is, I thought we were too, but you had to go and get greedy. Your snitch helped me understand the real Sakou." Mikey smiled at me.

"My snitch? What you mean, my snitch?"

Sakou looked me up and down before striking me in the jaw then wrestling me to the ground as if I was a man. We quickly jumped to our feet and stood away from one another when one of the wise guys fired a gunshot. Sakou gave me an "if we ever get out of this I'ma kill you" kind of expression. I wasn't worried. His ass wasn't going anywhere, and neither was Mikey.

"Bring them out to me," the driver of the luxury vehicle ordered. He snapped his fingers at one of his thugs, and moments later the thug returned with Sakou's wife and child. His son was in an uncontrollable fit of toddler rage, while his wife was totally in shock.

"Baby." Sakou rushed over to her.

"Get back over here," the driver said. "You don't get to do anything as of right now. Not until I say." The man walked over to Sakou's wife and took their son in his arms with care.

"Young life is such a beautiful thing, right?" he said, showing Sakou his own son.

Mikey said to the man, "Why don't you introduce yourself. I don't think he knows who you are."

"It doesn't matter who the fuck he is. Just don't hurt my son."

"Like you hurt mines?" the driver of the luxurious vehicle asked.

At this point, neither Sakou nor his wife had any idea what

the man was talking about, but I did. *When is Detective Shudemall and his cavalry gonna come save the day?*

"What in the hell are you talking about?"

"That's the sad part; you don't even remember."

Sakou's wife began pleading hysterically, "Please don't hurt my baby for something that he did."

"Your husband killed a child, darling," Mikey said to her. "Don't act like you don't know what he does for a living."

"I don't know anything. Please . . . my child," she said, holding out her arms.

"I don't care about your tears." The driver shot her in the head.

Sakou went wild and was quickly brought down by way of the bullet.

"You fucking piece of shit!" The driver spat down on a dying Sakou then finished him off with a point-blank shot to his head, another into his chest, and the last into his stomach.

And still no cavalry to the rescue.

Nine Italian gangsters surrounded me, and the only protection I had was Mikey Sarionni's word, and Detective Shudemall keeping his.

"Very good work, Mikey." The man placed Sakou's son down, and he ran over to his mother and fell on top of her, crying with confusion.

"Hey. Mikey Sarionni always makes good on his word." He smiled.

The driver stared at me. "Mikey, can I ask you a question?"

"Shoot." Mikey smiled.

"Why is this eggplant still breathing?" He motioned for one of his men to let a black bitch have it. "I hope you've learned your lesson when it comes to dealing with niggers. You just can't trust them. You know what's even worse?"

"What's that?" Mikey responded.

"If you'd done your own work instead of hiring that nigger, my son would still be here. God bless his soul."

"I thought we agreed all was forgiven if I delivered Sakou to you?"

Something told me to just drop, so I did. My instincts were correct, because shots started ringing out from both directions.

I crawled over to Sakou's son and covered his body with my own.

When the smoke finally cleared, everyone lay on the ground either dead or mortally wounded.

Not too long after, helicopters, squad cars, and my good buddy Detective Shudemall finally arrived, as if he'd just saved the day. Even as the officers and helicopter focused in on the small gangland fight, I continued protecting Sakou's son.

"You need a hand?" Detective Shudemall extended his down to me.

As he pulled me up, I reached down for the baby. That's when I saw the bullet fragment lodged in the top of his head. Apparently he'd been hit by the ricocheting gunfire.

"Damn." Detective Shudemall placed his arm around my shoulder. "When you clean house, you truly do clean it. I tell you what, though, Quiana. A promise is a promise. Everything's recorded, and once we do the paperwork, you'll be out of here. Oh. I've received some bad news earlier this evening," he said, sounding sad.

Anticipating what he was going to say, I almost didn't want to know. The tears had already begun leaking from my eyes the instant he said the words, *bad news.* "What?"

Grandma Thomasina's funeral and burial were held on the same day. She'd suffered from smoke inhalation, trying to save Jovan in the fire that brought her house down. All of our

family history and belongings had been either burned beyond recognition or waterlogged.

All of the kids who had survived the blaze, including Dana,
became wards of the state once more, since they no longer
had a guardian. I never thought Dana would cry. Her hurt
was undeniably authentic, and she couldn't even look at
Grandma's casket when they lowered it six feet below the
earth.

When the reverend asked if anyone would like to say a few
words before a final prayer, no one rose to the occasion. But
I couldn't let her leave without my heart being left atop the
casket.

"Good morning, everyone," I said to all the mourners surrounding Grandma's gravesite. "What can ever really be said
on a day like this?" I rubbed tears from my eyes. "I guess not
too much."

Dana wailed out loudly while looking down into the tomb.

"You know, when I was younger, Grandma used to tell me,
'Love the ones you care for while they're here because you
never know when the Lord's going to call them home. Be
sure they know you love them every day, even when you feel
like you don't, because once they're gone, they're gone.' I'm
never good with these things, so I'd just like to read a little
something I wrote down last night, and I'd like everyone here
to sign it when I'm done because I'll be leaving after today.
Leaving for good. And I'd like to leave this on top of her casket." I took out a piece of paper from the inside of my black
blazer and unfolded it. I started reading:

Grandma, my lady, I know you're still near
With each tear that I cry, you will always be here
Even though I can no longer touch you, you've
*   touched so many lives*
I may no longer have you on the outside, but on the
*   inside is where you remain alive*

It'll be difficult only dreaming of you
Talking to myself as if I'm still talking with you
And I don't see how I'm going to make it
Or go on without your perfect love
Or go on without your perfect hug
Pictures will never be enough
And—

I didn't have the strength to go on, so I cut it short. I signed my name on the paper then passed it around so the others could do the same.

Detective Shudemall was waiting on the street for me in his car outside the green iron gates of the cemetery. I did my last great deed and paid for the funeral service and made sure that the kids, including Dana, had a ride back to the agency in the limousine they'd come in.

I leaned against an oak tree as mourners comforted one another with hugs and kisses.

"Hey," Dana said softly, tapping my shoulder from behind.

Without even thinking, I spun around and hugged her then we both cried together.

"They don't care about her being dead. They're just waiting on the free meal after," Dana said of the alleged mourners. "I ain't never ever seen any of them folks over the house. Not one damn time since I've lived there."

"Despite all the bullshit, Dana, I've always considered you like the sister I never had."

She bit on her bottom lip. "Do you really have to leave?"

"Yeah, man. I don't need anybody hurting anybody I love no more."

"Stop blaming yourself. It was my boyfriend that started the fire."

"It's so much more than that, Dana. If I ever see you again in life, maybe one day we can sit down, and I can tell you all about it." I looked back at Detective Shudemall, who pointed down to his watch.

"That's your ride, huh?"

"Afraid so," I sadly responded. "You think you'll be all right out here on your own?"

"I'll be all right. I have to be. After all, in about another three months I'll be eighteen. A bitch gotta get up on the good foot."

"Yeah. While you're trying to get up on the good foot, you're going to need something to get around in." I dug into my pocket and handed her the keys to my truck.

Detective Shudemall parked in front of LaGuardia Airport. "Here's everything you'll need." He passed me a one-way ticket to Utah.

All I could think was, *What the hell will I do there? Learn how to mountain climb?*

"Listen to me carefully, Quiana. I don't ever want to see your ass here ever again. Do you understand me? If I see you in my city again, so help me God, I will arrest your ass and have you brought up on every charge ever created. I'll even make some up as I go along. Are we clear on that?"

"Whatever." I stepped out of the car just as an incoming airplane cast a shadow over me. I walked through the crowded lobby thinking what a dick the detective was.

Since my flight was to take off in an hour, I sat in one of the many comfortable seats in the waiting room. Just as I was about to stick the headphones to my iPod in my ears, a vagrant looking for spare change approached me.

"Excuse me, can you do me a favor?" he begged, holding out his hand.

"Naw. I don't think I'll be doing any more favors for any-one no time soon." I laughed and laughed, and the man walked away confused and upset.